THE BLACK TULIP

THE LOTUS LIBRARY

FULL LIST OF VOLUMES IN THE LIBRARY

THE BLACK TULIP

A Romance
by

ALEXANDRE DUMAS

Translated with an Introduction by
S. J. ADAIR FITZ-GERALD

NEW YORK: BRENTANO'S

Manufactured in Great Britain

CONTENTS

Introduction

FRIEDRICH FREIHERR VON FLOTOW, the volatile composer of many forgotten, and one almost remembered, opera, 'Martha,' was very fond of stating, when he was a popular figure in the *dilettante* world, that it was Prince George of Waldeck, the father of the present young Queen of the Netherlands, who first suggested the plot of *La Tulipe Noire* to Alexandre Dumas. If we are to trust the story, it would appear that when the author of *The Three Musketeers* was first presented to the King at Amsterdam, the royal host said, 'M. Dumas, you have written many brilliant stories dealing with distinguished Frenchmen, but have you not found any Dutchmen worthy of your consideration?'

'Your Majesty, I have not had time to make the necessary researches.'

'Oh! you need not trouble about that,' replied the King; 'I will tell you a story.'

Alexandre Dumas listened attentively to the King's recital until the end, and then ecstatically exclaimed, 'Ah! it is a fine subject for a novel!'

'Write it,' said the King.

'I will,' said Dumas.

'And your Majesty will appear on the title-page as part author,' slily suggested papa Dumas.

'Oh, no,' hastily rejoined the King, 'or my subjects might think there is more of fiction than fact in their monarch.'

So Dumas wrote the story, though he touches, it must be confessed, scarcely more than the fringe of the historical events of 1672-3, when William of Orange was so fearful of his position, which might have appealed to him. Many years after the above conversation, Flotow was complimented by the late King William of Holland upon the production of one of his operas. Flotow, in return, said he hoped to compose an opera dealing with Dutch history. The King told him the origin of Dumas's work, and the result was Flotow's opera on the same subject, which achieved some success in Italy.

Whatever truth there may be in this anecdote, it is certain that Dumas, except for the incarceration and wicked murders of the brothers De Witte, made little use of Dutch history, though there were many subjects to his hand. Of course, the period of unrest, and the singularly ungrateful disposition and character of the self-seeking Dutch, as exhibited on August 20th 1672, gave the French author a magnificent background for the infatuated tulip-grower, whose trials and misadventures are set forth in the following pages, and permitted him to cast into prison the hero of his work with every plausible reason and good conviction. Politically speaking, though the scenes are laid in stirring times, *The Black Tulip* has no interest; we only catch side glances of the complex nature of William of Orange, who became William III. of England, who might well have been termed William the Silent, like the first Prince of Orange, for his ways were mysterious and dark. Fear of the plotting French certainly conspired to make him over-suspicious; and through the anxiety he felt as to the safety of his own position, no doubt he was hurried into being the real murderer of the brothers De Witte. Owing to these shameful murders William was raised, through their blood, to the position of Stadtholder, which he ardently desired. For a full description of William and his ways history must be consulted. The present story will tell the reader little of Dutch intrigue and ambition. The chief point in *The Black Tulip* is the wonderful way which Dumas has contrived not only his local colour but the extraordinary art which he brings to bear, which compels an interest in a love-story of so slight and slender a texture as that of the tulip-grower and the jailer's daughter. He touches the human chord, and by his skilful drawing of the leading *dramatis personæ* the reader is carried on breathlessly from the beginning to the end. That *The Black Tulip* should be converted into a play speaks more for the stage instinct of Mr Sydney Grundy than for the dramatic intention of the master and the maker of many plays as well as romances. For it is common knowledge that Alexandre Dumas was a dramatist first and a novel-writer after. That is to say, at the beginning of his career, which, in his salad days, was somewhat erratic. His first play (after a volume of immature short stories had appeared and a couple of farces had been produced) was *Trois et sa Cour* in 1829. He wrote a number of plays after this and a vast quantity of travel matter, but it was as a story-teller that Dumas gained not only a large fortune but ever-enduring reputation. He was a magnificent receiver of ideas—no matter where they originated. He took whatever he could get from whomsoever he could get it, and minting it with his own die, gave it his immense, prodigious and radiant personality. In the shades Dumas should not lack for company, for a careful collector of detail has asserted that he had no less than ninety 'ghosts,' politely termed collaborators, whose names were always scrupulously unprinted on the title-pages of the works they assisted to write. But what does it signify? It is to Dumas we owe the publication of the finest series of romances the world has ever seen. Do we want to do more than refer to other masterpieces than *Monte Cristo*, *The Three Musketeers*, *La Dame de Monsoreau* and, lastly, *La Tulipe Noir* from the almost endless list of romances that came from the brain factory which he controlled? Alexandre Dumas was the grandson of Count Alexandre Davy de la Pailleterie and Marie-Cessette Dumas, a Haytian negress, and the son of General Alexandre Davy Dumas, and he was therefore a quadroon. He died full of honours at his celebrated son's house at Dieppe on December 5, 1870. And his life may be easily studied. It is a romance of itself. For the rest, his works may speak for themselves. It is not in my province, were I so inclined, to extol the talents of so brilliant a man. No man can justly praise Dumas justly. He can only be judged by each individual reader who finds that glorious satisfaction in the ideal realms of fiction which Dumas makes so real. Before he died he asked his son if he thought he should be forgotten. He inquired, 'Do you believe that anything I have written will survive me?' The son replied, 'You may rest in peace; much indeed will survive you.' And in 1894 the dutiful son wrote a letter to his father in the Elysian Fields, which is the most pathetic and beautiful production of its kind in literature. Its tender, nay, pathetic, simplicity should commend it to all Dumas's admirers. It was printed in English for the first time in Mr Beerbohm Tree's Souvenir of *The Three Musketeers* production. The answer as to Dumas's popularity is found in the fact that close upon three millions of his works have been sold in France alone since his death, and the number in England must be proportionately high. Dumas is not for an age but for all time. A dramatic version of 'The Black Tulip' by Mr Sydney Grundy was produced on October 28, 1899, at the Theatre Royal, Haymarket, under the management of Messrs Frederick Harrison and Cyril Maude. The play follows Dumas tolerably closely, though the action does not begin until the arrest of Cornelius van Baerle. Whatever liberties Mr Grundy has taken with the work for the purposes of his scheme, they are properly reverent and advisable, and even Dumas, were he alive, would admit the surprising ability brought to bear in the construction of the piece by the English writer. The play proved a very great and well-deserved success. It was admirably acted and sumptuously staged.

S. J. ADAIR FITZ-GERALD.

Cast of Characters.

DRAMATIS PERSONÆ IN THE WORK.

WILLIAM, PRINCE OF ORANGE, afterwards William III., King of England.
Captain VAN DEKEN, his *Aide-de-Camp*.
LOUIS XIV. OF FRANCE.
CORNELIUS DE WITTE, Inspector of Dykes at the Hague.
JOHN DE WITTE, his brother, Grand Pensionary of Holland.
COUNT TILLY, Captain of the Cavalry of the Hague.
Doctor CORNELIUS VAN BAERLE, a Tulip-Fancier, godson of Cornelius de Witte.
Mynheer ISAAC BOXTEL, *alias* JACOB GISELS, a rival Tulip-Grower.
Mynheer VAN SYSTENS, Burgomaster of Haarlem, and President of the Horticultural Society.
CRAEKE, John de Witte's Confidential Servant.
GRYPHUS, a Jailer.
Mynheer BOWELT ⎱ Deputies.
Mynheer D'ASPEREN ⎰
MARQUIS DE LOUVOIS.
THE RECORDER OF THE STATES.
Meester VAN SPENNEN, a Magistrate at Dort.
TYCKALAER, a Surgeon at the Hague.
ZUG, Doctor van Baerle's old Nurse.

AND

ROSA, daughter of Gryphus, in love with Cornelius van Baerle.

DRAMATIS PERSONÆ IN THE PLAY.

Written by SYDNEY GRUNDY.

Produced at the Haymarket Theatre by Messrs FREDERICK HARRISON and CYRIL MAUDE, Saturday, Oct. 28th 1899.

WILLIAM OF ORANGE	Mr FREDERICK HARRISON.
Doctor CORNELIUS VAN BAERLE	Mr CYRIL MAUDE.
CORNELIUS DE WITTE	Mr WILL DENNIS.
ISAAC BOXTEL	Mr MARK KINGHORNE.
Mynheer VAN SYSTENS	Mr F. H. TYLER.
Meester VAN SPENNEN	Mr SAMUEL JOHNSON.
GRYPHUS	Mr SYDNEY VALENTINE.
Captain VAN DEKEN	Mr CLARENCE BLAKISTON.
CRAEKE	Mr C. ST. AMORY.
RECORDER OF THE STATES	Mr J. S. BLYTHE.
CLERK	Mr J. H. BREWER.
AN ATTENDANT	Mr N. HOLTHOIR.
ZUG	Mrs E. H. BROOKE.
AN ATTENDANT	Miss MURIEL BEAUMONT.
AND	
ROSA	Miss WINIFRED EMERY.

xii

THE BLACK TULIP

CHAPTER I

A GRATEFUL PEOPLE

On the 20th of August 1672, the city of the Hague,
whose streets were usually so lively, neat and trim
that every day appeared like Sunday, with its
shady park, with its immense trees spreading over
its Gothic houses, its canals like mammoth mirrors,
in which were reflected its steeples and its almost
Eastern cupolas, the city of the Hague, the capital
of the Seven United Provinces, was swelling to
bursting in all its arteries with a black and red
stream of eager, panting and restless citizens, who,
with their knives in their girdles, muskets on their
shoulders, or sticks in their hands, were pushing on
to the Buytenhof, a fearful prison, the grated windows of which are still to be seen, where Cornelius
de Witte, the brother of the Grand Pensionary of
Holland, was languishing in confinement on the
charge of attempted murder, preferred against him
by the surgeon Tyckelaer.

If the history of that time, and more especially
that of the year in the middle of which our story
begins, were not indissolubly connected with the

two names just mentioned, the few explanatory pages which we are about to add might appear quite unnecessary; but we must apprise the reader that this explanation is as indispensable to the right understanding of our narrative as to that of the important event itself on which it is based.

Cornelius de Witte, Ruart de Pulten—that is to say, inspector of dykes, ex-burgomaster of Dort, his native town, and member of the Assembly of the States of Holland—was forty-nine years of age, when the Dutch people, weary of the Republic as administered by John de Witte, the Grand Pensionary of Holland, unexpectedly conceived a most violent affection for the Stadtholderate, which had been abolished forever in Holland by the Perpetual Edict forced by John de Witte upon the United Provinces.

As it rarely happens that public opinion, in its uncertain, capricious flights, invariably seeks to identify a principle with a man, the people saw the personification of the Republic in the two stern figures of the brothers De Witte, those Romans of Holland, who refused to pander to the fancies of the mob, and binding themselves with unbending fidelity to liberty without licentiousness, and prosperity without extravagance; on the other hand, the Stadtholderate recalled to the popular mind the grave, thoughtful image of the young Prince William of Orange, who was christened 'Taciturn.'

The brothers De Witte humoured Louis XIV., whose moral influence was felt throughout the whole of Europe, and the pressure of whose material power Holland had been made to feel in that marvellous campaign on the Rhine, made famous by the Comte de Guiche, which, in the space of three months, had laid the power of the United Provinces prostrate.

Louis XIV. had long been the enemy of the Dutch, who insulted or ridiculed him to their hearts' content, although it must be said that they generally made use of French refugees for the venting of their spite. Their national pride held him up as the Mithridates of the Republic. The brothers De Witte had therefore to strive against a double difficulty—against the force of national antipathy, and also against that feeling of weariness which is natural to all vanquished people, when they hope that a new leader will be able to save them from ruin and shame.

This new leader, who was quite ready to appear on the political horizon, and to measure himself against Louis XIV., however gigantic the fortunes of the Grand Monarch loomed in the future, was William, Prince of Orange, son of William II., and grandson, by his mother, Mary Stuart, of Charles I. of England. We have already referred to him as the person by whom the people expected to see the office of Stadtholder restored.

This young man was, in 1672, twenty-two years of age. John de Witte, who was his tutor, had brought him up with the view of making him a good citizen of the Republic. Loving his country better than he did his pupil, the master had, by the Perpetual Edict, extinguished the hope which the young Prince might have entertained of one day becoming Stadtholder. But God laughs at the presumption of man who attempts to raise and prostrate the powers on earth without consulting the King above; and the fickleness and caprice of the Dutch combined with the terror inspired by Louis XIV. in repealing the Perpetual Edict and re-establishing the office of Stadtholder in favour of William of Orange, for whom the hand of Providence had traced out lofty destinies on the hidden map of the future.

The Grand Pensionary bowed before the will of his fellow-citizens. Cornelius de Witte, however, was more obstinate; and notwithstanding all the threats of death from the Orangist rabble, who besieged him in his house at Dort, he firmly refused to sign the act by which the office of Stadtholder was restored. Moved by the tears and entreaties of his wife, he at last complied, only adding to his signature the two letters V. C. (*Vi Coactus*), notifying thereby that he only yielded to force.

It was only by a real miracle that he escaped that day from the doom intended for him.

John de Witte derived no advantage from his ready compliance with the wishes of his fellow-citizens. Only a few days later an attempt was made to stab him, in which he was severely although not mortally wounded.

This by no means suited the views of the Orange faction. The life of the two brothers being a constant obstacle to their plans, they changed their tactics, and tried to obtain by calumny that which they had not been able to effect by the aid of the poniard.

The wretched tool who was to be the criminal, in this instance, was Tyckelaer the surgeon. He lodged an information against Cornelius de Witte, setting forth that the warden—who, as he had shown by the letters added to his signature, was fuming at the repeal of the Perpetual Edict—had, being inflamed with hatred against William of Orange, hired an assassin to deliver the new Republic from its new Stadtholder; and he, Tyckelaer, was the person thus chosen; but that, horrified at the bare idea of the act which he was asked to perpetrate, he had preferred rather to reveal the crime than to commit it.

This disclosure was, indeed, well calculated to call forth a furious outbreak among the Orange faction. The Attorney-General caused, on the 16th of August 1672, Cornelius de Witte to be arrested ; and the noble brother of John de Witte had, like the vilest wretch, to undergo, in one of the apartments of the town prison, the preparatory degrees of torture, by means of which his judges expected to force from him the confession of his alleged plot against William of Orange.

But Cornelius was not only possessed of a great mind, but also of a great heart. He belonged to that race of martyrs who, indissolubly wedded to their political conviction, as their ancestors were to their faith, are able to bear pain with equanimity, and, while stretched on the rack, he recited, with a firm voice, and scanning the lines according to measure, the first strophe of the 'Justum ac tenacem' of Horace. But he made no confession, and soon tired, not only the strength, but even the fanaticism of his executioners.

The judges, nevertheless, acquitted Tyckelaer from every charge ; at the same time they sentenced Cornelius to be deposed from all his offices and dignities; to pay all the costs of the trial ; and to be banished from the soil of the Republic for ever.

This judgment against not only an innocent, but also a great man, was indeed some gratification to the passions of the people, to whose interests Cornelius de Witte had always devoted himself : but even this was not enough.

The Athenians, who, indeed, have left behind them a pretty tolerable reputation for ingratitude, have in this respect to yield precedence to the

Dutch. They, at least, contented themselves with banishing Aristides.

John de Witte, at the first intimation of the charge brought against his brother, had resigned his office of Grand Pensionary. He, too, received a noble recompense for his devotedness to the best interests of his country, taking with him, into the retirement of private life, the hatred of a host of enemies, and the scarcely healed wounds inflicted by assassins, only too often the sole guerdon obtained by honourable men who are guilty of having worked for their country, forgetful of their own private interests.

In the meanwhile, William of Orange urged on the course of events by every means in his power, eagerly waiting for the time when the people, by whom he was idolised, should have made of the bodies of the brothers the two steps over which he might ascend to the chair of Stadtholder.

Therefore, on the 20th of August 1672, as we have already stated, the whole town was crowding towards the Buytenhof, to witness the departure of Cornelius de Witte from prison, and driven into exile ; to see what traces the torture of the rack had left on the noble frame of the man who knew his Horace so well.

Yet all this multitude was not crowding to the Buytenhof with the innocent view of merely feasting their eyes with the spectacle : there were many who went there to play an active part in it, and to take upon themselves an office which they conceived had been badly filled—that of the executioner.

There were, indeed, others with less hostile intentions. All that they cared for was the spectacle, always so attractive to the mob, whose instinctive pride is gratified by the sight of greatness hurled down into the dust.

'Has not this Cornelius de Witte been locked up, and broken by the rack? Shall we not see him pale, streaming with blood, covered with shame?' were the questions asked. Indeed, this was a sweet triumph for the burghers of the Hague, whose envy even beat that of the common rabble; a triumph in which every honest citizen and townsman might be expected to share.

'Moreover,' hinted the Orange agitators, interspersed through the crowd, whom they hoped to manage like a sharp-edged and, at the same time, crushing instrument—' moreover, will there not be, from the Buytenhof to the gate of the town, an opportunity to throw some handfuls of dirt, or a few stones, at this Cornelius de Witte, who not only conferred the dignity of Stadtholder on the Prince of Orange merely *Vi Coactus*, but who also intended to have him assassinated?'

'Besides which,' the fierce enemies of France chimed in, 'if the work were done well and bravely at the Hague, Cornelius would certainly not be allowed to go into exile, where he will renew his intrigues with France, and live with his scoundrel of a brother, John, on the gold of the Marquis de Louvois.'

In such a temper people generally will run rather than walk—which was the reason why the inhabitants of the Hague were hurrying so fast towards the Buytenhof.

Honest Tyckelaer, with a heart full of spite and malice, and with no particular plan settled in his mind, was one of the foremost, being pushed forward by the Orange party like a model of probity, a hero of national honour and Christian charity.

This daring miscreant recounted, with all the embellishments and flourishes suggested by his base mind and his ruffianly imagination, the attempts which he pretended Cornelius de Witte had made to corrupt him, the sums of money which were promised, and all the diabolical stratagems planned beforehand to smooth for him, Tyckelaer, all the difficulties that he might commit murder.

Every phrase of his speech, eagerly listened to by the populace, called forth enthusiastic cheers for the Prince of Orange, and yells and imprecations of blind fury against the brothers De Witte.

The mob even began to vent its rage by inveighing against the iniquitous judges who had allowed such a detestable criminal as the villain Cornelius to get off so cheaply.

Some of the agitators whispered, ' He will be off; he will escape from us ! '   Others replied,—

' A vessel is waiting for him at Schevening, a French craft.   Tyckelaer has seen her.'

' Honest Tyckelaer !   Hurrah for Tyckelaer ! ' the mob cried in chorus.

' And let us not forget,' a voice exclaimed from the crowd, ' that at the same time with Cornelius, his brother John, who is as rascally a traitor as himself, will also make his escape.'

' And the two rogues will make merry in France with our money, with the money for our vessels, our arsenals and our dockyards, which they have sold to Louis XIV.'

' Well, then, why should we allow them to depart ? ' asked one of the patriots who had gained the start of the others.

' Forward to the prison, to the prison ! ' echoed the crowd.

Amid these cries, the citizens ran along faster and faster, cocking their muskets, brandishing their hatchets, with eyes flaming with fire and defiance.

No violence, however, had as yet been committed, and the file of horsemen who were guarding the approaches of the Buytenhof remained cool, unmoved, silent, much more threatening in their impassibility than all this crowd of burghers with their cries and their threats. The men on their horses, indeed, stayed like so many statues, under the eye of their leader, Count Tilly, the captain of the mounted troop of the Hague, who had his sword drawn, but held it with its point downwards, in a line with the straps of his stirrup.

This troop, the only defence of the prison, over-awed by its firm attitude not only the disorderly riotous mass of the populace, but also the detachment of the burgher-guard which, being placed opposite the Buytenhof to support the soldiers in keeping order, gave countenance to the seditious cries by shouting,—

'Hurrah for Orange! Down with the traitors!'

The presence of Tilly and his horsemen, indeed, exercised a salutary check on these civic warriors; but, by degrees, they waxed more and more angry by their own shouts, and as they were not able to understand how anyone could have courage without showing it by cries, they attributed the silence of the dragoons to cowardice, and advanced one step towards the prison, with all the turbulent mob following in their wake.

At this moment, Count Tilly rode forth towards them single-handed, merely lifting his sword slightly and contracting his brow as he demanded,—

'Well, gentlemen of the burgher-guard, why are you advancing, and what do you wish?'

The burghers brandished their muskets, repeating their cry,—

'Hurrah for Orange! Death to the traitors!'

'"Hurrah for Orange!" all well and good!'

replied Count Tilly, 'although I certainly am more partial to happy faces than to gloomy ones. "Death to the traitors," as much of it as you like so long as you show your wishes by cries only. But, as to putting them to death in good earnest, I am here to prevent that, and I shall prevent it.'

Then, turning round to his men, he gave the word of command,—

'Ready!'

The troopers obeyed orders with a precision which immediately caused the burgher-guard and the people to fall back in such haste and confusion as to excite the laughter of the cavalry officer.

'Halloa!' he exclaimed, with that bantering tone which is peculiar to men of his profession; 'be easy, my soldiers will not fire a shot; but, on the other hand, you will not advance by one step towards the prison.'

'And do you know, sir, that we have muskets?' roared the commandant of the burghers.

'By Jove! I can't help knowing it since you have made them glitter enough before my eyes; but I beg you to observe, also, that we on our side have pistols, that the pistol carries admirably to a distance of fifty yards, and that you are only twenty-five from us.'

'Death to the traitors!' cried the exasperated burghers.

'Bah,' growled the officer, 'you always cry the same thing over again. It is very wearisome.'

With this he resumed his post at the head of his troops, whilst the tumult grew fiercer and fiercer about the Buytenhof.

And yet, the furious crowd did not know that at the very moment when they were hot on the scent of one of their victims, the other, as if hurrying to meet his fate, passed, at a distance of not more than a hundred yards, behind the groups of people and the dragoons, on his way to the Buytenhof.

John de Witte, indeed, had alighted from his coach with a servant, and quietly walked across the courtyard of the prison.

Mentioning his name to the turnkey, who, however, knew him, he said,—

'Good morning, Gryphus, I am coming to take away my brother, who, as you know, is condemned to exile, and to carry him out of the city.'

Thereupon the jailer, a sort of bear, trained to lock and unlock the gates of the prison, greeted him and admitted him into the building, the doors of which were immediately closed again.

Ten yards farther on, John de Witte met a lovely young girl, of about seventeen or eighteen, dressed in the national costume of the Frisian women, who, with pretty demureness, dropped him a courtesey. Patting her cheek, he said to her,—

'Good morning, my good and fair Rosa; how is my brother?'

'Oh! Mynheer John, sir,' the young girl replied, 'I am not afraid of the harm which has been done to him. That's all over now.'

'But what is it you are afraid of?'

'I am afraid of the harm which they are going to do to him.'

'Oh! yes,' said De Witte, 'you speak of the people down below, don't you?'

'Do you hear them?'

'Yes, they are indeed in a state of great excitement; but when they see us, perhaps they will grow calmer, as we have never done them anything but good.'

'Unfortunately, that's no reason at all,' muttered the girl, as, seeing an imperative sign from her father, she withdrew.

' Indeed, child, what you say is only too true.'

Then, in pursuing his way, he said to himself,—-

' Here is a damsel who very likely does not know how to read, who, consequently, has never read anything; and yet, with one word, she has just told the whole history of the world.'

And with the same calm mien, but more melancholy than he had been on entering the prison, the Grand Pensionary proceeded towards the cell of his brother.

CHAPTER II

THE TWO BROTHERS

As the fair Rosa, with gloomy foreboding, had foretold, so it fell out. Whilst John de Witte was climbing the narrow winding stairs which led to the prison of his brother Cornelius, the burghers did their best to have the troops of Count Tilly, who were in their way, removed.

Seeing this disposition, the rabble, who fully appreciated the laudable intentions of their beloved militia, shouted most lustily,—

' Hurrah for the burghers!'

Count Tilly, who was as prudent as he was firm, began to parley with the burghers, under the protection of the cocked pistols of his dragoons, explaining to the valiant townsmen that his order from the States commanded him to guard the prison and its approaches with three companies.

' Why should there be such an order? Why guard the prison?' cried the Orangists,

'Stop,' replied the Count; 'there you at once ask me more than I can tell you. I was told,— "Guard the prison," and I guard it. You, gentlemen, who are almost military men yourselves, ought to know that an order must never be discussed.'

'But this order has been given to you that the traitors may be enabled to leave the town.'

'Very possibly, as the traitors are condemned to exile,' replied Tilly.

'But who has given this order?'

'The States, of course.'

'The States are traitors.'

'I don't know anything about that!'

'And you are a traitor yourself!'

'I?'

'Yes, you.'

'Well, as to that, let us understand each other, my friends. Whom should I betray? The States? Why, I cannot betray them, whilst, being in their pay, I faithfully obey orders.'

As the Count was so indisputably in the right, it was impossible to argue against him, the mob answered with redoubled clamour and extravagant threats, which the Count received with the most perfect urbanity.

'Gentlemen,' he said, 'uncock your muskets; one of them might go off by accident, and if the shot chanced to wound one of my men, it would certainly be the death of many of you. We should be very sorry for that, but you even more so; especially as such a thing is neither comtemplated by you nor by myself.'

'If you did that,' cried the burghers, 'we should return the compliment.'

'Of course you would, but suppose you killed every man of us, those whom we should have killed would be none the less dead.'

'Then leave the place to us and you will perform the part of a good citizen.'

'First of all,' said the Count, 'I am not a citizen, but an officer, which is a very different thing; and secondly, I am not a Hollander, but a Frenchman, which is still more different. I have to do with no one but the States, by whom I am paid; let me see an order from them to leave the place to you, and I shall only be too glad to wheel off in an instant, as I am confoundedly bored here.'

'Yes, yes!' cried a hundred voices; and the noise was immediately swelled by five hundred others; 'let us march to the Town Hall and see the deputies! Come along! come along!'

'That's it,' Tilly muttered between his teeth, as he saw the most violent among the crowd turning away; 'go and ask for a Court order at the Town Hall, and you will see whether they will grant it. Go, my fine fellows, go!'

The worthy officer relied on the honour of the magistrates, who, on their side, relied on his honour as a soldier.

'I suppose, Captain,' whispered the first lieutenant into the ear of the Count, 'the deputies will give these madmen a flat refusal; but, after all, it would do no harm if they would send us some reinforcement.'

Meanwhile John de Witte, whom we left climbing the stairs, after his conversation with the jailor Gryphus and his daughter Rosa, had reached the door of the cell, where, on a mattress, his brother Cornelius was resting, after having suffered the preliminary tortures. The sentence of banishment having been pronounced, there was no occasion for inflicting the torture extraordinary.

Cornelius lay prostrate on his couch, with broken wrists and crushed fingers. He had refused to confess to a crime of which he was guiltless; and now, after three days of agony, he once more breathed freely, on being informed that the judges, from whom he had expected death, were only condemning him to banishment.

Endowed with an iron frame and a stout heart, how would he have disappointed his enemies if they could only have seen, in the gloomy cell of the Buytenhof, his pale face lit up by the smile of the martyr who, having obtained a bright glimpse of the bright glory of heaven, forgets the dross of this earth.

The Ruart, indeed, had already recovered his full strength, more by the force of his own strong will than by actual aid ; and he was calculating how long the formalities of the law would still detain him in prison.

It was just at this moment that the mingled shouts of the burgher-guard and of the mob were raging against the two brothers and threatening Captain Tilly, who served as a living rampart to them. This uproar broke against the walls of the prison as the surf dashes against the rocks, and now reached the ears of the prisoner.

But threatening as it all sounded, Cornelius appeared not to deem it worth his while to inquire into the cause ; nor did he get up to look out of the narrow grated window, which gave access to the light and to the noise of the world without.

He was so benumbed by his never-ceasing pain, that it had almost become a habit with him. He felt with such intense delight the bonds, which connected his immortal being with his perishable frame, gradually loosening, that it seemed to him as if his spirit, freed from the trammels of the body, were floating in the air above it, like the expiring flame which rises from the half-extinguished embers.

He was also thinking of his brother; and whilst the latter was thus vividly present to his mind, the door opened, and John entered, and hurried to the bedside of the prisoner, who stretched out his broken limbs and his hands, tied up in bandages, towards that glorious brother, whom he now exceeded, not in services rendered to the country, but in the hatred which the Dutch bore him.

John tenderly kissed his brother on the forehead, and put his sore hands gently back on the mattress.

'Cornelius, my poor brother, you are suffering great pain, are you not?'

'I am suffering no longer, since I see you, my brother.'

'Oh! my poor, dear Cornelius, I feel distracted to see you in such a state.'

'Indeed, I have thought more of you than of myself; and while they were torturing me, I never thought of uttering a complaint, except once, to say, "Poor brother!" But now that you are here, let us forget all. You have to take me away, have you not?'

'I have.'

'I am quite healed; help me to get up, and you shall see how well I can walk.'

'You will not have to walk far, as I have my coach near the pond, behind Tilly's dragoons.'

'Tilly's dragoons! Why are they near the pond?'

'Well,' said the Grand Pensionary, with the melancholy smile which was habitual to him, 'the gentlemen at the Town Hall anticipate that the people of the Hague would like to see you depart, and there is some apprehension of a disturbance.'

'Of a disturbance?' inquired Cornelius, fixing his eyes on his perplexed brother; 'a disturbance?'

'Yes, Cornelius.'

'Oh! that's what I heard just now,' said the prisoner, as if speaking to himself. Then turning to his brother, he continued,—

'Are there many persons outside the prison?'

'Yes, my brother, there are.'

'But then, to come here to see me—'

'Well?'

'How is it that they have allowed you to pass?'

'You know well that we are not very popular, Cornelius,' said the Grand Pensionary, with gloomy bitterness. 'I have made my way through the back streets and alleys.'

'You hid yourself, John?'

'I wished to reach you without loss of time, and I did what people have to do in politics, or at sea when the wind is against them—I tacked.'

At this moment the tumult in the square below was heard to rise with increasing fury. Tilly was parleying with the burghers.

'Well, well,' said Cornelius, 'you are a very skilful pilot, John; but I doubt whether you will be able to guide your brother out of the Buytenhof in the midst of such a heavy sea, and through the raging surf of popular hatred, as cleverly as you did the fleet of Van Tromp past the shoals of the Scheldt to Antwerp.'

'With the help of God, Cornelius, we'll at least try,' answered John; 'but, first of all, a word with you.'

'What is it?'

The shouts began anew.

'Hark, hark!' continued Cornelius, 'how angry these people are. Is it against you, or against me?'

'I should say it is against us both, Cornelius. I
told you, my dear brother, that the Orange party,
while assailing us with their absurd calumnies, have
also made it a reproach against us that we have
negotiated with France.'

'What blockheads they are!'

'True, but nevertheless they charge us with it.'

'And yet, if these negotiations had been successful, they would have prevented the defeats of Rees,
Orsay, Wesel and Rheinberg; the Rhine would
not have been crossed, and Holland might still
consider herself invincible in the midst of her
marshes and canals.'

'All this is quite true, my dear Cornelius, but
still more certain it is that if at this moment our
correspondence with the Marquis de Louvois were
discovered, skilful pilot as I am, I should not be
able to save the frail bark which is to carry the
brothers De Witte and their fortunes out of Holland.
That correspondence, which might prove to honest
people how dearly I love my country, and what
sacrifices I have offered to make for its liberty
and glory, would be ruin to us if it fell into the
hands of the Orange party. I hope you burnt
the letters before you left Dort to join me at the
Hague.'

'My dear brother,' Cornelius answered, 'your
correspondence with M. de Louvois affords ample
proof of your having been of late the greatest, most
generous and most able citizen of the Seven United
Provinces. I dote on the glory of my country, and
your fame is dearer to me than all the world, John;
therefore I have taken good care not to burn that
correspondence.'

'Then we are lost, as far as this life is concerned,'
quietly observed the Grand Pensionary, approaching the window.

'On the contrary, John, we shall at the same time save our lives and regain our popularity.'

'But what have you done with the letters?'

'I have entrusted them to the care of Cornelius van Baerle, my godson, whom you know, and who lives at Dort.'

'Poor, honest, simple Van Baerle! the scholar who knows so much, and yet thinks of nothing but his flowers and of God who made them. You have entrusted him with this fatal packet; alas, it will be his ruin, poor soul!'

'His ruin?'

'Yes, for he will either be strong or he will be weak. If he is strong, he will, when he hears of what has happened to us, boast of our acquaintance; if he is weak, he will be afraid on account of his intimate connection with us; if he is strong, he will betray the secret by his boldness; if he is weak, he will allow it to be forced from him. In either case he is lost, and so are we. Let us, therefore, fly at once, if it is not already too late.'

Cornelius de Witte, raising himself on his couch, and grasping the hand of his brother, who shuddered at the touch of the linen bandages, replied,—

'Do not I know my godson? Have I not been able to read every thought in Van Baerle's mind and every sentiment in his heart? You ask whether he is strong or weak. He is neither the one nor the other; but that is not now the question. The principal point is, that he is sure not to divulge the secret, for the very good reason that he does not know it himself.'

John turned round in surprise.

'You must know, my dear brother, that the Ruart de Pulten has been trained in the school of that distinguished politician, John de Witte; and I repeat to you that Van Baerle is not aware of the

nature and importance of the deposit which I have
entrusted to him.'

'Quick, then!' cried John, 'as it is still time,
let us convey to him instructions to burn the
parcel.'

'Through whom?'

'Through my servant Craeke, who was to have
accompanied us on horseback, and who entered the
prison with me to assist you downstairs.'

'Consider well before ordering those precious
documents to be burnt, John!'

'I consider, above all things, that the brothers
De Witte must necessarily save their lives to be
able to save their character. If we are dead, who
will defend us? Who will have fully understood
our intentions?'

'Do you think, then, that they would kill us if
those papers were found?'

John, without answering, pointed with his hand
to the square, whence at that very moment fierce
shouts and savage yells were ominously heard.

'Yes, yes,' said Cornelius, 'I hear the shouts very
plainly, but what is their meaning?'

John opened the window.

'Death to the traitors!' howled the populace.

'Do you hear now, Cornelius?'

'To the traitors!—that means us?' said the
prisoner, raising his eyes to heaven and shrugging
his shoulders.

'Yes, it means us,' repeated John.

'Where is Craeke?'

'At the door of your cell, I expect.'

'Let him enter, then.'

John opened the door; the faithful servant was
waiting on the threshold.

'Come in, Craeke, and mind well what my brother
tells you.'

'No, John; it will not suffice to send a verbal messenger; unfortunately I shall be obliged to write.'

'Why?'

'Because Van Baerle will neither give up the parcel, nor burn it, without a special command to do so.'

'But will you be able to write, dear old fellow?' John asked, with a look at the scorched and bruised hands of the unfortunate sufferer.

'If I had pen and ink you would soon see,' said Cornelius.

'Here is a pencil, at anyrate.'

'Have you any paper? for they have left me nothing.'

'Here, take this Bible, and tear out the fly-leaf.'

'Very well, that will do.'

'But your writing will be illegible.'

'Not necessarily,' said Cornelius. 'The executioners, it is true, have pinched me badly enough, but my hand will not tremble in tracing the few lines which are requisite.'

And, truly, Cornelius took the pencil and began to write, whereupon through the white linen bandages drops of blood oozed out, which the pressure of the fingers against the pencil squeezed from the raw wounds.

A cold sweat stood on the brow of the Grand Pensionary.

Meantime Cornelius wrote :—

'AUGUST 20, 1672.

'MY DEAR GODSON,—Burn the parcel which I have entrusted to you. Burn it without looking at it and without opening it, so that its contents may for ever remain unknown to yourself. Secrets of this description are death to those with whom they are deposited. Burn it, and you will have

saved John and Cornelius de Witte.—Farewell,
and love me.   DE WITTE.'

John, with tears in his eyes, wiped off a drop of
the noble blood which had soiled the leaf; and,
having handed the dispatch to Craeke with a last
direction, returned to Cornelius, who seemed overcome by intense pain and near fainting.

'Now,' said he, 'when honest Craeke sounds his
old coxswain's whistle it will be a signal that he is
clear of the crowd and that he has reached the
other side of the pond. And then it will be our
turn to depart.'

Five minutes had not elapsed before a long and
shrill whistle was heard through the din and noise
of the square of the Buytenhof.

John gratefully raised his eyes to heaven.

'And now,' he said, 'Cornelius, let us be off.'

CHAPTER III

JOHN DE WITTE'S PUPIL

WHILE the clamour of the crowd in the square
of the Buytenhof, which grew more and more
menacing against the two brothers, determined
John de Witte to hasten the departure of his
brother Cornelius, a deputation of burghers had
gone to the Town Hall to demand the withdrawal
of Tilly's horse.

It was not far from the Buytenhof to the Hoogstraat (High Street); and a stranger, who since
the beginning of this scene had watched all its

incidents with intense interest, was seen to wend his way with, or rather in the wake of, the others toward the Town Hall, to hear, as soon as possible, the current news of the hour.

This stranger was a young man, of about twenty-two or three, with nothing about him that suggested any great vigour. He evidently had his good reasons for not making himself known, for he concealed his face in a handkerchief of fine Frisian linen, with which he constantly wiped his brow or his burning lips.

With an eye as keen as that of a bird of prey, a long aquiline nose, a finely-cut mouth, which he kept slightly open, and which gaped somewhat like a wound, this man would have presented to Lavater, if Lavater had lived at that time, a subject for physiognomical observations, which at the first blush would not have been very favourable to the person in question.

'What difference can be detected between the features of the conqueror and those of the successful pirate?' asked the ancients. The same difference that there is between the eagle and the vulture—serenity and restlessness.

And, in truth, the sallow physiognomy, the thin and sickly body, and the prowling ways of the stranger, were the very type of a suspecting master or an unquiet thief, and a police officer would certainly have decided in favour of the latter supposition on account of the great care which the mysterious person evidently took to hide his identity.

He was plainly dressed, and apparently unarmed; his arm was lean but wiry, and his hands dry, but of aristocratic whiteness and delicacy, and he leaned on the shoulder of an officer, who, with his hand on his sword, had watched the scenes in

the Buytenhof with eager curiosity, very natural in
a military man, until his companion left the square
and compelled him to follow.

On arriving at the square of the Hoogstraat, the
man with the sallow face pushed the other behind
an open shutter, and fixed his eye upon the balcony
of the Town Hall.

At the savage yells of the mob the window of
the Town Hall opened, and a man came forth to
parley with the people.

'Who is that on the balcony?' the young man
asked, glancing at the orator.

'It is the deputy Bowelt,' replied the officer.

'What sort of man is he? Do you know anything of him?'

'An honest man; at least I believe so, Monseigneur.'

Hearing this estimation given of Bowelt's
character, the young man showed signs of a strange
disappointment and such evident dissatisfaction
that the officer could not but remark it, and thereupon hastily added,—

'At least people say so, monseigneur. I cannot
say anything about it myself, as I have no personal
acquaintance with Mynheer Bowelt.'

'An honest man,' the young man muttered half
to himself and half to his companion; 'let us wait
and we shall soon see.'

The officer bowed his head in token of his
assent, and was silent.

'If this Bowelt is an honest man,' His Highness
continued, 'he will give to the demand of these
hot-headed petitioners a very queer reception.'

The nervous quiver of his hand, which moved
on the shoulder of his companion, as the fingers of
a player on the keys of a harpsichord, betrayed
his burning impatience, so ill-concealed at certain

times, and particularly at that moment, under the cold and sombre expression of his face.

The chief of the deputation of the burghers was then heard interrogating Mynheer Bowelt, and requested him to let them know where the other deputies, his colleagues, were.

'Gentlemen,' Bowelt repeated for the second time, 'I assure you that in this moment I am here alone with Mynheer d'Asperen, and I cannot take any resolution on my own responsibility.'

'The order! we want the order!' cried several thousand voices.

Mynheer Bowelt attempted to address the mob, but his words were not heard, and he was only seen moving his arms in all sorts of gestures, which plainly showed that he felt his position to be desperate. When, at last, he saw that he could not make himself heard, he turned round towards the open window, and called Mynheer d'Asperen.

The latter gentleman now made his appearance on the balcony, where he was saluted with shouts, even more energetic than those with which, ten minutes before, his colleague had been received.

This did not prevent him from undertaking the difficult task of haranguing the mob; but the mob preferred to try to force the guard of the States— which, however, offered no resistance to the sovereign people—rather than to listen to the speech of Mynheer d'Asperen.

'Come,' the young man coolly remarked, whilst the crowd was rushing into the principal gate of the Town Hall, 'it seems the question will be discussed indoors, Captain. Come along, and let us hear the debate.'

'Oh, Monseigneur! Monseigneur! take care!'

'Of what?'

'Among these deputies there are many who

have had dealings with you; and it would be
sufficient if only one of them should recognise
Your Highness.'

'Yes, that I might be charged with having been
the instigator of all this work; indeed, you are
right,' said the young man, colouring for a moment
from regret at having betrayed so much eagerness.
'From this place we shall see them return with or
without the order for the withdrawal of the
dragoons, and then we may judge which is greater,
Mynheer Bowelt's honesty or his courage.'

'Why,' replied the officer, looking with astonishment at the personage whom he addressed as
Monseigneur, 'why, Your Highness surely does
not suppose for one instant that the deputies will
order Tilly's horse to quit their post?'

'Why not?' asked the young man, cynically.

'Because to do so would simply mean the sign-
ing the death warrant of Cornelius and John de
Witte.'

'We shall see,' His Highness replied with the
utmost calm. 'God alone knows what is going on
within the hearts of men.'

The officer looked askance at the impassible
figure of his companion, and grew pale: *he* was an
honest man as well as a brave one.

From the spot where they stood, His Highness
and his attendant heard the tumult and the heavy
tramp of the crowd on the staircase of the Town
Hall. Then the noise sounded through the windows
of the hall, on the balcony of which Mynheers
Bowelt and d'Asperen had presented themselves.
These two gentlemen had retired into the building,
very likely from fear of being forced over the
balustrade into the street by the pressure of the
crowd.

After this, fluctuating shadows in tumultuous

confusion were seen flitting to and fro across the windows: the council hall was filling.

Suddenly the noise subsided; and as suddenly again it rose with redoubled intensity, and at last reached such a pitch that the old building shook to the very roof.

At length, the living stream poured back through the galleries and stairs to the arched gateway, from which it was seen issuing like water from a spout.

At the head of the first group, a man was flying rather than running, his face hideously distorted with Satanic glee: this man was the surgeon, Tyckelaer.

'We have it! we have it!' he cried, brandishing a paper in the air.

'They have got the order!' muttered the officer in amazement.

'Well, then,' His Highness quietly remarked, 'now I know what to believe with regard to Mynheer Bowelt's honesty and courage: he has neither the one nor the other.'

Then, looking with a steady glance after the crowd which was rushing along before him, he continued,—

'Let us now go to the Buytenhof, Captain; I expect we shall see a very strange sight there.'

The officer bowed, and, without making any reply, followed in the steps of his master.

There was an immense crowd in the square and about the neighbourhood of the prison. But Tilly's dragoons kept it in check, with the same success and with the same firmness as before.

It was not long before the Count heard the increasing din of the approaching multitude, the first ranks of which rushed on with the rapidity of a cataract.

At the same time, he observed the paper which was waving above the surface of clenched fists and glittering weapons.

'Aha!' he said, rising in his stirrups and touching his lieutenant with the knob of his sword; 'I really believe these rascals have got the order.'

'What dastardly ruffians they are!' cried the lieutenant.

It was indeed the order, which the burgher-guard received with a roar of triumph. They immediately sallied forth, with lowered arms and fierce shouts, to meet Count Tilly's dragoons.

But the Count was not the man to allow them to approach too near.

'Stop!' he cried, 'stop, and keep away from my horse, or I shall give the word of command to advance.'

'Here is the order,' a hundred insolent voices cried at once.

He took it in amazement, cast a rapid glance on it, and said aloud,—

'The men who signed this order are the real murderers of Cornelius de Witte. I would rather have my two hands cut off than have written one single letter of this infamous order.'

And, pushing back with the hilt of his sword the man who wanted to take it from him, he added,—

'Wait a minute, papers like this are of importance, and should be preserved.'

Saying this, he carefully folded up the document, and put it in the pocket of his doublet.

Then, turning round towards his troop, he gave the word of command,—

'Dragoons! Attention! Right wheel!'

After this he added in an undertone, yet loud enough for his words to be not altogether lost to those around him,—

'And now, butchers, do your work!'

A savage yell, in which all the keen hatred and ferocious triumph rife in the precincts of the prison simultaneously burst forth and shot after the dragoons as they quietly filed away.

The Count tarried behind to the last, facing the infuriated populace, which advanced at the same rate as the Count retired.

John de Witte, it will be seen, had by no means exaggerated the danger when he assisted his brother to rise and endeavoured to hasten his departure. Cornelius, leaning on the arm of the Grand Pensionary, descended the stairs which led to the courtyard. At the bottom of the staircase he found little Rosa trembling like a leaf in the wind.

'Oh! Mynheer John,' she said, 'what a misfortune!'

'What is it, my child?' asked De Witte.

'They say that they are gone to the Town Hall to fetch the order for Tilly's horse to withdraw.'

'You do not say so!' replied John. 'Indeed, my dear child, if the dragoons are withdrawn we shall be in a very sad plight.'

'I have some advice to give you,' Rosa said, trembling even more violently than before.

'Well, let us hear what you have to say, my child. Why should not God speak by your mouth?'

'Well, then, Mynheer John, if I were in your place, I should not go out through the High Street.'

'And why so, as the dragoons of Tilly are still at their post?'

'Yes, but their order, as long as it is not revoked, enjoins them to stop before the prison.'

'Undoubtedly.'

'Have you got an order for them to accompany
you out of the town?'

'We have not.'

'Well, then, at the very moment when you pass
the ranks of the dragoons you will fall into the
hands of the people.'

'But the burgher-guard?'

'Alas! the burgher-guard are the most enraged
and furious of all.'

'What are we to do, then?'

'If I were in your place, Mynheer John,' the
young girl timidly continued, 'I should leave by
the postern, which leads into a deserted bye-lane,
whilst all the people are waiting in the High Street
to see you come out by the principal entrance.
Thence I should try to reach the gate by which
you intend to leave the town.'

'But my brother is not able to walk,' said John.

'I shall try,' Cornelius said, with an expression
of most sublime fortitude.

'But have you not got your carriage?' asked the
girl.

'The carriage is down near the great entrance.'

'Not so,' she replied. 'I considered your coachman to be a faithful man, and I told him to wait
for you at the postern.'

The two brothers looked first at each other, and
then at Rosa, with a glance full of the most tender
gratitude.

'The question is now,' said the Grand Pensionary,
'whether Gryphus will open this door for us.'

'Indeed, he will do no such thing,' said Rosa.

'Then what are we to do?'

'I have foreseen his refusal, and just now, whilst
he was talking from the window of the porter's
lodge with a dragoon, I took away the key from
his bunch.'

' And you have got it ? '

' Here it is, Mynheer John.'

' My child,' said Cornelius, ' I have nothing to give you in exchange for the service you are rendering us but the Bible which you will find in my room : it is the last gift of an honest man ; I hope it will bring you good luck.'

' I thank you, Mynheer Cornelius ; it shall never leave me,' replied Rosa.

And then, with a sigh, she said to herself, ' What a pity I do not know how to read ! '

' The shouts and cries are growing louder and louder,' said John ; ' we have not a moment to lose.'

' Come along, gentlemen,' cried the girl, who now led the two brothers through an inner lobby to the back of the prison. Guided by her, they descended a staircase of about a dozen steps, traversed a small courtyard, which was surrounded by castellated walls ; and the arched door having been opened for them by Rosa, they emerged into a lonely street where their carriage was ready to receive them.

' Quick, quick, my masters, do you hear them ? ' cried the coachman, in a deadly fright.

Yet, after having made Cornelius get into the carriage first, the Grand Pensionary turned round towards the girl, to whom he said,—

' Goodbye, my child, words could never express our gratitude. God will reward you for having saved the lives of two men.'

Rosa took the hand which John de Witte proffered to her, and kissed it with every show of respect.

' Go—for Heaven's sake go,' she said ; ' they are going to force the gate.'

John de Witte hastily got in, sat himself down

by the side of his brother, and called out to the coachman,—

'To the Tol-Hek!'

The Tol-Hek was the iron gate leading to the harbour of Schevening, in which a small vessel was waiting for the two brothers.

The carriage drove off with the fugitives at the full speed of a pair of spirited Flemish horses. Rosa followed them with her eyes until they turned the corner of the street, upon which, closing the door after her, she went back and threw the key into a well.

The noise which had made Rosa suppose that the people were forcing the prison door, was, indeed, owing to the mob battering against it after the square had been deserted by the military.

Solid as the gate was, and although Gryphus, to do him justice, stoutly enough refused to open it, yet it could not evidently resist much longer, and the jailor, growing very pale, asked himself whether it would not be better to open the door than to allow it to be forced, when he felt someone gently pulling his coat.

He turned round and saw Rosa.

'Do you hear these madmen?' he said.

'I hear them so well, my father, that in your place—'

'You would open the door?'

'No; I should allow it to be forced.'

'But they will kill me!'

'Yes, if they see you.'

'How shall they not see me?'

'Hide yourself.'

'Where?'

'In the secret dungeon.'

'But you, my child?'

'I shall get into it with you. We shall lock the

door, and when they have left the prison, we can come forth from our hiding-place.'

'By Heaven, you are right there!' cried Gryphus; 'it's surprising how much sense there is in this little head!'

Then, as the gate began to give way amidst the triumphant shouts of the mob, she opened a little trap-door, and said,—

'Come, father, come along.'

'But what of our prisoners?'

'God will watch over them, and I shall watch over you.'

Gryphus followed his daughter, and the trap-door closed over his head just as the broken gate gave admittance to the populace.

The dungeon where Rosa had induced her father to hide himself, and where for the present we must leave the two, offered to them a perfectly safe retreat, being known only to those in power, who used to place there important prisoners of state, to guard against a rescue or an uprising.

The people rushed into the prison with the cry of,—

'Death to the traitors! To the gallows with Cornelius de Witte! Death! death!'

—————

CHAPTER IV

ROUGH JUSTICE

THE young man, with his hat still drawn over his eyes, still leaning on the arm of the officer, and still wiping from time to time his brow with his handkerchief, was watching in a corner of the Buytenhof, under the shades of the overhanging weatherboard of a closed shop, the antics of the infuriated mob, a spectacle which seemed to draw near its catastrophe.

'Indeed,' said he to the officer, 'indeed, I think you were right, Van Deken; the order which the deputies have signed is in reality the death-warrant of Mynheer Cornelius. Do you hear these people? They certainly bear great enmity towards the two De Wittes.'

'In truth,' replied the officer, 'I never heard such an uproar.'

'They must have found out the cell of the man. Look, look, is not that the window of the cell where Cornelius was incarcerated?'

A man had seized the iron bars of the window, in the room which Cornelius had left only ten minutes before, and with both hands was shaking them violently.

'Halloa, halloa,' the man called out, 'he has escaped.'

'How is that? escaped?' asked those of the mob who had not been able to get into the prison, crowded as it was with the mass of intruders.

'Gone, gone,' repeated the man in a rage, 'the bird has flown.'

'What does this man say?' asked His Highness, growing quite pale.

'Oh! Monseigneur, he says a thing which would be very fortunate if it should turn out true!'

'Certainly, it would be fortunate if it were true,' said the young man; 'unfortunately it cannot be true.'

'However, look—' said the officer.

And, indeed, some more faces, furious and contorted with rage, showed themselves at the windows, crying,—

'Escaped, gone, they have assisted them to fly!'

And the people in the street repeated with fearful imprecations,—

'Escaped! gone! Let us run after them and hunt them down like dogs!'

'Monseigneur, it seems that Mynheer Cornelius has really escaped,' said the officer.

'Yes, from prison perhaps, but not from the town; you will see, Van Deken, that the poor fellow will find the gate closed against him, which he hoped to find open.'

'Has an order been given to close the town gates, Monseigneur?'

'No, at least I do not think so; who could have given such an order?'

'Who, indeed? But what makes your Highness suppose—?'

'There are fatalities,' Monseigneur replied, in an off-hand manner; 'and the greatest men have sometimes fallen victims to them.'

At these words the officer felt his blood run cold, as somehow or other he was convinced that the prisoner's fate was sealed.

At this moment the roar of the multitude broke forth like thunder, for it was now quite certain that Cornelius de Witte was no longer in the prison.

Cornelius and John, after driving along the edge of the pond, had taken the main street which leads to the Tol Hek, giving directions to the coachman to slacken his pace in order not to excite any suspicion.

But when, on having proceeded half-way down that street, the man felt that he had left the prison and death behind, and before him there was life and liberty, he neglected every precaution, and set his horses off at a gallop.

All at once he stopped.

'What is the matter?' asked John, putting his head out of the coach window.

'Oh! my masters,' cried the coachman, 'it is—'

Terror choked the voice of the honest fellow.

'Well, say what you have to say!' urged the Grand Pensionary.

'The gate is closed, that's what it is.'

'How is this? It is not usual to close the gate by day.'

'Just look!'

John de Witte leaned out of the window, and indeed saw that the man was right.

'Never mind, drive on,' said John; 'I have with me the order for the commutation of the punishment, the gatekeeper will allow us to depart.'

The carriage moved onward again, but it was evident that the driver was no longer urging his horses with the same degree of confidence.

Moreover, as John de Witte put his head out of the carriage window, he was seen and recognised by a brewer, who, being behind his companions, was just shutting his door in all haste to join them at the Buytenhof. He uttered a cry of surprise, and ran after two other men before him, whom he overtook about a hundred yards further on, and told them what he had seen. The three men then stopped, and looked after the carriage, being, however, not yet quite sure whom it contained.

The carriage, in the meanwhile, arrived at the Tol-Hek.

'Open!' cried the coachman.

'Open!' echoed the gatekeeper, from the threshold of his lodge; 'it's all very well to say open, but what am I to do it with?'

'With the key, to be sure,' said the coachman.

'With the key! Oh, yes! but if one has not got it?'

'What! Have you not got the key?' demanded the coachman.

'No, I haven't.'

'What has become of it?'

'Well, they have taken it from me.'

'Who?'

'Some one, I should imagine, who had a mind that no one should leave the town.'

'My good man,' said the Grand Pensionary, putting his head out from the window, and risking all to gain all; 'my good man, it is for me, John de Witte, and for my brother Cornelius, whom I am taking away into exile.'

'Oh! Mynheer de Witte, I am indeed very much grieved,' said the gatekeeper, rushing towards the carriage; 'but, upon my sacred word, the key has been taken from me.'

'When?'

'This morning.'

'By whom?'

'By a pale and thin young man of about twenty-two.'

'But why did you give it up to him?'

'Because he showed me an order, signed and sealed.'

'By whom?'

'By the gentlemen of the Town Hall.'

'Well, then,' said Cornelius, calmly, 'our doom seems to be fixed.'

'Do you know whether the same precaution has been taken at all the other gates?'

'I do not.'

'Now, then,' said John to the coachman, 'God commands man to do all that is in his power to preserve his life; drive at once to another gate.'

While the servant was turning round the vehicle, the Grand Pensionary said to the gatekeeper,—

'Take our thanks for your good intentions; the will must count for the deed; you had the will to save us, and, in the eyes of the Lord, it is as if you had succeeded in doing so.'

'Alas!' said the gatekeeper, 'do you see what is taking place down there?'

'Drive at a gallop through that group,' John called out to the coachman, 'and take the street on the left; it is our only chance.'

The group to which John alluded had, for its nucleus, those three men whom we left looking after the carriage, and who, in the meantime, had been joined by seven or eight others.

These new-comers evidently meditated mischief towards the carriage.

When they saw the horses galloping down upon them, they placed themselves across the street, brandishing cudgels in their hands, and calling out,—

'Stop! stop!'

The coachman, however, lashed his horses into increased speed, until the coach and the men encountered.

The brothers De Witte, inclosed within the body of the carriage, were not able to see anything; but they felt a severe shock, occasioned by the rearing of the horses. The whole vehicle for a moment shook, and stopped; but immediately after, passing over something round and elastic, which seemed to be the body of a prostrate man, set off again amid a volley of the fiercest oaths.

'Alas!' said Cornelius, 'I am afraid we have hurt someone.'

'Faster! gallop faster!' called John.

But notwithstanding this order, the coachman suddenly came to a stop.

'Now then, what is the matter again?' inquired John.

'Look there!' said the coachman.

John looked. The whole mass of the people from the Buytenhof appeared at the extremity of the street along which the carriage was proceeding, and its stream came roaring and rapid, as if lashed on by a hurricane.

'Stop, and get down,' said John to the coachman; 'it is useless to go any further; we are lost!'

'Here they are! here they are!' five hundred voices were crying at the same time.

'Yes, here they are, the traitors, the murderers, the assassins!' answered the men who were running after the carriage to the people who were coming to meet it. The former carried in their arms the lifeless body of one of their companions, who, trying to seize the reins of the horses, had been trodden down by them.

This was the object over which the two brothers had felt their carriage pass.

The coachman stopped, but, however strongly his master urged him, he refused to get off and save himself.

In an instant the carriage was surrounded by those who followed and those who met it. It rose above the mass of moving heads like a floating island. But, in another instant, it came to a dead stop. A blacksmith had, with his hammer, struck down one of the horses, which fell in his traces.

At this moment the shutter of a window opened and disclosed the sallow face and the dark eyes of the young man, who, with intense interest, watched the scene which promised a tragic termination.

Behind him appeared the face of the officer, almost as pale as himself.

'Good heavens, Monseigneur, what is going to happen?' whispered the officer.

'Something very terrible, to a certainty,' replied the other.

'Don't you see, Monseigneur, they are dragging the Grand Pensionary from the carriage, they strike him, they tear him to pieces.'

'Indeed, these people must certainly be prompted by a most violent indignation,' said the young man, with the same impassible tone which he had preserved throughout.

'And here is Cornelius, whom they now likewise drag out of the carriage—Cornelius, who is already quite broken and mangled by the torture. Only look, look!'

'Indeed, it is Cornelius, beyond a doubt.'

The officer uttered a feeble cry, and turned his head away; the brother of the Grand Pensionary, before having set foot on the ground, whilst still on the bottom step of the carriage, was struck down with an iron bar which broke his skull. He rose once more, but immediately fell again.

Some fellows then seized him by the feet, and dragged him into the crowd, into the middle of which one might have followed his bloody track, and he was soon closed in among the savage yells of malignant exultation.

The young man—a thing which would have been thought impossible—grew even paler than before, and his eyes were, for a moment, veiled behind the lids.

The officer saw this sign of compassion, and,

wishing to avail himself of the softened mood of
his feelings, continued,—

'Come, come, Monseigneur, look, they are also
going to murder the Grand Pensionary.'

But the young man had already opened his eyes
again.

'To be sure,' he said. 'These people are really
implacable. It does little good to offend them.'

'Monseigneur,' said the officer, 'could we not
save this poor man, who was your Highness's
instructor? If there be a means, tell me, and
though I perish in the attempt—'

William of Orange—for he it was—knit his
brows in a very forbidding manner, restrained the
glance of gloomy malice which glistened in his
half-closed eye, and answered,—

'Captain van Deken, I request you to go and
look after my troops, that they may be armed for
any emergency.'

'But am I to leave your Highness here, alone,
almost in the clutch of all these murderers?'

'Go, and don't you trouble yourself about me
more than I do myself,' the Prince gruffly replied.

The officer started off with a speed which was
much less owing to his sense of military obedience
than to his pleasure at being relieved from the
necessity of witnessing the shocking spectacle of
the murder of the other brother.

He had scarcely left the room when John—who
with an almost superhuman effort had reached the
stone steps of a house nearly opposite that where
his former pupil concealed himself—began to
stagger under the blows which were inflicted on
him from all sides, calling out,—

'My brother—where is my brother?'

One of the ruffians knocked off his hat with a
blow of his clenched fist.

Another showed to him his bloody hands; for this vagabond had ripped open Cornelius and disembowelled him, and was now hastening to the spot in order not to lose the opportunity of serving the Grand Pensionary in the same manner, whilst they were dragging the dead body of Cornelius to the gibbet.

John uttered a cry of agony and grief, and put one of his hands before his eyes.

'Oh! you close your eyes, do you?' said one of the soldiers of the burgher-guard; 'well, I shall open them for you.'

And saying this, he stabbed him with his pike in the face, and the blood spurted forth.

'My brother!' cried John de Witte, trying to see, through the stream of blood which blinded him, what had become of Cornelius; 'my brother, my brother!'

'Go, and run after him!' bellowed another murderer, putting his musket to his temples, and pulling the trigger.

But the gun did not go off.

The fellow then turned his musket round, and, taking it by the barrel with both hands, struck John de Witte down with the butt-end. John staggered, and fell down at his feet, but raising himself, with a last effort, he once more called out, 'My brother!' with a voice so full of anguish that the young man opposite closed the shutter.

However, the end was near; a third murderer fired a pistol with the muzzle to his face; and as this time the shot took effect, blowing out his brains, John de Witte fell, to rise no more.

On this, every one of the miscreants, emboldened by his fall, wanted to fire his gun at him, or strike him with a sledge-hammer, or stab him with knife or sword; everyone wanted to draw a drop of blood from the fallen hero, and tear off a shred of his garments.

Then after they had mangled, and torn, and completely stripped the two brothers, the mob dragged their naked and bloody bodies to an extemporised gibbet, where amateur executioners hung them up by the feet.

Then came the most dastardly scoundrels of all, who, not having dared to strike the living flesh, cut the dead in pieces, and then went about in the town selling small slices of the bodies of John and Cornelius at ten sous a piece.

It cannot be definitely stated whether, through the almost imperceptible chink of the shutter, the young man witnessed the conclusion of this shocking scene; but at the very moment when they were hanging the two martyrs on the gibbet, he sped through the terrible mob, which was too much absorbed in their bloody task to take any notice of him, and unobserved he reached the Tol-Hek, which was still closed.

'Ah, Mynheer,' said the gatekeeper, 'have you brought me the key?'

'Yes, my man, here it is.'

'It is most unfortunate that you did not bring me the key only one quarter of an hour sooner,' said the gatekeeper, with a sigh.

'Why so?' asked the other.

'Because I might have opened the gate to Mynheers de Witte; whereas, finding the gate locked, they were obliged to retrace their steps.'

'Gate! gate!' cried a voice which seemed to be that of a man in a great hurry.

The Prince, turning round, observed Captain van Deken.

'Is that you, Captain?' he said, 'You are not

yet out of the Hague? This is executing my orders very slowly.'

'Monseigneur,' replied the Captain, 'this is the third gate at which I have presented myself; the two others were shut.'

'Well, this good man will open this one for you; do it, my friend.'

The last words were addressed to the gate-keeper, who stood quite thunderstruck on hearing Captain van Deken address by the title of Monseigneur this pale young man to whom he himself had spoken in such a familiar way.

Endeavouring to make up for his fault, he hastened to open the gate, which swung creaking on its hinges.

'Will Monseigneur avail himself of my horse?' asked the Captain.

'I thank you, Captain, but I have a mount awaiting me close at hand.'

And taking from his pocket a golden whistle, such as was generally used at that time for summoning servants, he sounded it with a shrill and prolonged call, on which an equerry on horseback speedily made his appearance, leading another horse by the bridle.

William, without touching the stirrup, vaulted into the saddle of the led horse, and, setting his spurs into its flanks, started off for the Leyden road. Having reached it, he turned round and beckoned to the Captain, who was far behind, to ride beside him.

'Do you know,' he then said, without stopping, 'that those rascals have killed John de Witte as well as his brother?'

'Alas! Monseigneur,' the Captain answered sadly. 'I should like it much better if these two obstacles still existed between your Highness's way and the actual Stadholderate of Holland.'

'Certainly, it would have been better,' said William, 'if what did happen had not happened. But it cannot be helped now, and we have had nothing to do with it. Let us push on, Captain, that we may arrive at Alphen before the message which the States-General are sure to send to me in camp.'

The Captain bowed, allowed the Prince to ride ahead, and, for the remainder of the journey, kept at the same respectful distance he had occupied before His Highness addressed him.

'Ah! how I should like,' William of Orange malignantly muttered to himself, with a dark frown, as he drove his spurs into his horse, 'to see the expression on Louis's face when he is apprised of the manner in which his dear friends De Witte have been served!'

CHAPTER V

THE TULIP-FANCIER AND HIS NEIGHBOUR

WHILE the burghers of the Hague were tearing the bodies of John and Cornelius de Witte to pieces, and while William of Orange, after having made sure that his two antagonists were really dead, was galloping on the Leyden road, followed by Captain van Deken, whom he found a little too compassionate to honour him any longer with his confidence, Craeke, the faithful servant, mounted on a good horse, and little suspecting what terrible events had taken place since his departure, proceeded along the high road lined with trees, until he was clear of the town and the neighbouring villages.

Being once safe, he, with a view of avoiding suspicion, left his horse at a livery stable, and tranquilly continuing his journey by the canal boats to Dort, soon descried that pleasant city at the foot of a hill dotted with windmills. He saw the fine red brick houses standing in white lines on the edge of the water with their balconies open towards the river, decked out with silk tapestry embroidered with gold flowers, and near these brilliant stuffs, large lines set to catch the voracious eels, which are attracted towards the houses by the food thrown every day from the kitchens into the river.

Craeke, standing on the deck of the boat, saw, across the moving sails of the windmills, on the slope of the hill, the red and pink house which was his goal. The outlines of its roof were concealed by the yellow foliage of a curtain of poplar trees, the whole habitation having for background a dark grove of gigantic elms.

Having disembarked unobserved amid the usual bustle of the city, Craeke at once directed his steps toward the house which—white, trim and tidy, even more cleanly scoured and more carefully waxed in the hidden corners than in the places which were exposed to view—domiciled a truly happy mortal.

This happy mortal, *rara avis*, was Doctor van Baerle, the godson of Cornelius de Witte. He had inhabited the same house ever since his childhood ; for it was the house in which his father and grandfather, old-established noble merchants of the princely city of Dort, were born,

Mynheer van Baerle, the father, had amassed, in the Indian trade, three or four hundred thousand guilders, which Mynheer van Baerle, the son, at the death of his dear and worthy parents, in 1688, found still quite new, although one set of them bore the date of coinage of 1640, and the other that of 1610, a fact which proved that they were guilders of Van Baerle the father, and of Van Baerle the grandfather; but we hasten to observe that these three or four hundred thousand guilders were only the pocket-money, or a sort of purse, for Cornelius van Baerle, the hero of this story, as his landed property in the province yielded him an income of about ten thousand guilders a year.

When the worthy citizen, the father of Cornelius, passed from time into eternity, three months after the decease of his wife, who seemed to have departed first to smooth for him the path of death as she had smoothed for him the path of life, he said to his son, as he embraced him for the last time,—

'Eat, drink, and spend your money if you wish to know what life really is; for as to toiling from morn to evening on a wooden stool, or a leathern chair, in a counting-house or a laboratory, that certainly is not living. Your time to die will come in due course; and if you are not then so fortunate as to have a son, you will let my name grow extinct, and my guilders, which no one has ever fingered but my father, myself and the coiner, will have to pass into unknown hands. Above all, avoid imitating the example of your godfather, Cornelius de Witte, who has plunged into politics, the most ungrateful of all careers, and who will certainly come to an untimely end.'

Having given utterance to this paternal advice

the worthy Mynheer van Baerle died, to the intense grief of his son Cornelius, who cared very little for the guilders, and very much for his father.

Thereafter, Cornelius lived alone in his large house. In vain his godfather offered him a place in the public service; in vain did he try to create in him a taste for glory. Cornelius van Baerle, who was present in De Ruyter's flagship, *The Seven Provinces*, at the battle of Southwold Bay, only calculated, after the fight was over, how much time a man, who likes to shut himself up within his own thoughts, is obliged to waste in closing his eyes and stopping his ears while his fellow-creatures indulge in the pleasure of shooting at each other with cannon balls. He, therefore, bade farewell to De Ruyter, to his godfather, and to glory, kissed the hands of the Grand Pensionary, for whom he felt a profound veneration, and retired to his house at Dort, where he possessed every element of what alone was happiness to him.

He studied plants and insects, collected and classified the Flora of all the Dutch islands, arranged the whole entomology of the province, on which he wrote a treatise, with plates drawn by his own hands; and at last, being at a loss what to do with his time, and especially with his money, which went on accumulating at a most alarming rate, he took it into his head to select for himself, from all the follies of his country and of his age, one of the most elegant and expensive of all fads —that of tulip fancier.

It was the time when the Dutch and the Portuguese, rivalling each other in this branch of horticulture, had begun to idolise and almost worship that flower, which had originally come from the East.

Soon people from Dort to Mons began to talk

of Mynheer van Baerle's tulips; and his beds, pits,
drying-rooms and drawers of bulbs were visited, as
the galleries and libraries of Alexandria in olden
times were by illustrious Roman travellers.

Van Baerle began by expending his yearly
revenue in laying the ground-work of his collec-
tion, after which he broke in upon his new guilders
to bring it to perfection. His exertions, indeed,
were crowned with a most magnificent result : he
produced three new tulips, which he called the
'Jane,' after his mother ; the 'Van Baerle,' after his
father ; and the 'Cornelius,' after his godfather ; the
other names have escaped us, but amateurs will be
sure to find them in the catalogues of the period.

In the beginning of the year 1672, Cornelius de
Witte came to Dort for three months, to live at his
old family mansion; for not only was he born in
that city, but his family had dwelt there for
centuries.

Cornelius, at that time, as William of Orange
said, began to enjoy the most perfect unpopularity.
To his fellow-citizens, the good burghers of Dort,
however, he did not appear in the light of a
criminal who deserved to be hung. It is true, they
did not particularly like his somewhat too austere
republicanism, but they were proud of his valour ;
and when he made his entrance into their town,
the cup of honour was offered to him, readily
enough, in the name of the city.

After having thanked his fellow-citizens, Cornelius
proceeded to his old paternal house, and gave
directions for some repairs, which he wished to
have executed before the arrival of his wife and
children ; and thence he wended his way to the
house of his godson, who, perhaps, was the only
person in Dort as yet unacquainted with the
presence of Cornelius in his native town.

In the same degree as Cornelius de Witte had excited the hatred of the people, by sowing those evil seeds which are called political passions, Van Baerle had gained the affections of his fellow-citizens by completely shunning the pursuit of politics, absorbed as he was in the peaceful pursuit of cultivating tulips.

Van Baerle was truly beloved by his servants and labourers; nor had he any conception that there was in this world a man who could wish ill to another.

And yet it must be said, to the disgrace of mankind, that Cornelius van Baerle, without being aware of the fact, had a much more ferocious, fierce, and implacable enemy than the Grand Pensionary and his brother had among the Orange party.

At about the time when Cornelius van Baerle began to devote himself to tulip-growing, expending on this hobby his yearly revenue and the guilders of his father, there was at Dort, living next door to him, a citizen of the name of Isaac Boxtel, who, from the age when he was able to think for himself, had indulged the same fancy, and who was in ecstacies at the mere mention of the word tulip.

Boxtel had not the good fortune of being rich like Van Baerle. He had, therefore, with great care and patience, and by dint of strenuous exertions, laid out, near his house at Dort, a garden fit for the culture of his cherished flower; he had mixed the soil according to the most approved prescriptions, and given to his hotbeds just as much heat and fresh air as the strictest rules of horticulture exact.

Isaac knew the temperature of his frames to the twentieth part of a degree. He knew the strength of the current of air, and tempered it so as to adapt it to the motion of the stems of his flowers. His productions also began to meet with the favour of the public. They were beautiful and much sought after. Several fanciers visited Boxtel to see his tulips. At last he planted a tulip which bore his name, and which, after having travelled all through France, had found its way into Spain, and penetrated as far as Portugal; and the King, Don Alphonso VI.—who, being expelled from Lisbon, retired to the Island of Terceira, where he amused himself, not, like the Great Condé, with watering his carnations, but with growing tulips—had, on seeing the Boxtel tulip, exclaimed, 'Not so bad, by the mass.'

All at once, Cornelius van Baerle, who, after all his learned pursuits, had been seized with the tulipomania, made some changes in his house at Dort, which, as we have stated, was next door to that of Boxtel. He raised a certain building in his courtyard by a storey, which, shutting out the sun, took half a degree of warmth from Boxtel's garden, and, on the other hand, returned half a degree of cold in winter; not to mention that it cut the wind, and disturbed all the horticultural calculations and arrangements of his neighbour.

After all, this mishap appeared to Boxtel of no great consequence. Van Baerle was but a painter, a sort of fool who tried to reproduce, and disfigure on canvas, the wonders of nature. The painter, he thought, had raised his studio by a storey to get better light, and thus he had only been in the right. Mynheer van Baerle was a painter, as Mynheer Boxtel was a tulip-grower; he wanted somewhat more sun for his paintings, and he took half a degree from his neighbour's tulips.

The law was with Van Baerle, and Boxtel had to make the best of it.

Moreover, Isaac discovered that too much sun was injurious to tulips, and that this delicate flower grew quicker, and had a better colouring, with the temperate warmth of morning than with the powerful heat of the midday sun. He, therefore, felt almost grateful to Cornelius van Baerle for having given him a screen gratis.

Maybe this was not quite in accordance with the true state of things in general, and of Isaac Boxtel's feelings in particular. But great minds find rich comfort in the midst of terrible catastrophes, which they derive from the consolations of philosophy.

But, alas! what was the agony of the unfortunate Boxtel on seeing the windows of the new storey set out with bulbs and seedlings of tulips in full bloom, and tulips in pots; in short, with everything dear to the tulip-fancier.

There were bundles of labels, pigeon-holes, and drawers with compartments, and wire-guards for the cupboards, to allow free access to the air whilst keeping out slugs, mice, dormice, and rats, all of them very curious and inquisitive fanciers of tulips at two thousand francs a bulb.

Boxtel was quite amazed when he saw all this apparatus, but he was not as yet aware of the full extent of his misfortune. Van Baerle was known to be fond of everything that pleases the eye. He studied nature in all her aspects for the benefit of his paintings, which were as minutely finished as those of Gerard Dow, his master, and of Mieris, his friend. Was it not possible that, having to paint the interior of a tulip-grower's, he had collected in his new studio all the accessories of decoration?

Yet, although thus somewhat consoling himself with illusory suppositions, Boxtel was not able to resist the burning curiosity which was devouring him. In the evening, therefore, he placed a ladder against the partition-wall between the two gardens, and, looking into that of his neighbour Van Baerle, he convinced himself that the soil of a large square bed, which had formerly been occupied by different plants, had been dug up, and the ground disposed in beds of loam mixed with river mud (a combination which is particularly favourable to the tulip), and the whole surrounded by a border of turf to keep the soil in its place. Besides this, the bed was so arranged as to receive the rays of the rising and setting sun, and sufficiently shaded to temper the noon-day heat; water in abundant supply was close at hand ; and, in short, every requirement to ensure not only success but also progress. There could not be a doubt that Van Baerle had become a tulip-grower.

Boxtel at once pictured to himself this learned man, with a capital of four hundred thousand, and a yearly income of ten thousand guilders, devoting all his intellectual and financial resources to the cultivation of the tulip. He foresaw his neighbour's success, and he felt such a pang at the mere idea of this success, that his hands dropped powerless, his knees trembled, and he fell in despair from the ladder.

Thus it was not for the sake of painted tulips, but for real ones, that Van Baerle took from him half a degree of warmth. And thus Van Baerle was to have the most admirably-fitted aspect, and besides, a large, airy and well-ventilated chamber in which to preserve his bulbs and seedlings ; whilst he, Boxtel, had been obliged to give up for this purpose his bedroom, and, lest his sleeping in the same apartment might injure his bulbs and seedlings, had taken up his abode in a miserable garret.

Boxtel, then, was to have next door to him a
rival and successful competitor; and his rival,
instead of being some unknown, obscure gardener,
was the godson of Mynheer Cornelius de Witte,
that is to say, a celebrity.

Boxtel, as a reader may see, was not possessed
of the spirit of Porus, who, on being conquered by
Alexander, consoled himself with the celebrity of
his conqueror.

And how if Van Baerle produced a new tulip,
and named it the John de Witte, after having
named one the Cornelius? It was indeed enough
to choke poor Isaac with rage.

Thus Boxtel, with jealous foreboding, became
the prophet of his own misfortune. And, after
having made this melancholy discovery, he passed
the most wretched night imaginable.

CHAPTER VI

THE HATRED OF A TULIP-FANCIER

From that moment Boxtel's interest in tulips was
of a mixed nature and he grew anxious, nervous
and afraid. Henceforth all his thoughts ran only
upon the injury which his neighbour would cause
him, and thus his favourite occupation was changed
into a constant source of misery to him.

Van Baerle, as may easily be imagined, had no
sooner begun to apply his naturally keen interest
to his new fancy, than he succeeded in growing the
very finest tulips. Indeed, he knew better than
any one else at Haarlem or Leyden—the two

towns which boast the best soil and the most congenial climate—how to vary the colours, to modify the shape, and to produce new species.

Mynheer van Baerle and his tulips, therefore, were in the mouth of everybody; so much so, that Boxtel's name disappeared for ever from the list of the notable tulip-growers in Holland, and those of Dort were now represented by Cornelius van Baerle, the modest and inoffensive savant.

Engrossed, heart and soul, in his pursuits of sowing, planting and gathering, Van Baerle, caressed by the whole fraternity of tulip-growers in Europe, entertained not the least suspicion that there was at his very door a pretender whose throne he had usurped.

He went on in his career, and consequently in his triumphs; and, in the course of two years, he covered his borders with such marvellous productions as no mortal man, following in the tracks of the Creator, except, perhaps, Shakespeare and Rubens, has ever equalled in point of numbers.

If Dante had wished for a new type to be added to his characters of the Inferno, he might have chosen Boxtel during this period of Van Baerle's successes. Whilst Cornelius was weeding, manuring, watering his beds; whilst, kneeling on the turf-border, he analysed every vein of the flowering tulips, and meditated on the modifications which might be effected by crosses of colour or otherwise, Boxtel, concealed behind a small sycamore which he had trained at the top of the partition-wall in the shape of a fan, watched, with his eyes starting from their sockets, and with foaming mouth, every step and every gesture of his neighbour; and, whenever he thought he saw him look happy, or descried a smile on his lips, or a flash of contentment glistening in his eyes, he poured out towards him such a volley of maledictions and furious threats as to make it indeed a matter of wonder that this venomous breath of envy and hatred did not carry a blight on the innocent flowers which had excited it.

When the evil spirit has once taken hold of the heart of man, it urges him on without letting him stop. Thus Boxtel soon was no longer content with watching Van Baerle. He wanted to see his flowers too; he had the feelings of an artist; the masterpiece of a rival engrossed his interest.

He therefore bought a telescope, which enabled him to watch, as accurately as did the owner himself, every progressive development of the flower, from the moment when, in the first year, its pale seed-leaf begins to peep from the ground, to that glorious one when, after five years, its petals at last reveal the hidden treasures of its calyx. How often did the miserable jealous man observe, in Van Baerle's beds, tulips which dazzled him by their beauty and almost choked him by their perfection of form and colour.

And then, after the first wave of admiration which he could not resist, he began to be tortured by the pangs of envy, by that slow fever which creeps over the heart and changes it into a nest of vipers, each devouring the other and ever born anew. How often did Boxtel, in the midst of tortures which no pen is fully able to describe— how often did he feel an inclination to jump down into the garden, during the night, to destroy the plants, to tear the bulbs with his teeth, and to sacrifice to his wrath the owner himself, if he should venture to stand to defend his own tulips.

But to destroy a tulip was a horrible crime in the eyes of a genuine tulip-fancier; killing a man would not have mattered half so much.

Yet Van Baerle made such progress in the science of growing tulips, which he seemed to master instinctively, that Boxtel at last was maddened to such a degree as to seriously think of casting stones and sticks into the flower-stands of his neighbour. But remembering that he would be sure to be found out, and that he would not only be punished by law, but also dishonoured for ever in the face of all the tulip-growers of Europe, he had recourse to stratagem; and, to gratify his hatred, tried to devise a plan by means of which he might gain his ends without compromising himself.

He considered a long time, and at last his meditations were crowned with success.

One evening he tied two cats together by their hindlegs with a string about six feet in length, and threw them from the wall into the midst of that noble, that princely, that royal bed, which contained not only the 'Cornelius de Witte,' but also the 'Beauty of Brabant,' milkwhite, edged with purple and pink; the 'Marble of Rotterdam,' flax-coloured, and feathered red and flesh-colour; and the 'Wonder of Haarlem,' dark dove-colour, tinged with a lighter shade of the same and several others.

The frightened animals, alighting on the ground, first tried to fly from each other in a different direction, until the string by which they were tied together was tightly stretched across the bed; then, however, feeling that they were not able to get off, they began to pull to and fro, and to wheel about with heart-rending caterwaulings, mowing down with the string the flowers among which they were disporting themselves, until, after a furious strife of about a quarter of an hour, the string broke and the combatants vanished.

Boxtel, hidden behind his sycamore, could not

see anything, as it was pitch dark ; but the piercing cries of the cats told the whole tale, and his heart, overflowing with gall, was now throbbing with triumphant joy.

Boxtel was so· eager to ascertain the extent of the damage, that he remained at his post until morning to feast his eyes on the sorry state in which the two cats had left the flower-beds of his neighbour. The mists of the morning chilled his frame, but he did not feel the cold, the hope of revenge keeping his blood at fever heat. The chagrin of his rival was to pay for all the inconvenience which he incurred himself.

At the earliest dawn the door of the white house opened, and Van Baerle made his appearance, approaching the flower-beds with the smile of a man who had passed the night comfortably in his bed, and has had happy dreams.

All at once he perceived furrows and little mounds of earth on the beds, which only the evening before had been as smooth as a mirror ; all at once he perceived the symmetrical rows of his tulips in awful and harrowing disorder, like the ranks of a battalion in the midst of which a shell has fallen.

He ran up to them with blanched cheek.

Boxtel trembled with joy. Fifteen or twenty tulips, torn and crushed, were lying about, some of them bent, others completely broken and already withering ; the sap was oozing from their bleeding wounds. How gladly would Van Baerle have redeemed that precious sap with his own blood !

But what were his surprise and his delight ! what was the disappointment of his rival ! Not one of the four tulips which the latter had meant to destroy was injured at all. They proudly raised their noble heads above the corpses of their slain

companions. This was enough to console Van
Baerle, and enough to fan the rage of the horticultural murderer, who tore his hair at the sight of
the effects of the crime which he had committed in
vain.

Van Baerle could not imagine the cause of the
mishap, which, fortunately, was of far less consequence than it might have been. On making
inquiries, he learned that the whole night had been
disturbed by terrible caterwaulings. He, besides,
found traces of the cats, their footmarks and hairs
left behind on the battle-field ; to guard, therefore,
in future against a similar outrage, he gave orders
that henceforth one of the under-gardeners should
sleep in the garden in a sentry-box near the
flower-beds.

Boxtel heard him give the order, and saw the
sentry-box put up that very day ; but he deemed
himself lucky in not having been suspected, and,
being more than ever incensed against the
successful horticulturist, he resolved to await his
opportunity.

About this period the Tulip Society of Haarlem
offered a prize for the discovery or production of a
large black tulip without a spot of colour, a feat
which had not yet been accomplished, and was considered impossible, as at that time there did not
exist a flower of that species approaching even to
so dark a shade as bistre. It was, therefore,
generally said that the founders of the prize might
just as well have offered two millions as a hundred
thousand guilders, since no one would be able to
gain it.

The tulip-growing world, nevertheless, was
thrown by the offer into a state of most active
commotion. Some fanciers caught at the idea
without believing it practicable ; but such is the

power of imagination among florists, that, although
considering the undertaking as certain to fail, all
their thoughts were engrossed by that grand black
tulip, which was looked upon as chimerical, as the
black swan of Horace or the white blackbird of old
time tradition.

Van Baerle was one of the tulip-growers who
was struck with the idea ; Boxtel thought of it in
the light of a speculation. Van Baerle, as soon as
the idea had once taken root in his clear and
ingenious mind, slowly began the necessary sow-
ings and operations to reduce the tulips, which he
had grown already, from red to brown, and from
brown to dark brown.

By the next year he had obtained flowers of a
perfect nut-brown, and Boxtel espied them in the
border, whereas he had himself, as yet, only succeeded in producing the light brown.

Boxtel, once more worsted by the superiority
of his hated rival, was now completely disgusted
with tulip-growing, and, being driven half mad,
devoted himself entirely to observation.

The house of his rival was quite open to view ;
a garden exposed to the sun, cabinets with glass
walls, shelves, cupboards, boxes and ticketed
pigeon-holes, which could easily be surveyed by
the telescope. Boxtel allowed his bulbs to wither
in the pits, his seedlings to dry up in their cases,
and his tulips to rot in the borders, and hence-
forward occupied himself with nothing else but the
doings of Van Baerle.

But the most curious part of the operations was
not performed in the garden.

At one o'clock in the morning, Van Baerle
went up to his laboratory, into the glazed cabinet
whither Boxtel's telescope had easy access ; and
here, as soon as the lamp illuminated the walls and

windows, Boxtel saw the inventive genius of his rival at work.

He beheld him sorting his seeds, and soaking them in liquids which were destined to modify or to deepen their colours. He knew what Cornelius was aiming at when he saw him heating certain grains, then moistening them, then combining them with others by a sort of grafting—a minute and marvellously delicate manipulation. After this he shut up in darkness those which were expected to furnish the black colour; exposed to the sun or to the lamp those which were to produce red; and placed between the endless reflection of two water-mirrors those intended to be white, the pure representation of the limpid element.

This innocent magic, the fruit at the same time of childlike musings and of manly genius—this patient, untiring labour, of which Boxtel knew himself to be incapable—made him, gnawed as he was with envy, centre all his life, all his thoughts, and all his hopes in his telescope.

For, strange to say, the love and interest of horticulture had not deadened in Isaac his fierce envy and thirst for revenge. Sometimes, whilst covering Van Baerle with his telescope, he deluded himself into a belief that he was levelling a never-failing musket at him; and then, with his finger, he would seek for the trigger to fire the shot which was to end his neighbour's life. But it is time that we should show the connection between the operations of the one and the espionage of the other, and the visit which Cornelius de Witte paid to his native town at this epoch.

CHAPTER VII

THE HAPPY MAN MAKES ACQUAINTANCE
WITH MISFORTUNE

CORNELIUS DE WITTE, after having attended to
his family affairs, arrived at the house of his godson, Cornelius van Baerle, one evening in the
month of January 1672.

De Witte, although not greatly interested in
horticulture, or much of an artist, went over the
whole establishment from the studio to the greenhouse, inspecting everything from the pictures down
to the tulips. He thanked his godson for having
joined him on the deck of the Admiral's ship, *The
Seven Provinces*, during the battle of Southwold
Bay, and for having given his name to a magnificent tulip; and whilst he thus, with the kindness
and affability of a father to a son, visited Van
Baerle's treasures, a crowd gathered with curiosity,
not unmingled with respect, before the door of the
happy man.

All this hubbub excited the attention of Boxtel,
who was just taking his meal by his fireside. He
inquired what it meant, and on being informed of
the cause of all the stir, climbed up to his post of
observation, where, in spite of the cold, he took his
stand, with his eye to his beloved telescope.

This telescope had not been of great service to
him since the autumn of 1671. The tulips, like
true daughters of the East, averse to cold, will not
live in the open ground in winter. They need the
shelter of the house, the soft bed on the shelves,
and the congenial warmth of the stove. Van
Baerle, therefore, passed the whole winter in his
laboratory, in the midst of his books and pictures,

He only went on rare occasions to the room where
he kept his bulbs, unless it were to allow some
fugitive rays of the sun to enter, by opening one of
the moveable sashes of the glass front.

On the evening of which we are speaking, after
the two Corneliuses together had visited all the
apartments of the house, followed by a train of
domestics, De Witte said, in a low voice, to Van
Baerle,—

'My dear son, send these people away, and let
us be alone for some minutes.

The younger Cornelius, bowing assent, said
aloud,—

'Would you now care to see my drying-room?'

The drying-room, this pantheon, this sanctum
sanctorum of the tulip-fancier, was, as Delphi of
old, interdicted to the profane uninitiated.

Never had any of his servants been bold enough
to set his foot within those sacred precincts.
Cornelius admitted only the inoffensive broom of
an old Frisian housekeeper, who had been his
nurse, and who, from the time when he had devoted
himself to the culture of tulips, ventured no longer
to put onions in his stews, in case she might by
accident pull to pieces and mince the idols of her
foster child.

At the mere mention of the *drying-room*, therefore, the servants, who were carrying the lights,
respectfully fell back. Cornelius, taking the candlestick from the hands of the foremost, conducted
his godfather into that room, which was no other
than that very cabinet with a glass front, into
which Boxtel was continually prying with his
telescope.

The envious spy was watching more intently
than ever.

First of all he saw the walls and windows lit up

Then two dark figures appeared.

One of them tall, majestic, stern, sat down near the table on which Van Baerle had placed the taper.

In this figure, Boxtel recognised the pale features of Cornelius de Witte, whose long hair, parted in front, fell over his shoulders.

De Witte, after having said some few words to Cornelius, the meaning of which the prying neighbour could not read in the movement of his lips, took from his breast pocket a white parcel, carefully sealed, which Boxtel, judging from the manner in which Cornelius received it, and placed it in one of the presses, supposed to contain papers of the greatest importance.

His first thought was that this precious deposit inclosed some newly-imported bulbs from Bengal or Ceylon ; but he soon reflected that Cornelius de Witte was very little addicted to tulip-growing, and that he only occupied himself with the affairs of man, a pursuit by far less peaceful and agreeable than that of the florist. He, therefore, came to the conclusion that the parcel contained simply some papers, and that these papers related to politics.

But why should papers of political import be entrusted to Van Baerle, who not only was, but also boasted of being, an entire stranger to that science which, in his opinion, was more occult than alchemy itself?

It was undoubtedly a packet of important documents which Cornelius de Witte, already threatened by the unpopularity with which his countrymen were going to honour him, was placing in the hands of his godson ; a contrivance so much the more cleverly devised, as it certainly was not at all likely that it would be sought for at the house of one who had always stood aloof from every sort of intrigue.

And, besides, if the parcel had been made up of bulbs, Boxtel knew his neighbour too well not to expect that Van Baerle would not have lost one moment in satisfying his curiosity and feasting his eyes on the present which he had received.

But, on the contrary, Cornelius received the parcel from the hands of his godfather with every mark of respect, and put it by with the same respectful manner in a drawer, stowing it away so that it should not take up too much of the room which was reserved for his bulbs.

The parcel thus being secreted, Cornelius de Witte got up, pressed the hand of his godson, and turned towards the door. Van Baerle seized the candlestick and lighted his godfather on his way down to the street, which was still crowded with people who wished to see the Ruart get into his coach.

Boxtel had not been mistaken in his supposition. The deposit entrusted to Van Baerle, and carefully locked up by him, was nothing more nor less than John de Witte's secret correspondence with the Marquis de Louvois, the war-minister of the King of France ; the godfather, however, forebore giving to his godson the least intimation concerning the political importance of the packet, merely desiring him not to deliver it to anyone but to himself, or to whomsoever he should send to claim it in his name.

And Van Baerle, as we have seen, locked it up with his most precious bulbs, to think no more of it after his godfather had left him ; unlike Boxtel, who looked upon this parcel as a clever pilot does on the distant and scarcely perceptible cloud which increases on its way, and which is fraught with a storm.

Quite unaware of the jealous hatred of his neighbour, Van Baerle had proceeded step by step towards gaining the prize offered by the Horticultural Society of Haarlem. He had progressed from bistre to the shade of roasted coffee; and on the very day when the frightful events took place at the Hague, which we have related in the preceding chapters, we find him, about one o'clock in the day, gathering from the beds the young bulbs raised from tulips of the colour of roasted coffee; which, being expected to flower for the first time in the spring of 1673, would, undoubtedly, produce the large black tulip required by the Haarlem Society.

On the 20th of August 1672, at one o'clock, Cornelius was, therefore, in his drying-room, with his feet resting on the foot-bar of the table, and his elbows on the cover, looking with intense delight at three suckers which he had just detached from the mother bulb, pure, perfect and entire, and from which was to grow that wonderful produce of horticulture which would render the name of Cornelius van Baerle for ever illustrious.

'I shall find the black tulip,' said Cornelius to himself, whilst detaching the baby bulbs. 'I shall obtain the hundred thousand guilders offered by the Society. I shall distribute them among the poor of Dort; and thus the hatred which every rich man has to encounter in times of civil disturbances will be soothed down, and I shall be able, without fearing any harm either from Republicans or Orangists, to keep my beds as heretofore in splendid condition. I need no more be afraid lest, on the day of a riot, the shopkeepers of the town, and the sailors of the port, should come and tear out my bulbs to boil them as onions for their families, as they have sometimes quietly threatened when

they happened to remember my having paid two
or three hundred guilders for one bulb. It is,
therefore, settled I shall give the hundred thousand
guilders of the prize Haarlem to the poor. And
yet—'

Here Cornelius stopped, and heaved a sigh.

'And yet,' he continued, 'it would have been so
very delightful to spend the hundred thousand
guilders on the enlargement of my tulip-bed, or
even on a journey to the East, the country of
beautiful flowers. But, alas! these are no thoughts
for the present times, when muskets, standards,
proclamations and beating of drums are the order
of the day.'

Van Baerle raised his eyes to heaven, and sighed
again. Then turning his glance towards his bulbs
—objects of much greater importance to him than
all those muskets, standards, drums and proclamations, which he conceived only to be fit to disturb
the minds of fighting people—he said,—

'These are, indeed, beautiful bulbs; how smooth
they are, how well formed! there is that air of
melancholy about them which promises to produce
a flower of the colour of ebony. On their skin one
cannot even distinguish the veins with the naked
eye. It is certain I think that not a light spot will
disfigure the tulip which I have called into existence. And by what name shall we call this off-
spring of my sleepless nights, of my labour and
my thought? *Tulipa nigra Barlœensis.*

'Yes, *Barlœensis;* a fine name. All the tulip-
fanciers—that is to say all the intelligent people of
Europe—will feel a thrill of excitement when the
rumour spreads to the four quarters of the globe:
THE GRAND BLACK TULIP IS FOUND! "How is it
called?" the fanciers will ask. — "*Tulipa nigra
Barlœensis!*" "Why *Barlœensis?*"—"After its

grower, Van Baerle," will be the answer. "And who is this Van Baerle?"—"It is the same man who has already produced five new tulips: The Jane, the John de Witte, the Cornelius de Witte, etc." Well, that is my ambition. It will cause no one to shed a tear. And people will still talk of my *Tulipa nigra Barlæensis* when, perhaps, my godfather, this sublime politician, is only known from the tulip to which I have given his name.

'Oh! these darling bulbs!'

'When my tulip has flowered,' Baerle continued in his soliloquy, 'and when tranquillity is restored in Holland, I shall give to the poor only fifty thousand guilders, which, after all, is a goodly sum for a man who is under no obligation whatever. Then, with the remaining fifty thousand guilders, I shall make experiments. With them I shall succeed in imparting scent to the tulip. Ah! if I succeeded in giving it the odour of the rose or the carnation, or, what would be still better, a completely new scent; if I restored to this queen of flowers its natural distinctive perfume, which she has lost in passing from her Eastern to her European throne, and which she must have in the Indian Peninsula at Goa, Bombay and Madras, and especially in that island which in olden times, as is asserted, was the terrestrial paradise, and which is called Ceylon—oh, what glory! I must say, I would then rather be Cornelius van Baerle than Alexander, Cæsar or Maximilian.

'Oh, these admirable bulbs!'

Thus Cornelius indulged in the delights of contemplation, and was carried away by the sweetest dreams.

Suddenly the bell of his cabinet was rung much more violently than usual.

Cornelius, startled, laid his hands on his bulbs, and turned round.

'Who is here?' he asked. 'Sir,' answered the servant, 'it is a messenger from the Hague.'

'A messenger from the Hague! What does he want?'

'Sir, it is Craeke.'

'Craeke! the confidential servant of Mynheer John de Witte? Good, let him wait.'

'I cannot wait,' said a voice in the lobby.

And at the same time Craeke forced his way, and rushed into the drying-room.

This abrupt entrance was such an infringement on the established rules of the household of Cornelius van Baerle, that the latter, at the sight of Craeke, convulsively moved his hand which covered the bulbs, so that two of them fell on the floor, one of them rolling under a small table and the other into the fireplace.

'Deuce take it!' said Cornelius, eagerly picking up his precious bulbs, 'what's the matter?'

'The matter, sir!'—said Craeke, laying a paper on the large table, on which the third bulb was lying—'the matter is, that you are requested to read this paper without losing a moment.'

And Craeke, who thought he had remarked in the streets of Dort symptoms of a tumult similar to that which he had witnessed before his departure from the Hague, ran off without even looking behind him.

'All right! all right! my dear Craeke,' said Cornelius, stretching his arm under the table for the bulb; 'your paper shall be read, indeed it shall.'

Then, examining the bulb which he held in the hollow of his hand, he said, 'Well, here is one of them uninjured. That confounded Craeke! to rush into my drying-room so impetuously; let us now look after the other.'

And without laying down the bulb which he already held, Baerle went to the fireplace, knelt down, and stirred with the tip of his finger the ashes, which fortunately were quite cold.

He at once felt the other bulb.

'Well, here it is,' he said. And looking at it with almost fatherly affection, he exclaimed, 'Uninjured, like the other one!'

At this very instant, and whilst Cornelius, still on his knees, was examining his pets, the door of the drying-room was so violently shaken, and opened in such a brusque manner, that Cornelius felt rising in his cheeks and his ears the glow of that evil counsellor which is called wrath.

'What is it now?' he demanded; 'are people going mad in this house?'

'Oh, Mynheer!' cried the servant, rushing into the drying-room, with a much paler face and with much more frightened mien than Craeke had shown.

'Well!' asked Cornelius, anticipating some trouble from this double breach of the strict rule of his house.

'Oh, sir, fly! fly, quick!' cried the servant.

'Fly! and what for?'

'Sir, the house is full of the guards of the States.'

'What do they want?'

'They want you.'

'What for?'

'To arrest you.'

'Arrest me? Arrest me, do you say?'

'Yes, sir, and they are headed by a magistrate.'

'What's the meaning of all this?' said Van Baerle, grasping in his hands the two bulbs, and directing his terrified glance towards the staircase.

'They are coming up! they are coming up!' cried the servant.

'Oh, my dear child, my worthy master!' cried the old housekeeper, who now likewise made her appearance in the drying-room, 'take your gold, your jewellery, and fly! fly!'

'But how shall I make my escape, nurse?' said Van Baerle.

'Jump out of the window.'

'Twenty-five feet from the window!'

'But you will fall on six feet of soft soil.'

'Yes, but I should fall on my tulips.'

'Never mind, jump out.'

Cornelius took the third bulb, approached the window, and opened it, but seeing what havoc he would necessarily cause in his borders, and, more than this, what a height he would have to jump, he called out, 'Never!' and fell back a step.

At this moment they saw across the banister of the staircase the points of the halberds of the soldiers rising.

The housekeeper raised her hands to heaven.

As to Cornelius van Baerle, it must be stated to his honour, not as a man, but as a tulip-fancier, his only thought was for his priceless bulbs.

Looking about for a paper in which to wrap them up, he noticed the fly-leaf from the Bible, which Craeke had laid upon the table, took it without, in his confusion, remembering whence it came, folded in it the three bulbs, secreted them in his bosom, and waited.

At this very moment the soldiers, preceded by a magistrate, entered the room.

'Are you Doctor Cornelius van Baerle?' demanded the magistrate (who, although knowing the young man very well, put his questions according to the forms of justice, which gave his proceedings a much more dignified air).

'I am that person, Mynheer van Spennen,' answered Cornelius, politely bowing to his judge, 'and you know it very well.'

'Then give up to us the seditious papers which you secrete in your house.'

'The seditious papers!' repeated Cornelius, quite dumfounded at the imputation.

'Now don't look astonished, if you please.'

'I vow to you, Master van Spennen,' Cornelius replied, 'that I am completely at a loss to understand what you want.'

'Then I shall put you in the way, doctor,' said the judge; 'give up to us the paper which the traitor Cornelius de Witte deposited with you in the month of January last.'

A sudden light came into the mind of Cornelius.

'Halloa!' said Van Spennen, 'you begin now to remember, don't you?'

'Indeed I do; but you spoke of seditious papers, and I have none of that sort.'

'You deny it then?'

'Certainly I do.'

The magistrate turned round, and took a rapid survey of the whole cabinet.

'Where is the apartment you call your dryingroom?' he asked.

'The very same where you now are, Mynheer van Spennen.'

The magistrate cast a glance at a small note at the top of his papers.

'All right,' he said, like a man who is sure of his ground.

Then, turning round towards Cornelius, he continued, 'Will you give up those papers to me?'

'But I cannot, Mynheer van Spennen; those papers do not belong to me; they have been deposited with me as a trust, and a trust is sacred.'

'Doctor Cornelius,' said the judge, 'in the name of the States I order you to open this drawer, and to give up to me the papers which it contains.'

Saying this, the judge pointed with his finger to the third drawer of the press near the fireplace.

In this very drawer, indeed, the papers deposited by the Ruart de Pulten with his godson were lying; a proof that the police had received very exact information.

'Ah! you will not,' said Van Spennen, when he saw Cornelius standing immovable and bewildered; 'then I shall open the drawer myself.'

And, pulling out the drawer to its full length, the magistrate at first alighted on about twenty bulbs carefully arranged and ticketed, and then on the paper parcel, which had remained in exactly the same state as it was when delivered by the unfortunate Cornelius de Witte to his godson.

The magistrate broke the seals, tore off the envelope, cast an eager glance on the first leaves which met his eye, and then exclaimed with a terrible voice,—

'Well, justice has been rightly informed after all!'

'How,' said Cornelius, 'how is this?'

'Don't pretend to be ignorant, Mynheer van Baerle,' answered the magistrate, 'follow me.'

'What do you mean?' cried the doctor.

'In the name of the States I arrest you.'

Arrests were not as yet made in the name of William of Orange, he had not been Stadtholder long enough for that.

'Arrest me?' cried Cornelius; 'pray, what have I done?'

'That's no affair of mine, doctor, you will explain all that before your judges.'

'Where?'

'At the Hague.'

Cornelius, in mute stupefaction, embraced his old nurse Zug, who was in a swoon, shook hands with his weeping servants, and followed the magistrate, who put him in a coach, as a prisoner of State, and ordered him to be driven at full gallop to the Hague.

CHAPTER VIII

CORNELIUS VAN BAERLE ARRESTED

THE incident just related was, of course, the mischievous work of Mynheer Isaac Boxtel.

It will be remembered that, with the help of his telescope, not even the least detail of the private meeting between Cornelius de Witte and Van Baerle had escaped him. He had, indeed, heard nothing; but he had seen everything and had rightly concluded that the papers entrusted by the warden to the doctor must have been of great importance, as he saw Van Baerle so carefully secreting the parcel in the drawer where he kept his most precious bulbs.

The upshot of all this was, that when Boxtel— who watched the course of political events much more attentively than his neighbour Cornelius did —heard the news of the brothers De Witte being

arrested on a charge of high treason against the
States, though he knew within his heart that if
he, Boxtel, only said one word the godson would
be arrested as well as the godfather.

Yet, full of hatred as was Boxtel's heart, he at
first shrank with horror from the idea of informing
against a man whom this information might lead
to the scaffold.

But the most terrible about evil thoughts is that
evil minds grow soon familiar with them.

Mynheer Isaac Boxtel encouraged himself with
the following sophism :—

'Cornelius de Witte is a bad citizen, as he is
charged with high treason and arrested.

' I, on the contrary, am a good citizen, as I am
not charged with anything in the world, and I am
as free as the air of heaven.

' If, therefore, Cornelius de Witte is a bad
citizen—of which there can be no doubt, for he is
charged with high treason and arrested—his accomplice, Cornelius van Baerle, is no less a bad citizen
than himself.

' Therefore, as I am a good citizen, and as it is
the duty of every good citizen to inform against
the bad ones, it is my duty to inform against
Cornelius van Baerle.'

Specious as this mode of reasoning might sound,
it would not, perhaps, have taken so complete a
hold of Boxtel, nor would he, perhaps, have yielded
to the mere desire of vengeance which was gnawing
at his heart, had not the demon of envy been joined
by that of cupidity.

Boxtel was quite aware of the progress which
Van Baerle had made towards producing the
wonderful black tulip.

Doctor Cornelius, notwithstanding all his modesty,
had not been able to hide from his most intimate

friends that he was all but certain to win, in the year of grace 1673, the prize of a hundred thousand guilders offered by the Horticultural Society of Haarlem.

It was just this seeming certainty of Cornelius van Baerle that caused the fever which raged in the heart of Isaac Boxtel.

If Cornelius should be arrested, there would necessarily be a great upset in his house, and during the night after his arrest no one would think of keeping watch over the tulips in his garden.

Now, during that night, Boxtel would climb over the wall, and, as he knew where the bulb which was to produce the grand black tulip was planted, he would annex it ; and instead of flowering for Cornelius, it would flower for him, Isaac. He also, instead of Van Baerle, would have the prize of a hundred thousand guilders, not to speak of the sublime honour of calling the new flower *Tulipa nigra Boxtellensis*—a result which would satisfy not only his vengeance, but also his cupidity and his ambition.

Awake, he thought of nothing but the grand black tulip; asleep, he dreamed of it.

At last, on the 19th of August, about two o'clock in the afternoon, the temptation grew so strong that Mynheer Isaac was no longer able to resist it.

Accordingly he wrote an anonymous information, the minute exactness of which made up for its want of authenticity, and dispatched his letter.

Never did a venomous paper, slipped into the jaws of the bronze lions at Venice, produce a more prompt and terrible effect.

On the same evening the communication reached the principal magistrate, who, without a moment's delay, called upon his colleagues to meet early next day. On the following morning, therefore, they assembled, and decided on Van Baerle's arrest, placing the order for its execution in the hands of Mynheer van Spennen, who, as we have seen, performed his duty like a true Hollander, and had the doctor arrested at the very hour when the Orange party at the Hague were roasting the bleeding shreds of flesh torn from the corpses of Cornelius and John de Witte.

But, whether from a feeling of shame or from craven weakness, Isaac Boxtel did not venture that day to point his telescope either into the garden, or the laboratory, or the drying-room.

He knew too well what was about to happen in the house of the poor doctor, so that he had no desire to look into it. He did not even get up when his only servant—who envied the lot of the servants of Cornelius just as bitterly as Boxtel did that of their master—entered his bedroom. He said to the man,—

'I shall not get up to-day; I am ill.'

About nine o'clock he heard a great noise in the street, which made him tremble; at this moment he was paler than a real invalid, and shook more violently than a man in the height of fever.

His servant entered the room; Boxtel hid himself under the counterpane.

'Oh, sir!' cried the servant, not without some inkling that, whilst deploring the mishap which had befallen Van Baerle, he was announcing agreeable news to his master—'oh, sir! you do not know, then, what is happening at this moment?'

'How can I know it?' answered Boxtel, with an almost unintelligible voice.

'Well, Mynheer Boxtel, at this moment your neighbour, Cornelius van Baerle, is arrested for high treason.'

'Nonsense!' Boxtel muttered, with a faltering voice; 'the thing is impossible.'

'Faith! sir, at anyrate that's what people say; and, besides, I have seen Judge van Spennen with the archers entering the house.'

'Well, if you have seen it with your own eyes, that's a different matter altogether.'

'At all events,' said the servant, 'I shall go and inquire once more; I will let you know all about it, mynheer.'

Boxtel contented himself with signifying his approval of the zeal of his servant by pantomime.

The man went out, and returned in half an hour.

'Oh, mynheer! all that I told you is indeed quite true.'

'Indeed?'

'Mynheer van Baerle is arrested, and has been put into a carriage, and they are driving him to the Hague.'

'To the Hague?'

'Yes, to the Hague; and if what people say is true, it won't do him much good.'

'And what do they say?' Boxtel asked.

'Well, they say—but it is not quite certain—that by this hour the burghers must be murdering Mynheer Cornelius and Mynheer John de Witte.'

'Oh!' muttered Boxtel, closing his eyes from the dreadful picture which presented itself to his imagination.

'Why,' said the servant to himself as he left the room, 'Mynheer Isaac Boxtel must be very sick not to have jumped out of bed on hearing such good news.'

And, in reality, Isaac Boxtel was very sick, like a man who has murdered another.

But he had murdered his man with a double

object; the first was attained, the second was still to be attained.

Night closed in. It was the night which Boxtel had anxiously longed for.

As soon as it was dark he got up.

He then climbed into his sycamore.

He had judged accurately. No one thought of keeping watch over the garden; the house and the servants were in a state of the utmost confusion.

He heard the clock strike ten, eleven, twelve.

At midnight, with a beating heart, trembling hands, and a livid countenance, he descended from the tree, took a ladder, leaned it against the wall, mounted it to the last step but one, and listened.

All was perfectly quiet, not a sound broke the silence of the night; one solitary light, that of the housekeeper, was burning in the old nurse's room.

This silence and this darkness emboldened Boxtel; he got astride of the wall, stopped for an instant, and, after having ascertained that there was nothing to fear, he put his ladder from his own garden into that of Cornelius, and descended.

After this, knowing to an inch where the bulbs which were to produce the black tulip were planted, he ran towards the spot, following, however, the crisp, gravelled walks in order not to be betrayed by his footprints, and on arriving at the precise spot, he rushed, with the eagerness of a tiger, to plunge his hand into the soft ground.

He found nothing, and thought he was mistaken.

In the meanwhile the cold sweat stood on his brow.

He rummaged close by it—nothing.

He rummaged on the right and on the left—nothing.

He rummaged in front and at the back—nothing.

He was nearly mad, when at last he satisfied

himself that on that very morning the earth had been turned.

In fact, whilst Boxtel was lying in bed, Cornelius had gone down to his garden, had taken up the parent-bulb, and, as we have seen, divided it into three.

Boxtel could not bring himself to leave the place. He dug with his hands more than ten square feet of the ground.

At last no doubt remained of his bad luck.

Mad with rage, he returned to his ladder, mounted the wall, drew up the ladder, flung it into his own garden, and jumped after it.

All at once a last ray of hope presented itself to his mind : the seedling bulbs might be in the drying-room ; it was therefore only necessary to make his entry there as he had done into the garden.

There he would find them ; and, moreover, it was not at all difficult, as the sashes of the drying-room might be raised like those of a greenhouse. Cornelius had opened them on that morning, and no one had thought of closing them again.

Everything, therefore, depended upon whether he could procure a ladder of sufficient length—one of twenty-five feet, instead of ten.

Boxtel had noticed in the street where he lived a house which was being repaired, and against which a very tall ladder was placed.

This ladder would do admirably, unless the workmen had taken it away.

He ran to the house, the ladder was there. Boxtel took it, carried it after great exertion to his garden, and with even greater difficulty raised it against the wall of Van Baerle's house, where it just reached the ledge of the window.

Boxtel put a lighted dark lantern into his

pocket, mounted the ladder, and slipped into the drying-room.

On reaching this sanctuary of the florist he stopped, supporting himself against the table; for his legs failed him, and his heart beat as if it would choke him. Here it was even worse than in the garden: there Boxtel was only a trespasser, here he was a thief.

However, he took courage again; he had gone too far to turn back with empty hands now.

But in vain he searched the room from end to end, to open and shut all the drawers, even that particular one where the parcel which had been so fatal to Cornelius had been deposited, took no time; he found ticketed, as in a botanical garden, the 'Jane,' the 'John de Witte,' the hazel nut, and the roasted coffee-coloured tulip; but of the black tulip, or rather of the seedling bulbs within which it was still sleeping, not a trace was to be found.

And yet, on looking over the register of seeds and bulbs, which Van Baerle kept, if possible, even with greater exactitude and care than the first commercial houses of Amsterdam kept their ledgers, Boxtel read the following entry:—

'To-day, 20th of August 1672, I have taken up the mother bulb of the grand black tulip, which I have divided into three perfect bulbs.'

'Oh, these bulbs, these bulbs!' cried Boxtel, turning over everything in the dry-room. 'Where could he have hidden them?'

Then suddenly striking his forehead in his frenzy, he called out, 'Oh, wretch that I am! Would anyone be separated from his bulbs? Would one leave them at Dort when one goes to the Hague? Could one live far from one's bulbs, when they inclose the grand black tulip? He had time to get hold of them, the scoundrel,

he has them about him, he has taken them to the
Hague!'

It was like a flash of lightning which showed to
Boxtel the abyss of the crime which he had un-
successfully committed.

Boxtel sank absolutely paralysed on that very
table, and on that very spot where, some hours
before, the unfortunate Van Baerle had so leisurely,
and with such intense delight, contemplated his
darling bulbs—the bulbs of the black tulip.

'Well, after all,' said the envious Boxtel—raising
his livid face from his hands in which it had been
buried—'if he has them, he can keep them only as
long as he lives, and—'

The rest of this detestable thought merged in a
hideous smile.

'The bulbs are at the Hague,' he said, 'therefore
I can no longer live at Dort. For them, to the
Hague! to the Hague! for the bulbs,' he cried
deliriously.

And, without taking any notice of the treasures
about him—so entirely were his thoughts absorbed
by another inestimable treasure—Boxtel let himself out by the window, slid down the ladder,
carried it back to the place whence he had taken
it, and, like a beast of prey, returned growling to
his house.

CHAPTER IX

THE FAMILY CELL

It was about midnight when poor Van Baerle was
locked up in the prison of the Buytenhof.

What Rosa foresaw had come to pass. On finding the cell of Cornelius de Witte empty, the wrath of the people ran very high, and had Gryphus fallen into the hands of those madmen, he would certainly have lost his life through the escape of the prisoner.

But this fury had vented itself and been satisfied by the murder of the two brothers when they were overtaken by the blood-seekers, thanks to the precaution which William, the man of precautions, had taken in having the gates of the city closed.

A momentary lull had therefore set in whilst the prison was empty, and Rosa availed herself of this favourable moment to come forth from her hiding-place, which she also induced her father, who was somewhat of a coward, to leave.

The prison was therefore completely deserted. Why should people remain in the jail whilst murder was going on at the Tol-Hek?

Gryphus came forth trembling behind the courageous Rosa. They went to close the great gate, at least as well as it would close, considering that it was half demolished. It was easy to see that a hurricane of mighty wrath had been spent upon it.

About four o'clock a return of the uproar was heard, but of no threatening character to Gryphus and his daughter. The people were only dragging in the two corpses, which they brought back to gibbet at the usual place of execution.

Rosa hid herself again, but only that she might not see the ghastly spectacle.

At midnight, people were knocking at the gate of the jail, or rather at the barricade which served in its stead; it was Cornelius van Baerle whom they were bringing this time.

When the jailer received this new inmate, and

saw from the warrant the name and station of his
prisoner, he muttered with this turnkey smile,—

'Godson of Cornelius de Witte! Well, young
man, we have here your family cell, and you shall
occupy it.'

Immensely pleased with his joke, the ferocious
Orangeman took his cresset and his keys to
conduct Cornelius to the cell, which, on that very
morning, Cornelius de Witte had left to go into
exile, or what, in revolutionary times, is meant by
'exile' by those sublime philosophers who lay it
down as an axiom of impregnable policy, 'It is
only the dead who do not return.'

On his way to the cell the unhappy tulip-
fancier heard nothing but the barking of a dog,
and saw nothing but the face of a young girl.

The dog rushed forth from a niche in the wall,
shaking his heavy chain, and sniffing all round
Cornelius in order that he might be able to recognise him should he be ordered to pounce upon
him.

The young girl, while the prisoner was mounting
the staircase, appeared at the narrow door of her
chamber, which opened on the same flight of steps ;
and, holding the lamp in her right hand, she at the
same time lit up her pretty, blooming face, surrounded by a profusion of rich, wavy, golden
locks, while with her left she held her white night-
dress closely over her breast, having been roused
from her first slumber by the unexpected arrival of
Van Baerle.

It would have made a fine picture, worthy of
Rembrandt, the gloomy winding stairs illuminated
by the reddish glare of the cresset of Gryphus,
with his scowling jailer's countenance at the top,
the melancholy figure of Cornelius bending over
the banister to look down upon the sweet face of

Rosa, standing, as it were, in the bright frame of the door of her chamber, with flurried mien at being thus seen by a stranger.

Further down, quite in the shade, where the details were deepened by the darkness, the mastiff, with his eyes glistening like carbuncles, and shaking his chain, on which the double light from the lamp of Rosa and cresset of Gryphus threw a brilliant glitter.

The sublime master would, however, have been altogether unable to render the sorrow expressed in the face of Rosa when she saw this pale, handsome young man slowly climbing the stairs, and thought of the full import of the words which her father had just spoken, '*You will have the family cell.*' This vision lasted but a moment, and Gryphus proceeded on his way, Cornelius following him, and five minutes after he entered his cell, which it is unnecessary to describe, as the reader is already acquainted with it.

Gryphus pointed with his finger to the bed on which the martyr had suffered so much, who on that day had rendered his soul to God. Then, taking up his cresset, he quitted the cell.

Thus left alone, Cornelius threw himself on the bed with sleepless sobs; he kept his eye fixed on the narrow window, barred with iron, which looked on the Buytenhof; and in this way saw from behind the trees that first pale beam of light which morning casts over the earth like a white mantle.

Now and then, during the night, horses had galloped at a smart pace over the Buytenhof, the heavy tramp of the patrols had resounded from the pavement, and the slow matches of the arquebuses, flaring in the cold wind, had thrown up at intervals a sudden glare as far as the panes of his window.

But when the rising sun began to gild the coping

stones at the gable ends of the houses, Cornelius, eager to know whether there was any living creature about him, approached the window, and gazed sorrowfully round the prison yard.

At the end of the enclosure a dark mass, tinted with a melancholy blue by the morning dawn, rose before him, its irregular outlines standing out in contrast to the houses already illuminated by the pale light of early morning.

Cornelius recognised the gibbet.

On it were suspended two shapeless trunks, which indeed were no more than bleeding skeletons.

The good people of the Hague had chopped off the flesh of their victims, but faithfully carried the remainder to the gibbet, in order to have a pretext for a double inscription, written on a huge placard, on which Cornelius, with the keen sight of a young man of twenty-eight, was able to read the following lines, daubed by the coarse brush of a sign-painter,—

'Here are hanging the great rogue of the name of John de Witte, and the little rogue, Cornelius de Witte, his brother, two enemies of the people but great friends of the King of France.'

Cornelius uttered a cry of horror, and in the agony of his frantic terror banged with his hands and feet at his door so violently and continuously that Gryphus, with his huge bunch of keys in his hand, ran furiously up to him.

The jailer opened the door, with terrible imprecations against the prisoner for disturbing him at such an early hour.

'Upon my word, I believe this new De Witte is mad,' he cried ; 'but all those De Wittes have the devil in them.'

'Master, master,' cried Cornelius, seizing the

jailer by the arm, and dragging him towards the
window; 'master, what do I read down there?'

'Where, down where?'

'On that placard.'

And trembling, pale and gasping for breath, he
pointed to the gibbet, with the cynical inscription
surmounting it at the other side of the yard.

Gryphus broke out in a laugh.

'Ho! ho!' he answered, 'so you have read it.
Well, my good mynheer, that's what people get for
corresponding with the enemies of His Highness,
the Prince of Orange.'

'The brothers De Witte are murdered!' Cornelius
muttered, with beads of cold sweat on his brow, as
he sank on his bed, his arms hanging by his side,
and his eyes closed.

'The brothers De Witte have been judged by
the people,' said Gryphus; 'you call that murder,
do you? Well, I call it execution.'

Seeing that the prisoner had grown calm again,
and, indeed, prostrate and senseless, he started
from the cell, violently slamming the door, and
noisily fixing the bolts.

Recovering his consciousness, Cornelius found
himself alone, and recognised the room where he
was—'the family cell,' as Gryphus called it—as
the fatal passage leading to ignominious death.

And as he was a philosopher, and, more than
that, as he was a Christian, he began to pray for
the soul of his godfather, then for that of the
Grand Pensionary, and at last submitted with
resignation to all the sufferings which might be in
store for him.

Then turning again to earthly affairs, having
satisfied himself that he was alone in his dungeon,
he drew from his breast the three bulbs of the
black tulip, and concealed them behind a block of

stone, on which the traditional water-jug of the prison was standing, in the darkest corner of his cell.

Useless labour of so many years! such sweet hopes crushed. His discovery was, after all, to lead to nought, just as his own career was likely to end in an early and ignominious death. Here, in his cell, there was not a trace of vegetation, not an atom of soil, not a ray of sunshine.

At this thought Cornelius fell into gloomy despair, from which he was only roused by an extraordinary circumstance.

What was the circumstance?

This will be discovered in due course.

CHAPTER X

THE JAILER'S DAUGHTER

ON the same evening Gryphus, as he brought the prisoner his mess, slipped on the damp flags whilst opening the door of the cell, and fell in the attempt to steady himself on his hand, but as it was turned the wrong way he broke his arm just above the wrist.

Cornelius rushed forward towards the jailer, but Gryphus, who was not yet aware of the serious nature of his injury, called out to him,—

'It is nothing, keep where you are.'

He then tried to support himself on his arm, but the bone gave way; then he felt the pain, and uttered a sick cry.

When he discovered that his arm was broken, this man, so harsh to others, coward - like, fell swooning on the threshold, where he remained motionless and cold as if dead.

During all this time the door of the cell stood open, and Cornelius found himself almost free. But the thought of profiting by this accident never entered his mind ; he had seen from the manner in which the arm was turned, and from the noise it made in bending, that the bone was fractured, and that the patient must be in extreme pain ; and now he thought of nothing but of administering relief to the sufferer, however little gracious the man had shown himself during their short interview.

At the noise of Gryphus's fall, and at the cry which escaped him, a hasty step was heard on the staircase, and immediately after a lovely apparition presented itself to the eyes of Cornelius.

It was the beautiful young Frisian, who, seeing her father stretched on the ground, and the prisoner bending over him, uttered a faint sob, as, in the first fright, she thought Gryphus, whose brutality she well knew, had fallen in consequence of a struggle between him and the prisoner.

Cornelius understood what was passing in the mind of the girl, almost at the very moment when the suspicion arose in her heart.

In one second, however, she learned the true state of the case, and, ashamed of her first thoughts, she cast her beautiful eyes, wet with tears, on the young man, and said to him,—

'I beg your pardon, and thank you, mynheer ; the first for what I have thought, and the second for what you are doing.'

Cornelius coloured, and said, 'I am only doing my duty as a Christian in assisting a neighbour.'

'Yes, and affording him your help this evening, you have forgotten the abuse which he heaped upon you this morning. Oh, sir! this is more than humanity—this is indeed Christian charity.'

Cornelius cast his eyes on the beautiful girl, quite astonished to hear from the mouth of one so humble such a noble and feeling speech.

But he had no time to express his surprise. Gryphus recovered from his swoon, opened his eyes, and as his brutality was returning with his senses, he growled,—' That's it, a fellow is in a hurry to bring a prisoner his supper, and falls and breaks his arm, and is left lying on the ground.'

' Hush, my father,' said Rosa, ' you are unjust to this gentleman, whom I found endeavouring to give you his aid.'

' His aid?' Gryphus replied, with a doubtful air.

' It is quite true, mynheer; I am quite ready to help you still more.'

' You!' said Gryphus, ' are you a medical man?'

' It was formerly my profession.'

' And so you would be able to set my arm?'

' Perfectly.'

' And what would you need to do it?'

' Two splinters of wood, and some linen for a bandage.'

' Do you hear, Rosa?' said Gryphus, ' the prisoner is going to set my arm, that's a saving; come, give me a hand to get up, I feel as heavy as lead.'

Rosa lent the sufferer her shoulder; he put his unhurt arm round her neck, and making an effort, got on his legs, whilst Cornelius, to save his steps, pushed a chair towards him.

Gryphus sat down; then, turning towards his daughter, he said,—

' Well, didn't you hear? Go and fetch what is wanted.'

Rosa went down, and immediately afterwards

returned with two staves of a small barrel and a large roll of linen binding.

Cornelius had made use of the intervening moments to take off the man's coat, and to turn up his shirt sleeve.

'Is this what you require, sir?' asked Rosa.

'Yes, jufvrouw,' answered Cornelius, looking at the things which she had brought; 'yes, that's right. Now, push this table whilst I support the arm of your father.'

Rosa pushed the table, Cornelius placed the broken arm on it, so as to make it flat, and with easy skill set the bone, adjusted the splinters, and fastened the bandages.

At the last touch the jailer fainted a second time.

'Go and fetch some vinegar, please,' said Cornelius; 'we must bathe his temples, and he will soon recover.'

But instead of acting up to the doctor's prescription, Rosa, after having assured herself that her father was still unconscious, approached Cornelius and said,—

'Service for service, sir.'

'What do you mean, my dear?' said Cornelius.

'I mean to say, sir, that the judge who is to examine you to-morrow has inquired to-day for the room in which you are confined, and on being told that you were occupying the cell of Mynheer Cornelius de Witte, laughed in a very strange and disagreeable manner, which makes me fear that some evil may await you.'

'But what harm can they do me?' asked Cornelius.

'Look at that gibbet!'

'I am not guilty of any crime.' said Cornelius.

'Were they guilty whom you see down there, gibbeted, mangled, and torn to pieces?'

'That's true,' said Cornelius, gravely.

'And besides,' continued Rosa, 'the people want to find you guilty. But whether innocent or guilty, your trial begins to-morrow, and the day after you will be condemned. Matters are settled very quickly in these times.'

'Well, and what do you conclude from all this?'

'I conclude that I am alone, that I am weak, that my father is lying in a swoon, that the dog is muzzled, and that consequently there is nothing to prevent you from making your escape. Fly, then, that's what I mean.'

'What do you say? Do you mean that?'

'I say that I was not able to save Mynheer Cornelius or Mynheer John de Witte, and that I should like to save you. Only be quick, don't think of me; there, my father is regaining his breath; one minute more and he will open his eyes and it will be too late. Why do you hesitate?'

Cornelius stood immovable, looking at Rosa, yet looking at her as if he did not hear her.

'Don't you understand me?' said the young girl, with some impatience.

'Yes, I do,' said Cornelius, 'but—'

'But?'

'I will not; they would accuse you.'

'Never mind,' said Rosa, blushing, 'never mind that.'

'You are very good, my dear child,' replied Cornelius, 'but I stay.'

'You stay, oh, sir! oh, sir! don't you understand that you will be condemned to death, executed on the scaffold, perhaps assassinated and torn to pieces, just like Mynheer John and Mynheer Cornelius. For Heaven's sake don't think of me, but fly from this place. Take care, it bears ill luck to the De Wittes!'

'Holloa!' cried the jailer, recovering his senses, 'who is talking of those rogues, those wretches, those villains, the De Wittes?'

'Don't be angry, my good man,' said Cornelius, with his good-tempered smile; 'the worst thing for a fracture is excitement, by which the blood is heated.'

Thereupon he said in an undertone to Rosa, 'My child, I am innocent, and I shall await my trial with tranquillity and an easy mind.'

'Hush,' said Rosa.

'Why hush?'

'My father must not suppose that we have been talking to each other.'

'What harm would that do?'

'What harm? He would never allow me to come here any more,' said Rosa.

Cornelius received this innocent confidence with a smile; he felt as if a ray of good fortune was breaking over his path.

'Now, then, what are you two jabbering about?' demanded Gryphus, rising and supporting his right arm with his left.

'Nothing,' said Rosa. 'Mynheer is explaining to me what diet you are to have.'

'Diet, diet for me? Well, my fine girl, I shall put you on diet too.'

'On what diet, my father?'

'To keep away from the cells of the prisoners; and if ever I catch you visiting them, you will regret it. Come, off with you, lead the way, and be quick.'

Rosa and Cornelius exchanged glances.

That of Rosa tried to express,—

'There, you see how it is?'

That of Cornelius answered,—

'Let it be as the Lord will.'

CHAPTER XI

CORNELIUS VAN BAERLE'S WILL

ROSA was not mistaken; the judges arrived on the following day at the Buytenhof, and proceeded with the trial of Cornelius van Baerle. The examination, however, did not last long, it having been proved indisputably that Cornelius had secured at his house the fatal correspondence of the brothers De Witte with France.

He did not deny it.

The only point about which there seemed any difficulty was, whether this correspondence had been entrusted to him by his godfather Cornelius de Witte.

But as, since the two martyrs were dead, Van Baerle had no longer any reason for withholding the truth, therefore he did not deny that the parcel had been delivered to him by Cornelius de Witte himself, but also stated all the circumstances under which it was done.

This confession involved the godson in the crime of the godfather; for manifest complicity was concluded to exist between Cornelius de Witte and Cornelius van Baerle.

The honest doctor did not confine himself to this avowal, but told the whole truth with regard to his own tastes, habits and daily life. He spoke of his indifference to politics, his love of study, of the fine arts, of science and of flowers. He vowed that, since the day Cornelius de Witte handed him the parcel at Dort, he himself had never touched, nor even noticed it.

To this it was objected, that in this respect he could not possibly be speaking the truth, since the papers had been deposited in a press which he was constantly using.

Cornelius answered that that was certainly true ; that, however, he never put his hand into the press but to ascertain whether his bulbs were dry, and that he never looked into it but to see if they were beginning to sprout.

To this again it was objected that his pretended indifference respecting his charge was not to be reasonably entertained, as he could not have received such valuable papers from the hand of his godfather without being made acquainted with their important character.

He replied that his godfather Cornelius loved him too well to have communicated to him any-thing of the contents of the parcel, well knowing that such a confidence would only have caused anxiety to him who received it.

To this it was objected that if De Witte had wished to act in such a way, he would have added to the parcel, in case of accidents, a certificate, setting forth that his godson was an entire stranger to the nature of this correspondence, or at least he would, during his trial, have written a letter to him, which might be produced as his justification.

Cornelius replied that undoubtedly his godfather could not have thought that there was any risk for the safety of his deposit, hidden as it was in a press which was looked upon as sacred as the Ark of the Covenant by the whole household of Van Baerle ; and that, consequently, he had considered the certificate as useless. As to a letter, he certainly had some remembrance that some moments previous to his arrest, while he was absorbed in the contemplation of one of the rarest of his bulbs, John de Witte's servant entered his dry-room, and handed to him a paper, but the whole matter was

to him only like a vague dream; the servant had
disappeared, and as to the paper, perhaps it might
be found if a proper search was made.

As far as Craeke was concerned, it was impossible to find him, as he had left Holland.

The paper also was not very likely to be found,
as no one gave himself the least trouble to look
for it.

Cornelius himself did not much press this point,
because even if the paper should turn up, it would
not be likely to have any direct connection with
the correspondence which constituted the charge.

The judges wished to appear as though they
wanted to urge Cornelius to make a better defence;
they displayed that benevolent patience which is
generally a sign of the magistrates being interested
for the prisoner; or of a man's having so completely got the better of his adversary that he
no longer needs any oppressive means to destroy
him.

Cornelius did not acknowledge this hypocritical
protection, and in his final answer, which he set
forth with the noble bearing of a martyr, and the
calm serenity of a righteous man, he said,—

'You ask me things, gentlemen, to which I can
only give the exact truth. Hear it. The parcel
was put into my hands in the way I have described; I declare before God that I was, and am
still, ignorant of its contents, and that it was not
until my arrest that I learned that this deposit was
the correspondence of the Grand Pensionary with
the Marquis de Louvois. And, lastly, I protest
that I do not understand how anyone should have
known that this parcel was in my house; and,
above all, how I can be deemed criminal for having
received what my illustrious and unfortunate godfather brought to me.'

This was the extent of Van Baerle's defence, after which the judges began to deliberate on the verdict.

They considered that every offshoot of civil discord is dangerous, because it revives the contest which it is the interest of all to put down.

One of them, who bore the character of a profound observer, laid down as his opinion that this young man, so phlegmatic in appearance, must in reality be cynically mischievous, as, under his icy exterior, he was sure to conceal an ardent desire to revenge his friends the De Wittes.

Another observed that the love of tulips agreed perfectly well with that of politics, and that it was proved in history that many very dangerous men were engaged in gardening, just as if it had been their profession, whilst really they occupied themselves with perfectly different concerns. For example, Tarquin the Elder, who grew poppies at Gabii, and the Great Condé, who watered his carnations at the palace of Vincennes, at the very moment when the former meditated his return to Rome, and the latter his escape from prison.

The judge therefore summed up with the following complex reasoning:—

'Either Cornelius van Baerle is a great lover of tulips, or a great lover of politics; in either case he has told us a falsehood, first, because his having occupied himself with politics is proved by the letters which were found at his house; and secondly, because his having occupied himself with tulips is proved by the bulbs, which leave no doubt of the fact. Finally, and herein lies the enormity of the case—As Cornelius van Baerle was concerned in the growing of tulips and in the pursuit of politics at one and the same time, the prisoner is of a hybrid character, of versatile organisation, working with equal ardour at politics and at tulips, which proves him to belong to the class of men most dangerous to public tranquillity, and shows a certain, or rather a complete, analogy between his character and that of those master minds, Tarquin the Elder and the Great Condé, which have been felicitously quoted as examples.'

The upshot of all these paradoxes was, that His Highness, the Prince Stadtholder of Holland, would decidedly feel greatly obliged to the magistracy of the Hague if they simplified for him the government of the Seven Provinces by destroying even the least germ of conspiracy against his authority.

This argument capped all the others, and in order so much the more effectually to destroy the germ of conspiracy, sentence of death was unanimously pronounced against Cornelius van Baerle, accused and convicted of having, under the innocent appearance of a tulip-fancier, participated in the detestable intrigues and abominable plots of the brothers De Witte against Dutch nationality, and in their secret relations with their French enemy.

The sentence concluded to the effect that 'the aforesaid Cornelius van Baerle should be led from the prison of the Buytenhof to the scaffold in the square of the same name, where the public executioner would duly cut off his head.'

As this deliberation was a most serious affair, it lasted a full half-hour, during which the prisoner was remanded to his cell.

There the Recorder of the States went to read the sentence to him.

The grim Gryphus was detained in bed by the fever caused by the fracture of his arm. His keys had passed into the hands of one of his assistants.

Behind this turnkey, who introduced the Recorder, Rosa, the fair Frisian maid, had slipped into the recess of the door, with a handkerchief to her mouth to stifle her sobs.

Cornelius listened to the sentence with an expression rather of surprise than of sadness.

After the sentence was read, the Recorder asked him whether he had anything to answer.

'Indeed, I have not,' he replied. 'Only I confess that among all the causes of death against which a cautious man may guard, I should never have supposed this could possibly be imagined.'

Upon this answer, the Recorder saluted Van Baerle with all that consideration which such functionaries generally bestow upon great criminals of every kind.

When he was about to withdraw, Cornelius inquired, 'By-the-bye, Mr Recorder, when will the sentence be carried out?'

'Why, to-day,' answered the Recorder, a little surprised by the self-possession of the condemned man.

A sob was heard from behind the door, and Cornelius turned round to learn from whom it came; but Rosa, who had foreseen such a movement, had fallen back.

'What hour is appointed?' continued Cornelius.

'Twelve o'clock, sir.'

'The deuce!' said Cornelius. 'I think I heard the clock strike ten about twenty minutes ago; I have not much time to spare.'

'Indeed you have not, if you wish to make your peace with God,' said the Recorder, bowing to the ground. 'You may ask for any clergyman you please.'

Saying these words he bowed himself out backwards, and the assistant turnkey was going to follow him, and to lock the door of Cornelius's cell, when a white and trembling arm interposed between him and the heavy door.

Cornelius saw nothing but the golden brocade cap, daintly tipped with lace, such as Frisian girls wore; he heard nothing but someone whispering into the ear of the turnkey. And the latter put his heavy keys into the white hand which was stretched out to receive them, and, descending some steps, sat down on the staircase, which thus was guarded above by himself, and below by the dog. The head-dress turned round, and Cornelius beheld the face of Rosa, blanched with grief, her beautiful eyes streaming with tears.

She went up to Cornelius, crossing her arms on her heaving breast.

'Oh, mynheer!' she said, but her sobs choked all further utterance.

'My good girl,' Cornelius replied with emotion, 'what do you wish? My time on earth is short.'

'I come to ask a favour of you,' said Rosa, extending her arms partly towards him and partly towards heaven.

'Don't weep so, Rosa,' said the prisoner, 'for your tears touch my heart more deeply than my approaching doom; and you know, the less guilty a man is, the more necessary is it for him to die calmly, and even joyfully, for he dies a martyr. Come, there's a dear, weep no more, and tell me what you wish, my pretty Rosa.'

She fell on her knees. 'Forgive my father,' she said.

'Your father, your father?' said Cornelius, astonished.

'Yes, he has been so harsh with you, but it is his nature; he is so to everyone, and you are not the only one whom he has bullied.'

'He is punished, my dear Rosa, more than punished, by the accident that has befallen him, and I forgive him.'

'I thank you, sir,' said Rosa. 'And now tell me —oh, tell me—can I do anything for you?'

'You can dry your beautiful eyes, my dear child,' answered Cornelius, with a gentle smile.

'But what can I do for you—for you?'

'A man who has only one hour longer to live must be a great Sybarite still to want anything, my dear Rosa.'

'The clergyman whom they have proposed to you?'

'I have worshipped God all my life, I have worshipped Him in His works, and praised Him always. I am at peace with Him, and do not wish for a clergyman. The last thought which occupies my mind, however, has reference to the glory of the Almighty. Help me, my dear, to carry out my last thought.'

'Oh, Mynheer Cornelius, speak, speak!' exclaimed Rosa, still bathed in tears.

'Give me your hand, and promise me not to laugh, my dear child.'

'Laugh,' exclaimed Rosa, frantic with grief, 'laugh, at this moment!. Do you not see my tears?'

'Rosa, I have looked at you, and know you, and appreciate your character. I have never seen a woman more fair or more pure than you are, and if from this moment I take no more notice of you, forgive me; it is only because, on leaving this world, I do not wish to die with any further regret.'

Rosa felt a shudder creeping over her frame, for, whilst the prisoner pronounced these words, the belfry clock of the Buytenhof struck eleven.

Cornelius understood her. 'Yes, yes, let us make haste,' he said, 'you are right, Rosa.'

Then, taking the paper with the three bulbs from his breast, where he had again put it, since he had no longer any fear of being searched, he said,—

'My dear girl, I have been very fond of flowers. That was at a time when I did not know that there was anything else to be loved. Don't blush, Rosa, nor turn away; even though I were to make you a declaration of love. Alas! my dear, it would be of no more consequence. Down there in the square there is an instrument of steel which in sixty minutes will put an end to my boldness. Well, Rosa, I loved flowers dearly, and I have found, or at least I believe so, the secret of the grand black tulip, which it has been considered impossible to grow, and for which, as you may or may not know, a prize of a hundred thousand guilders has been offered by the Horticultural Society of Haarlem. These hundred thousand guilders—and Heaven knows I do not regret them—these hundred thousand guilders I have here in this paper; for they are won by the three bulbs wrapped up in it, which you may take, Rosa, as I make you a present of them.'

'Mynheer Cornelius!'

'Yes, yes, Rosa, you may take them, you are not wronging anyone, my child. I am alone in this world; my parents are dead; I never had a sister or brother. I have never had a thought of loving anyone with what is called love, and if anyone has loved me, I have not known it. However, you see well, Rosa, that I am abandoned by everybody, as in this sad hour you alone are with me in my prison, consoling and assisting me.'

'But, sir, a hundred thousand guilders!'

'Now, let us talk seriously, my dear child. Those hundred thousand guilders will be a nice marriage portion, with your pretty face ; you shall have them, for I am quite sure of my bulb. You shall have them, Rosa, dear Rosa, and I ask nothing in return but your promise that you will marry a fine young man, whom you love, and who will love you as sincerely as I loved my flowers. Don't interrupt me, Rosa, dear, I have only a few minutes more.'

The poor girl was nearly choking with her sobs.

Cornelius took her by the hand.

'Listen to me,' he continued ; ' I'll teach you how to manage it. Go to Dort and ask Butruysheim, my gardener, for soil from my border number six, fill a deep box with it, and plant in it these three bulbs. They will flower next May, that is to say in seven months ; and when you see the flower forming on the stem, be careful at night to protect them from the wind, and by day to screen them from the sun. They will flower black ; I am quite sure of it. You must then communicate with the President of the Haarlem Society. He will cause the colour of the flower to be proved before the committee, and those hundred thousand guilders will be paid to you.'

Rosa heaved a deep sigh.

'And now,' continued Cornelius, wiping away a tear which was glistening in his eye, and which was shed much more for that marvellous black tulip which he was not to see than for the life which he was about to lose, ' I have no wish left, except that the tulip should be called " *Rosa Barlænsis*," that is to say, that its name should combine yours and mine ; and as, of course, you do not understand Latin, and might therefore forget this name, try to get for me pencil and paper, that I may write it down for you,'

Rosa sobbed afresh, and handed to him a book, bound in shagreen, which bore the initials C. W.

'What is this?' asked the prisoner.

'Alas!' replied Rosa, 'it is the Bible of your poor godfather Cornelius de Witte. From it he derived strength to endure the torture, and to bear his sentence without flinching. I found it in this cell after the death of the martyr, and have preserved it as a relic. To-day I brought it to you, for it seemed to me that this book must possess in itself a power which is divine. Write in it what you have to write, Mynheer Cornelius; and though, unfortunately, I am not able to read, I will take care that what you desire shall be accomplished.' Cornelius took the Bible and kissed it reverently.

'With what shall I write?' asked Cornelius.

'There is a pencil in the Bible,' said Rosa.

This was the pencil which John de Witte had lent to his brother, which he had forgotten to take away back.

Cornelius took it, and on the second fly-leaf (for it will be remembered that the first was torn out), drawing near his end like his godfather, he wrote, with a firm hand,—

'On this day, the 23rd of August 1672, being about to render, although innocent, my soul to God on the scaffold, I bequeath to Rosa Gryphus the only worldly goods which have remained to me of all that I have possessed in this world, the rest having been confiscated; I bequeath, I say, to Rosa Gryphus three bulbs, which I am convinced must produce, in the next May, the Grand Black Tulip, for which a prize of a hundred thousand guilders has been offered by the Haarlem Society, requesting that she may be paid the same sum in my stead, as my sole heiress, under the only condition of her marrying a respectable young man of about my age, who loves her, and whom she loves, and of her giving the grand black tulip, which will constitute a new species, the name of *Rosa Barlæensis*, that is to say, her name and mine combined.

'So may God grant me mercy; and to her health and long life!

'CORNELIUS VAN BAERLE.'

The prisoner, then giving the Bible to Rosa, said,—

'Read.'

'Alas!' she answered, 'I have already told you I cannot read.'

Cornelius then read to Rosa the testament which he had just made.

The agony of the poor girl almost overpowered her.

'Do you accept my conditions?' asked the prisoner, with a melancholy smile, kissing the trembling hands of the afflicted girl.

'Oh, I don't know, sir,' she stammered.

'You don't know, child, and why not?'

'Because there is one condition which I am afraid I cannot keep.'

'Which? I thought that all was settled between us.'

'You give me the hundred thousand guilders as a marriage-portion, don't you?'

'Yes.'

'And under the condition of my marrying a man whom I love?'

'Certainly.'

'Well, then, sir, this money cannot belong to me. I shall never love anyone; neither shall I marry.'

And after having with difficulty uttered these

words, Rosa almost swooned away in the violence of her grief.

Cornelius, frightened at seeing her so pale and inanimate, was going to take her in his arms, when a heavy step, followed by other foreboding sounds, was heard on the staircase, mingled with the continued barking of the dog.

'They are coming to fetch you. Oh, God! oh, God!' cried Rosa, wringing her hands. 'Have you nothing more to tell me?'

Again she fell on her knees, with her face buried in her hands, weeping hysterically.

'I have only to say that I wish you to preserve these bulbs as the most precious treasure, and carefully to treat them according to the directions I have given you! Do it for my sake, and now farewell, Rosa.'

'Yes, yes,' she said, without raising her head, I will do anything you bid me, except marry,' she added in a low voice, 'for that, oh! that is impossible for me now.'

She then placed the cherished treasure in her breast.

The noise on the staircase which Cornelius and Rosa had heard was caused by the Recorder, who was coming for the prisoner. He was followed by the executioner, by the soldiers who were to form the guard round the scaffold, and by the usual hangers-on of the prison.

Cornelius, without exhibiting any weakness, and without any bravado, received them rather as friends than as persecutors, and quietly submitted to all those preparations which these men were obliged to make in the performance of their duty.

Then, casting a glance into the yard through the narrow iron-barred window of his cell, he perceived the scaffold, and, at twenty paces distant from it, the gibbet, from which, by order of the Stadtholder, the outraged remains of the two brothers De Witte had been taken down.

When the moment came to descend, to follow the guards, Cornelius sought with his eyes the angelic expression in Rosa's face, but he saw, behind the swords and halberds, only a form lying outstretched near a wooden bench, and a death-like face, half covered with long golden locks.

But, as she fell, Rosa, still obeying her friend, had pressed her hand on her velvet bodice, instinctively grasping the precious packet which Cornelius had entrusted to her care.

Leaving the cell, the young man could still see, in the convulsively-clenched fingers of Rosa, the yellowish leaf from that Bible on which Cornelius de Witte had with such difficulty and pain written those few lines which, if Van Baerle had read them, would undoubtedly have been the salvation of a man and a tulip.

CHAPTER XII

THE EXECUTION

CORNELIUS had not three hundred paces to walk outside the prison to reach the foot of the scaffold. At the bottom of the staircase the dog quietly looked at him while he was passing: Cornelius even fancied he saw in the eyes of the monster a certain expression which savoured of compassion.

The dog, perhaps, knew by instinct the condemned prisoners, and only bit those who left as free men.

The shorter the way from the door of the prison
to the foot of the scaffold, the more fully, of course,
it was crowded with curious people.

They were the same who, not satisfied with the
blood which they had shed three days before, were
now craving for a new victim.

Scarcely had Cornelius made his appearance
than a fierce groan ran through the whole street,
spreading all over the yard, and re-echoing from
the roads which led to the scaffold, which were
crowded with spectators.

The scaffold seemed like an islet at the confluence of several rivers.

In the midst of these threats, groans and yells,
Cornelius, very likely in order not to hear them,
had lost himself in oblivion.

And what did he think of, with death staring
him in the face?

Not of his enemies, nor of his judges, nor of his
executioners.

He was thinking of the beautiful tulips which he
would see from paradise, at Ceylon, or Bengal, or
elsewhere, when he would be able to look with
pity on this earth, where John and Cornelius de
Witte had been murdered for having thought too
much of politics, and where Cornelius van Baerle
was about to be murdered for having loved tulips
too ardently.

'It is only one stroke of the axe,' said the
philosopher to himself, 'and my beautiful dream
will begin to be realised.'

Only there was still a doubt, as in the case
before of M. de Chalais and M. de Thou and
other badly-executed people, for the headsman
might inflict more than one stroke, that is to say,
more than one martyrdom, on the poor tulip-
fancier.

Yet, notwithstanding all this, Van Baerle mounted the scaffold not the less resolutely, proud of having been the friend of that illustrious John and godson of that noble Cornelius de Witte whom the ruffians, who were now crowding to witness his own doom, had torn to pieces and burnt three days before.

He knelt down, said his prayers, and observed, not without a feeling of sincere joy, that laying his head on the block, and keeping his eyes open, he would be able, to his last moment, to see the grated window of the Buytenhof.

At last the fatal moment arrived, and Cornelius placed his chin on the cold, damp block. As he did so his eyes closed involuntarily, to receive more resolutely the terrible avalanche which was about to fall on his head and to end his life.

A gleam, like that of lightning, fell across the scaffold as the executioner raised his sword.

Van Baerle bade farewell to the grand black tulip, hoping to awake in another world full of light and glorious tints and radiance.

Three times he felt, with a shudder, a cold current of air from the knife passing over his neck, yet he neither felt pain nor shock.

He saw no change in the colour of the clouds nor the world around him.

Then suddenly Van Baerle felt gentle hands raising him, and he soon stood on his feet again, although trembling a little.

He opened his eyes. There was someone by his side, reading a large parchment, sealed with a huge seal of red wax.

And the same sun, yellow and pale, as Dutch sun generally is, was shining in the skies; and the same grated window looked down upon him from the Buytenhof.

And the same rabble, no longer yelling, but completely thunderstruck, was staring at him from the streets below.

Van Baerle began to be sensible of what was going on around him.

His Highness, William, Prince of Orange, somewhat afraid that Van Baerle's blood would turn the scale of judgment against him, had compassionately taken into consideration his good character and the seeming proofs of his innocence.

His Highness, accordingly, had granted him his life.

Cornelius at first hoped that the pardon would be complete, and that he would be restored to his full liberty and to his flower-borders at Dort.

But Cornelius was mistaken. To use an expression of Madame de Sevigné, 'there was a postscript to the letter'; and the most important point of the letter was contained in the postscript.

By this postscript, William of Orange, Stadtholder of Holland, condemned Cornelius van Baerle to imprisonment for life. He was not sufficiently guilty to suffer death, nor sufficiently innocent to be set at liberty.

Cornelius heard this postscript in amazement, but the first feeling of vexation and disappointment over, he said to himself,—

'Never mind, all is not lost yet, there is some good in this perpetual imprisonment. Rosa will be there, and I shall have my three bulbs of the black tulip.'

But Cornelius forgot that the Seven Provinces had seven prisons, one for each; and that the board of the prisoner is anywhere else less expensive than at the Hague, which is a capital.

His Highness of Orange, who, as it seemed, was disinclined to feed Van Baerle at the Hague, sent him to undergo his perpetual imprisonment at the fortress of Lœwestein, close to Dort, but, alas! also very far from it; for Lœwestein is situated at the point of the islet which is formed by the confluence of the Waal and the Meuse, opposite Gorcum.

Van Baerle was sufficiently versed in the history of his country to know that the celebrated Grotius was confined in that castle after the death of Barneveldte; and that the States, in their generosity to the illustrious publicist, jurist, historian, poet and divine, had granted to him for his daily maintenance the sum of twenty-four Dutch sous.

'I,' said Baerle to himself, 'who am of much less importance than Grotius, shall be lucky if they give me twelve stivers, which will be bad enough, but anyhow I shall live.'

Then, suddenly, a terrible thought occurred to him.

'Ah!' he exclaimed, 'how damp and misty that part of the country is; and the soil is so bad for the tulips. And then there is Rosa, she will not be at Lœwestein!'

CHAPTER XIII

WHAT ONE OF THE SPECTATORS WAS THINKING ALL THIS TIME

WHILE Cornelius was reflecting upon his misfortunes, a coach had driven up to the scaffold. This vehicle was for the prisoner. He was invited to enter it, and he obeyed.

His last look was towards the Buytenhof. He hoped to see the face of Rosa at the window. But the coach was drawn by quick horses who soon carried Van Baerle away from the shouts which the rabble roared in honour of the most magnanimous Stadtholder, intermingled with it a spice of abuse against the brothers De Witte and the godson of Cornelius, who had just now been rescued from death.

Van Baerle's reprieve suggested to the worthy spectators remarks such as the following :—

' It's very fortunate that we used such speed in having justice done to that great villain John, and to that little rogue Cornelius, otherwise His Highness might have snatched them from us, just as he has done this fellow.'

Among all the spectators whom Van Baerle's execution had attracted to the Buytenhof, and whom the sudden turn of affairs had disagreeably surprised, undoubtedly the one most disappointed was a certain respectably-dressed burgher, who, from early morning, had made such a good use of his feet and elbows that he at last was separated from the scaffold only by the file of soldiers which surrounded it.

Many had shown themselves eager to see the perfidious blood of the guilty Cornelius flow, but not one had shown such keen anxiety and persistency as the individual alluded to.

The most furious had come to the Buytenhof at daybreak to secure a better place ; but he, outdoing even them, had passed the night at the threshold of the prison, whence, as we have already said, he had advanced to the very foremost rank, *unguibus et rostro*, that is to say, coaxing some and kicking others.

When the executioner had brought the prisoner to the scaffold, this burgher, who had mounted on

the stone of the pump, the better to see and be
seen, made a sign to the executioner, as much as
to say,—

'It's a bargain, isn't it?'

The executioner answered by another sign, which
was meant to say,—

'Never fear, it's all right.'

This burgher was no other than Mynheer Isaac
Boxtel, who, since the arrest of Cornelius, had
come to the Hague to try if he could not get hold
of the three bulbs of the black tulip.

Boxtel had at first tried to buy over Gryphus to
his interest, but the jailer had not only the snarl-
ing fierceness, but likewise the fidelity, of a dog.
He had therefore bristled up at Boxtel's apparent
spite, whom he suspected to be a warm friend of
the prisoner making trifling inquiries to contrive,
with more certainty, some means of escape for him.

Therefore, to the very first proposals which
Boxtel made to Gryphus to steal the bulbs, which
Cornelius Van Baerle must be supposed to conceal,
if not in his breast, at least in some corner of his
cell, the surly jailer had only answered by showing Mynheer Isaac the door, and setting the dog
to attend him down the staircase.

The mastiff managed to secure a piece of his
hose, but this did not discourage Boxtel.   He
returned to the charge, but this time Gryphus was
in his bed, feverish, and with a broken arm.   He
therefore was not able to admit the petitioner, who
then addressed himself to Rosa, offering to buy for
her a head-dress of pure gold if she would but get the
bulbs for him.   On this, the generous girl, although
not yet knowing the value of the object of the
robbery which was to be so well remunerated, had
directed the tempter to the executioner as the heir
of the prisoner.

Meanwhile, the sentence had been pronounced. Thus Isaac had no more time to bribe anyone. He therefore seized upon the idea which Rosa had suggested, and he went to the executioner.

Isaac had not the least doubt but that Cornelius would die with his bulbs next his heart.

But there were two things which Boxtel did not calculate upon.

Rosa, that is to say—love ; and—

William of Orange, that is to say—clemency.

But for Rosa and William the calculations of the envious neighbour would have been accurate.

But for William, Cornelius would have died.

But for Rosa, Cornelius would have died with his bulbs next his heart.

Mynheer Boxtel went to the headsman, to whom he gave himself out as a great friend of the condemned man, and bought from him all the clothes of the dead man that was to be for the exorbitant sum of one hundred guilders, as he engaged to leave all the trinkets of gold and silver to the executioner.

But what was the sum of a hundred guilders to a man who was all but sure to receive with it the prize of the Haarlem Society ?

It was money lent at a thousand per cent., which was really a very agreeable investment.

The headsman, on the other hand, had scarcely anything to do to earn his hundred guilders. He needed only, as soon as the execution was over, to allow Mynheer Boxtel to ascend the scaffold with his servants to remove the inanimate remains of his friend.

The thing was, moreover, quite customary among the ʿfaithful brethren' when one of their masters died a public death in the yard of the Buytenhof.

A fanatic like Cornelius might very easily have found another fanatic who gave a hundred guilders for his remains.

The executioner also readily acquiesced in the proposal, making only one condition—that of being paid in advance.

Boxtel, like the people who enter a show at a fair, might not be pleased and refuse to pay on going out.

So Boxtel had to pay in advance; then he waited.

After this the reader may imagine how excited Boxtel was; with what anxiety he watched the guards, the Recorder and the executioner; and with what intense interest he surveyed the movements of Van Baerle. How would he place himself on the block? how would he fall? and would he not, in falling, crush those inestimable bulbs? had not he at least taken care to enclose them in a golden box? as gold is the hardest of all metals.

Every trifling delay irritated him. Why did that stupid executioner thus lose his time in brandishing his sword over the head of Cornelius, instead of cutting that head off?

But when he saw the Recorder take the hand of the condemned man, and raise him as he drew the parchment from his pocket; when he heard the pardon of the Stadtholder publicly read out—then Boxtel was no longer a human being. The rage and malice of the tiger, of the hyena, and of the serpent glistened in his eyes, and vented itself in his yell and his movements. Had he been able to get at Van Baerle, he would have pounced upon and murdered him.

And so, then, Cornelius was to live, and was to go to Lœwestein, and thither to his prison he would take his bulbs; and perhaps he would even find a garden where the black tulip would flower for him.

Boxtel, overcome by his frenzy, fell from the stone upon some Orangemen, who, like him, were sorely vexed at the turn which affairs had taken. They, mistaking the frantic cries of Mynheer Isaac for demonstrations of joy, began to belabour him with kicks and cuffs, such as could not have been administered in better style on the other side of the Channel.

Blows were, however, nothing to him. He wanted to run after the coach which was carrying away Cornelius with his bulbs. But in his hurry he overlooked a paving-stone in his way, stumbled, lost his centre of gravity, rolled over to a distance of some yards, and only rose again, bruised and begrimed, after the whole rabble of the Hague with their muddy feet had passed over him.

One would think that this was enough for one day, but Mynheer Boxtel did not seem to think so, as in addition to having his clothes torn, his back bruised, and his hands scratched, he inflicted upon himself the further punishment of tearing out his hair as an offering to that smaller goddess, Envy, who, as mythology tells us, wears a head-dress of hissing serpents.

CHAPTER XIV

THE PIGEONS OF DORT

IT was, indeed, in itself a great honour for Cornelius van Baerle to be confined in the same prison which had once received the learned master, Grotius.

But, on arriving at the prison, he met with an honour even greater. As chance would have it, the cell formerly occupied by the illustrious Barneveldte happened to be vacant when the clemency of the Prince of Orange sent the tulip-fancier, Van Baerle, there.

The cell had a very bad character at the castle since the time when Grotius, by means of the device of his wife, made escape thence in that famous book-chest which his guards forgot to examine.

On the other hand, it seemed to Van Baerle an auspicious omen that this very cell was assigned to him; for, according to his ideas, a jailer ought never to have given to a second pigeon the cage from which the first had so easily flown.

The cell is historical. In it was still the alcove which was contrived for the use of Madame Grotius. Otherwise it differed in no respect from the other cells of the prison; except, perhaps, that it was a little higher, and had a splendid view from the grated window.

Cornelius himself felt perfectly indifferent as to the place where he had to lead an existence which was little more than vegetation. There were only two things now for which he cared, and the possession of which was a happiness which he could only enjoy in imagination.

A flower and a woman. Both of them, as he believed, lost to him for ever.

But the prisoner was mistaken. In his prison cell the most adventurous life which ever fell to the lot of any tulip-fancier was reserved for him.

One morning, while standing at his window, inhaling the fresh air which came from the river, and casting longing looks towards the windmills of his dear old native Dort, which stood out in the distance behind a forest of chimneys, he saw flocks

of pigeons coming from that quarter, to perch
fluttering on the pointed gables of Lœwestein.

'These pigeons,' Van Baerle muttered, 'come
from Dort, and consequently may return there.
By fastening a little note to the wing of one of
these birds, I might have a chance of sending
a message back.' Then, after a few moments
consideration, he exclaimed,—

'I will do it.'

At twenty-eight a man condemned to a prison
for life grows philosophical. That is to say, doomed
to something like twenty-two or twenty-three thousand days of captivity.

Van Baerle, ever thinking of his darling bulbs,
made a snare for catching the pigeons. He
tempted the birds with all the resources of his
limited kitchen, such as it was for about sixpence
(English) a day; and, after a month of unsuccess-
ful attempts, he at last caught a female bird.

It cost him two more months to catch a male
bird. He then shut them up together; and having
about the beginning of the year 1673 obtained some
eggs from them, he released the female, which,
leaving the male behind to hatch the eggs in her
absence, flew joyously back to Dort, with the note
under her wing.

She returned in the evening with the note
intact.

Thus it went on for fifteen days, at first to the
disappointment, and then to the great grief of Van
Baerle.

On the sixteenth day, however, she came back
without it.

Van Baerle had addressed it to his nurse, the
old Frisian woman, and implored any charitable
soul who might find it to convey it to her as safely
and speedily as possible.

In this letter there was a little note enclosed for Rosa.

Van Baerle's nurse had received the letter in the following way.

On leaving Dort, Mynheer Isaac Boxtel had abandoned not only his house, his servant, his observatory, and his telescope, but also his pigeons.

The servant, having been left without wages, first lived on his little savings, and then on his master's pigeons.

Seeing this, the pigeons emigrated from the roof of Isaac Boxtel to that of Cornelius van Baerle.

The nurse was a kind-hearted woman, who could not live without having something to love. She conceived an affection for the pigeons which had thrown themselves on her hospitality; and when Boxtel's servant demanded them, having eaten the first fifteen, with culinary intentions towards the other fifteen, she offered to buy them from him for a consideration just double their value, and the nurse found herself in undisputed possession of the pigeons of her master's envious neighbour.

The note, as we have said, had reached Van Baerle's nurse.

And so it befell that one evening in the beginning of February, just when the stars were beginning to twinkle, Cornelius heard on the staircase of the little turret a voice which thrilled through him.

He put his hand to his heart, and listened.

It was the sweet, melodious voice of Rosa.

Let us confess that Cornelius was not so stupefied with surprise, or so beyond himself with joy as he would have been but for the pigeon, which,

in answer to his letter, had brought back hope to
him under her empty wing ; and, knowing Rosa,
he expected, if the note had ever reached her, to
hear of her whom he loved, and also of his three
precious bulbs.

He rose, listened once more, and bent toward
the door.

Yes, they were indeed the accents which had
fallen so sweetly on his heart at the Hague.

The question now was, whether Rosa, who had
made the journey from the Hague to Lœwestein,
and who—Cornelius did not understand how—had
succeeded even in penetrating into the prison,
would also be fortunate enough in making her
way to his cell.

While Cornelius, debating this point within
himself, was building all sorts of castles in the
air, and was struggling between hope and fear, the
shutter of the grating in the door opened, and
Rosa, beaming with joy, and beautiful in her
pretty national costume—but still more beautiful
from the grief which for the last five months had
blanched her cheeks—pressed her little face against
the wire grating of the window, saying to him,—

'Oh! mynheer, mynheer, here I am!'

Cornelius stretched out his arms, and, looking
toward heaven, uttered a cry of joy,—

'Oh, Rosa, Rosa!'

'Hush! let us speak low; my father is close at
hand,' said the girl.

'Your father?'

'Yes, he is in the courtyard at the bottom of the
staircase, receiving the instructions of the Governor.
He will presently come up.'

'The instructions of the Governor?'

'Listen to me, and I'll try to tell you everything
in a few words. The Stadtholder has a country

house one league distant from Leyden—properly speaking, a kind of large dairy—and my aunt, who was his nurse, has the management of it. As soon as I received your letter, which, alas! I could not read myself, but which your housekeeper read to me, I hastened to my aunt. There I remained until the Prince came to the dairy; and when he came, I asked him, as a favour, to allow my father to exchange his post at the prison of the Hague with the jailer of the fortress of Lœwestein. The Prince, of course, did not suspect my object; otherwise, naturally, he would have refused my request.'

'And so you are here?'

'As you see.'

'And I shall see you every day?'

'As often as I can manage it.'

'Oh, Rosa, my beautiful Rosa, do you love me a little?'

'A little?' she said. 'Mynheer Cornelius, you don't ask enough.'

Cornelius tenderly stretched out his hands towards her, but they were only able to touch each other with the tips of their fingers through the wire grating.

'Here is my father,' said she.

Rosa then abruptly drew back from the door, and ran to meet old Gryphus, who had just reached the top of the staircase.

CHAPTER XV

THE LITTLE GRATED WINDOW

GRYPHUS was followed by the mastiff.

The turnkey took the animal round the jail, so

that, in case of need, he might recognise the prisoners.

'Father,' said Rosa, 'here is the famous prison from which Mynheer Grotius escaped. You know about Mynheer Grotius?'

'Oh, yes, that rogue Grotius; a friend of that villain Barneveldte, whom I saw executed when I was a child. Ah! Grotius; and that's the cell from which he escaped. Well, I'll answer for it no one will get a chance to follow his example.'

And opening the door, he began in the dark to talk to the prisoner.

The dog, on his part, went up to the prisoner, and growled and sniffed at his legs, just as though to ask him what right he had still to be alive, after having left the prison in the company of the Recorder and the executioner.

But the fair Rosa called him to her side.

'Well, mynheer,' said Gryphus, holding up his lantern to throw a little light around, 'you see in me your new jailer. I am head turnkey, and have all the cells under my care. I'm not vicious, but I'm not to be trifled with as far as discipline goes.'

'My good Mynheer Gryphus, I know you perfectly well,' said the prisoner, approaching to within the circle of light cast around by the lantern.

'Halloa! is that you, Mynheer van Baerle,' said Gryphus. 'That you; well, I declare, it's astonishing what a small place the world of prisons is.'

'Yes, and it's really a great pleasure to me, good Mynheer Gryphus, to see that your arm is doing well, as I see you are able to hold your lantern with it.'

Gryphus frowned. 'It's always the way,' he said; 'people will make blunders in politics. His Highness has granted you your life; I'm sure I should never have done so,'

'Don't say so,' replied Cornelius. 'Why not?'

'Because you are the very man to conspire again. You learned people have dealings with the devil.'

'Nonsense, Mynheer Gryphus. Are you dissatisfied with the manner in which I have set your arm, or with the price that I asked you?' said Cornelius, laughing.

'Oh, no,' growled the jailer, 'you set it only too well. There is some witchcraft in this. After six weeks I was able to use it as if nothing had happened; so much so, that the doctor of the Buytenhof, who knows his trade well, wanted to break it again, to set it in the regular way, and promised me that I should go three months without being able to move it.'

'And you did not want that?'

'I said, "Nay, as long as I can make the sign of the cross with that arm" (Gryphus was a Roman Catholic), "I can laugh at the devil."'

'But if you laugh at the devil, Mynheer Gryphus, you ought with so much more reason to laugh at learned people.'

'Ah, learned people, learned people. Why, I would rather have to guard ten soldiers than one scholar. The soldiers smoke, guzzle and get drunk; they are as gentle as lambs if you only give them brandy or Moselle; but scholars, and drink, smoke and fuddle—ah, yes, that's altogether different. They keep sober, spend nothing, and have their heads always clear to think of conspiracies. But I tell you, at the very outset, it won't be such an easy matter for you to conspire here. First of all, you will have no books, no paper, and no conjuring works. It was books that helped Mynheer Grotius to get off.'

'I assure you, Mynheer Gryphus,' replied Van

Baerle, 'that if I have entertained the idea of escaping, I most decidedly have abandoned it now.'

'All right,' said Gryphus, 'keep sharp; that's what I shall do also. But, for all that, I say His Highness has made a great mistake.'

'Not to have cut off my head? thank you, Mynheer Gryphus.'

'Just so. See how quiet the Mynheers de Witte keep now.'

'What you say is horrible, Mynheer Gryphus,' cried Van Baerle, turning away his head to conceal his disgust. 'You forget that one of those unfortunate gentlemen was my friend, and the other my second father.'

'Yes, but I also remember that they were both conspirators. And, moreover, I am speaking Christianly.'

'Oh, indeed, explain that a little to me, my good Mynheer Gryphus. I do not quite understand it.'

'Well, then, if you had remained on the block of Mynheer Harbruck—'

'What?'

'You would not suffer any longer; whereas, I will not disguise it from you, I shall lead you a devil of a life of it.'

'Thank you for the promise, Mynheer Gryphus.'

While the prisoner smiled ironically at the old jailer, Rosa, from the outside, answered by a bright smile, which carried sweet consolation to the heart of Van Baerle.

Gryphus stepped towards the window.

It was still light enough to see, although indistinctly, through the grey haze of the evening, the vast expanse of the horizon.

'What view has one from here?' asked Gryphus.

'Why, a very fine one,' said Cornelius, glancing at Rosa.

'Yes, yes, too much of a view, too much.'

At this moment the two pigeons, scared by the sight, and especially by the voice of the stranger, left their nest, and disappeared, quite frightened, in the evening mist.

'Halloa! what's this?' cried Gryphus.

'My pigeons,' answered Cornelius.

'Your pigeons,' cried the jailer, 'your pigeons! Has a prisoner anything of his own?'

'Why, then,' said Cornelius, 'the pigeons which a merciful Father in Heaven has lent to me.'

'So here's a breach of the rules already,' replied Gryphus. 'Pigeons! ah, young man, young man; I'll tell you one thing, that before to-morrow is over your pigeons will boil in my pot.'

'First of all you must catch them, Master Gryphus. You won't allow these pigeons to be mine. Well, I vow they are even less yours than mine.'

'We shall see,' growled the jailer. 'I shall certainly wring their necks before twenty - four hours are over.'

'While giving utterance to this ill - natured promise, Gryphus put his head out of the window to examine the nest. This gave Van Baerle time to run to the door and squeeze the hand of Rosa, who whispered to him,—

'At nine o'clock this evening.'

Gryphus, quite taken up with the desire of catching the pigeons next day, as he had promised he would do, saw and heard nothing of this love interlude; and having closed the window, he took the arm of his daughter, left the cell, turned the key twice, drew the bolts, and went off to make similar kind promises to the other prisoners.

He had scarcely gone when Cornelius went to the door to listen to the sound of his footsteps, and as soon as they had died away, he ran to the window and completely demolished the nest of the pigeons.

Rather than expose them to the tender mercies of the great bully, he drove away for ever those gentle messengers to whom he owed the happiness of having back his Rosa again.

This visit of the jailer, his brutal threats, and the gloomy prospect of the harshness which, he knew, he was likely to experience, made Cornelius very downhearted and soon cast out the sweet hope which the presence of Rosa had re-awakened in his heart.

He waited eagerly to hear the tower clock of Lœwestein strike nine.

The last chime was still vibrating through the air when Cornelius heard on the staircase the light step and the rustle of the flowing dress of the fair Frisian maid, and soon after a light appeared at the little wicket in the door, on which the prisoner fixed his earnest gaze.

The shutter was opened from the outside.

'Here I am,' said Rosa, out of breath from running up the stairs; 'here I am.'

'Oh, my good Rosa!'

'You are then glad to see me?'

'Can you ask? But how did you contrive to come? tell me.'

'I will tell you. My father falls asleep every evening, almost immediately after his supper; I then make him lie down, a little stupefied with his schnapps. Don't say anything about it, because, thanks to this nap, I shall be able to come every evening and chat for an hour with you.'

'Oh, I thank you, Rosa, dear Rosa.'

Saying these words, Cornelius put his face so near the little window that Rosa withdrew hers.

'I have brought your bulbs to you.'

Cornelius's heart leaped with joy. He had not yet dared to ask Rosa what she had done with the precious treasure which he had entrusted to her.

'Oh! you have preserved them, then?'

'Did you not give them to me as a thing which was dear to you?'

'Yes, but as I have given them to you, it seems to me that they belong to you.'

'They would have belonged to me after your death, but, fortunately, you are alive now. Oh! how I blessed His Highness in my heart. If God grants to him all the happiness that I have wished him, certainly Prince William will be the happiest man on earth. When I looked at the Bible of your godfather Cornelius, I was resolved to bring your bulbs back to you, only I did not know how to accomplish it. I had, however, already formed the plan of going to the Stadtholder to ask from him, for my father, the appointment of jailer at Lœwestein, when your housekeeper brought me your letter. Oh, how we wept together. But your letter only confirmed me the more in my resolution. I then left for Leyden, and the rest you know.'

'What! my dear Rosa, you thought, even before receiving my letter, of coming to meet me again?'

'Did I think of it?' said Rosa, allowing her love to get the better of her bashfulness. 'I thought of nothing else.'

And, saying these words, Rosa looked so exceedingly pretty, that for the second time Cornelius placed his forehead and lips against the wire grating, no doubt with the laudable desire to thank the young lady.

Rosa, however, drew back as before.

'In truth,' she said, with that coquetry which somehow or other is in the heart of every young girl, ' I have often been sorry that I am not able to read, but never so much so as when your house-keeper brought me your letter. I kept the paper in my hands, which spoke to other people, and which was dumb to poor stupid me.'

' So you have often regretted not being able to read,' said Cornelius. ' On what occasions, pray?'

' Troth,' said she, laughing, ' to read all the letters which were written to me.'

' Oh, you received letters, Rosa?'

' By hundreds.'

' But who wrote to you?'

' Who! Why, in the first place, all the students who passed over the Buytenhof, all the officers who went to parade, all the clerks, and even the merchants who saw me at my little window.'

' And what did you do with all these notes, my dear Rosa?'

' Formerly,' she answered, ' I got some friend to read them to me, which was capital fun; but since a certain time—well, what use is it to attend to all this nonsense?—since a certain time I have burnt them.'

' Since a certain time!' exclaimed Cornelius, with a look beaming with love and joy.

Rosa blushingly cast down her eyes. In her sweet confusion she did not observe the lips of Cornelius, which, alas! only met the cold wire grating. Yet, in spite of this obstacle, they com-municated to the lips of the young girl the glowing breath of the most tender kiss.

At this sudden outburst of tenderness Rosa grew as pale, and perhaps paler than she had been on the day of the execution. She uttered a plaintive sob, closed her fine eyes, and fled, trying in vain to still the beating of her heart.

And so Cornelius was again alone,

Rosa fled so precipitately that she completely forgot to return to Cornelius the three bulbs of the Black Tulip.

———

CHAPTER XVI

MASTER AND PUPIL

THE worthy Gryphus was far from sharing the kindly feelings of his daughter for the godson of Cornelius de Witte.

There being only five prisoners at Lœwestein, the post of turnkey was not a very onerous one, but rather a sort of sinecure, given after a long period of service.

But the worthy jailer, in his zeal, had magnified, with all the power of his imagination, the importance of his office. To him Cornelius assumed the gigantic proportions of a criminal of the first order. He looked upon him, therefore, as the most dangerous of all his prisoners. He watched all his steps, and always spoke to him with an angry countenance; punishing him for what he called his dreadful rebellion against the kind-hearted Stadtholder.

Three times a day he entered Van Baerle's cell, expecting to find him breaking some of the rules; but Cornelius had ceased to correspond since his correspondent was at hand. It is even probable that if Cornelius had obtained his full liberty, with permission to go wherever he liked, the prison, *with* Rosa and his bulbs, would have appeared to

him preferable to any other habitation in the world
without Rosa and his bulbs.

Rosa, in fact, had promised to come and see him
every evening, and from the first she had kept her
word.

On the following evening she went up as before,
with the same mysteriousness and the same precaution. But she had resolved within herself not
to approach too near the grating. In order, however, to engage Van Baerle in a conversation from
the very first, which would seriously occupy his
attention, she tendered to him through the grating
the three bulbs, which were still wrapped up in the
same paper.

But to the great astonishment of Rosa, Van
Baerle pushed back her white hand with the tips
of his fingers.

The young man had been thinking the matter
over.

' Listen to me,' he said. ' I think we should risk
too much by embarking our whole fortune in one
ship.   Only think, my dear Rosa, that the question
is to carry out an enterprise, which until now has
been considered impossible, namely, that of making
the grand Black Tulip flower. Let us, therefore,
take every possible precaution, so that, in case of
a failure, we may not have anything to reproach
ourselves with.   I will now tell you the way I think
the safest for us both.'

Rosa listened attentively to all that he had to
say, more on account of the importance which the
unfortunate tulip-fancier attached to it than from
any real faith in the affair herself.

' I will explain to you, Rosa,' he said. ' I daresay you have in this fortress a small garden, or
some courtyard, or, if not that, at least some sort
of terrace.'

'We have a very nice garden,' said Rosa; 'it runs along the bank of the Waal, and is full of fine old trees.'

'Could you bring me some soil from the garden, that I may judge?'

'I will do so to-morrow.'

'Take some from a sunny and some from a shady spot, so that I may judge of its properties in a dry and in a moist state.'

'Rest assured I shall.'

'After having chosen the soil, and, if it be necessary, modified it, we will divide our three bulbs; you will take one and plant it, on the day that I shall tell you, in the soil chosen by me. It is sure to flower, if you tend it according to my directions.'

'I will not lose sight of it for a minute.'

'You will give me another, which I will try to grow here in my cell, and which will help me to beguile the long, weary hours when I cannot see you. I confess to you I have very little hope for the latter one, and I look beforehand on this unfortunate bulb as sacrificed to my selfishness. However, the sun sometimes visits me. I will, besides, try to convert everything into an artificial aid, even the heat and the ashes of my pipe; and lastly we, or rather you, will keep in reserve the third bulb as our last resource, in case our first two experiments prove a failure. In this way, my dear Rosa, it is impossible that we should not succeed in gaining the hundred thousand guilders for our marriage-portion; and how dearly shall we enjoy that supreme happiness of seeing our work brought to a successful issue!'

'I know it all now,' said Rosa. 'I will bring you the soil to-morrow, and you will choose it for your bulb and for mine. As to that in which yours is to grow, I shall have several journeys to convey it to you, as I cannot bring much at a time.'

'There is no hurry for it, dear Rosa; our tulips need not be put into the ground for a month at least. So you see we have plenty of time before us. Only I hope that, in planting your bulb, you shall strictly follow all my instructions.'

'I promise you I will.'

'And when you have once planted it, you will communicate to me all the circumstances which may interest our nursling; such as change of weather, footprints on the walks, or footprints in the borders. You will listen at night to ascertain if the garden is resorted to by cats. A couple of those wretched animals laid waste two of my borders at Dort.'

'I will listen.'

'On moonlight nights, have you ever looked at your garden, then, my dear child?'

'The window of my sleeping-room overlooks it.'

'Well, on moonlight nights you will observe whether any rats come out from the holes in the wall. The rats are most mischievous, for they gnaw everything; and I have heard unfortunate tulip-growers complain most bitterly of Noah for having put a couple of rats in the ark.'

'I will observe, and if there are cats or rats—'

'You will apprise me of it—that's right. And, moreover,' Van Baerle, having become mistrustful in his captivity, continued, 'there is an animal much more to be feared than even the cat or the rat.'

'What animal?'

'Man. You understand, my dear Rosa, a man may steal a guilder and risk the prison for such a trifle, and, consequently, it is much more likely that some one might steal a bulb worth a hundred thousand guilders.'

'No one ever enters the garden but myself.'

'Thank you, thank you, my dear Rosa. All the joy of my life comes from you.'

And as the lips of Van Baerle approached the grating with the same ardour as the day before, and as, moreover, the hour for retiring had struck, Rosa drew back her head, and stretched out her hand.

In this pretty little hand, of which the coquettish damsel was particularly proud, was the bulb.

Cornelius kissed most tenderly the tips of her fingers. Did he do so because his hand kept one of the bulbs of the Grand Black Tulip, or because this hand was Rosa's?

Rosa withdrew with the two other bulbs, pressing them to her heart.

Did she press them to her heart because they were the bulbs of the Grand Black Tulip, or because she had them from Cornelius?

However, from that moment life became sweet, and again full of interest to the prisoner.

Rosa, as we have seen, had returned to him one of the bulbs.

Every evening she brought to him, handful by handful, a quantity of soil from that part of the garden which he had found to be the best, and which, indeed, was excellent.

A large jug, which Cornelius had skilfully broken, did service as a flower-pot. He had filled it, and mixed the earth of the garden with a small portion of dried river-mud, a mixture which formed a capital soil.

Then, at the beginning of April, he planted his first bulb.

Not a day passed that Rosa did not come to have her chat with Cornelius.

The tulips, concerning whose cultivation Rosa

was taught all the mysteries of the art, formed the principal topic of the conversation; but, interesting as the subject was, people cannot always talk about tulips.

They, therefore, began to chat about other things, and the tulip-fancier found out, to his great astonishment, what a vast range of subjects a conversation may comprise.

But Rosa had made it a rule to keep her pretty face invariably six inches distant from the grating, having, perhaps, become mistrustful of herself.

There was one thing especially which gave Cornelius almost as much anxiety as his bulbs— a subject to which he always returned—the dependence of Rosa on her father.

Of a verity Van Baerle's happiness depended on the whim of this man. He might one day find Lœwestein dull, or the air of the place unhealthy, or the gin bad, and leave the fortress, and take his daughter with him, when Cornelius and Rosa would again be separated.

'Of what use would the carrier-pigeons then be?' said Cornelius to Rosa, 'as you, my dear girl, would not be able to read what I should write to you, nor to write to me your thoughts in return.'

'Well,' answered Rosa, who, in her heart, was as much afraid of a separation as Cornelius himself, 'we have one hour every evening, let us make the most of it.'

'I don't think we make such a bad use of it as it is.'

'Let us employ it even better,' said Rosa, smiling. 'Teach me to read and to write. I shall learn quickly, and in this way we shall never be separated any more, except by our own will.'

'Oh, then, we have eternity before us,' said Cornelius.

Rosa smiled, and made a gesture of dissent.

'Will you remain for ever in prison?' she said; 'and, after having granted you your life, will not His Highness also grant you your liberty? And will you not then recover your fortune, and be a rich man; and then when you are driving in your own coach, riding your own horse, will you still look at poor Rosa, scarcely better than the daughter of a hangman?'

Cornelius protested with all his heart, and with all the sincerity of a soul full of love.

She, however, smilingly interrupted him, saying, 'How is your tulip going on?'

To speak to Cornelius of his tulip was an expedient resorted to by her to make him forget everything, even Rosa herself.

'Very well indeed,' he said; 'the coat is growing black; the sprouting has commenced; the veins of the bulb are swelling; in eight days hence, and perhaps sooner, we may distinguish the first buds of the leaves protruding—and yours, Rosa?'

'Oh, I have done things on a large scale, and according to your directions.'

'Now let me hear, Rosa, what you have done,' said Cornelius, with as tender an anxiety as he had lately shown to herself.

'Well,' she said, smiling, for in her own heart she could not help studying this double love of the prisoner for herself and for the black tulip, 'I have done things on a large scale; I have prepared a bed as you described it to me, on a clear spot, far from trees and walls, in a soil slightly mixed with sand, rather moist than dry, without a fragment of stone or pebble.'

'Well done, Rosa, well done!'

'I am now only waiting for your further orders to put in the bulb; you know that I must be

behindhand with you, as I have in my favour all
the chances of good air, of the sun, and abundance
of moisture.'

'All true, all true,' exclaimed Cornelius, clapping
his hands with joy, 'you are a good pupil, Rosa,
and you are sure to gain your hundred thousand
guilders.'

'Don't forget,' said Rosa, smiling, 'that your
pupil, as you call me, has still other things to
learn besides the cultivation of tulips.'

'Yes, yes, and I am as anxious as you are, Rosa,
that you should learn to read.'

'When shall we begin?'

'At once.'

'No, to-morrow.'

'Why to-morrow?'

'Because to-day our hour is expired, and I must
leave you.'

'Already? but what shall we read?'

'Oh,' said Rosa, 'I have a book—a book which I
hope will bring us luck.'

'To-morrow, then.'

'Yes, to-morrow.'

On the following evening Rosa returned with
the Bible of Cornelius de Witte.

———

CHAPTER XVII

THE FIRST BULB

ON the following evening, as we have said, Rosa
returned with Cornelius de Witte's Bible.

Then began between the master and the pupil

one of those charming scenes which are a delight to describe.

The grated wicket, the only opening through which the two lovers were able to communicate, was too high for conveniently reading a book, although it had been quite sufficient for them to read each other's faces.

Rosa, therefore, had to press the open book against the grating edgeways, holding it on a level with the light, and Cornelius hit upon the lucky idea of fixing it to the bars, so as to afford her a little rest. Rosa was then enabled to follow with her finger the letters and syllables, which she was to spell for Cornelius, who with a straw pointed out the letters to his attentive pupil, through the holes of the grating.

The light of the lamp illuminated the rich complexion of Rosa, her blue liquid eye, and her golden hair under her head-dress of gold brocade; with her fingers held up, and showing in the blood, as it flowed downwards in the veins, that pale pink hue which shines before the light, owing to the living transparency of the flesh tint.

Rosa's intellect rapidly developed itself under the animating influence of the mind of Cornelius, and when the difficulties appeared too arduous, the sympathy of two loving hearts seemed to smooth them away.

And Rosa, after having returned to her room, repeated in her solitude the reading lessons, recalling at the same time the delight which she had felt whilst receiving them.

One evening she came half-an-hour later than usual. This was too extraordinary an incident not to call forth Cornelius's inquiries after its cause.

'Oh! do not be angry with me,' she said, 'it is

not my fault. My father has renewed an acquaintance with an old crony who used to visit him at the Hague, and to ask him to let him see the prison. He is a good sort of fellow, fond of his bottle, tells funny stories, and, moreover, is very free with his money, and always ready to stand a treat.'

'You don't know anything further of him?' asked Cornelius, surprised.

'No,' she answered, 'it's only for about a fortnight that my father has taken such a fancy to this friend who visits him so assiduously.'

'Ah, so,' said Cornelius, shaking his head uneasily as every new incident seemed to him to forebode some catastrophe, 'very likely some spy, one of those who are sent into jails to watch both prisoners and their keepers.'

'I don't believe that,' said Rosa, smiling. 'If that worthy person is spying after anyone, it is certainly not after my father.'

'After whom, then?'

'Me, for instance.'

'You?'

'Why not?' said Rosa, smiling.

'Ah, that's true,' Cornelius observed, with a sigh. 'You will not always have suitors in vain, this man may wish to become your husband.'

'I don't say anything to the contrary.'

'What cause have you to entertain such a happy prospect?'

'Rather say, what fear, Mynheer Cornelius.'

'Thank you, Rosa, you are right; well, I will say, then, fear?'

'I have only this reason—'

'Tell me, I am anxious to hear.'

'This man came several times before to the Buytenhof, at the Hague. I remember now, it was just about the time when you were confined there. When I left, he left too; when I came here, he came after me. At the Hague his pretext was that he wanted to see you.'

'See me?'

'Yes, it must have undoubtedly been only a pretext; for now, when he could plead the same reason, as you are my father's prisoner again, he does not care any longer for you; quite the contrary. I heard him say to my father only yesterday that he did not know you.'

'Go on, Rosa, pray do, that I may guess who this man is, and what he wants.'

'Are you quite sure, Mynheer Cornelius, that none of your friends can interest himself for you?'

'I have no friends, Rosa; I have only my old nurse, whom you know, and who knows you. Alas! poor Zug, she would come herself, and use no roundabout ways. She would at once say to your father, or to you, "My good sir, or my good miss, my child is here, see how grieved I am, let me see him only for one hour and I'll pray for you as long as I live." No, no,' continued Cornelius, 'with the exception of poor old Zug I have no friends in this world.'

'Then I come back to what I thought before; and the more so as last evening at sunset, while I was arranging the border where I am to plant your bulb, I saw a shadow gliding between the elder trees and the aspens. I did not appear to see him, but it was this man. He concealed himself and saw me digging the ground, and certainly it was *me* whom he followed, and *me* whom he was spying after. I could not move my rake, or touch one atom of soil, without his noticing it.'

'Oh! I see, he is in love with you,' said Cornelius. 'Is he young? Is he handsome?'

Saying this, he looked anxiously at Rosa, eagerly waiting for her answer.

'Young? handsome?' cried Rosa, bursting into a laugh. 'He is hideous to look at; crooked, nearly fifty years of age, and never dares to look me in the face, or to speak, except in an undertone.'

'And his name?'

'Jacob Gisels.'

'I don't know him.'

'Then you see that, at all events, he does not come after you.'

'At anyrate, if he loves you, Rosa, which is very likely, for to see you is to love you, at least you don't love him.'

'To be sure I don't.'

'Then you wish me to keep my mind easy.'

'I should certainly advise you to do so.'

'Well, then, now as you begin to know how to read, you will read all that I write to you of the pangs of jealousy and of absence, won't you, Rosa?'

'I will, if you write with good big letters.'

Then, as the turn which the conversation took began to make Rosa uneasy, she asked,—

'By-the-bye, how is your tulip going on?'

'Oh, Rosa, only imagine my delight. This morning I looked at it in the sun, and after having moved the soil aside which covers the bulb, I saw the first sprouting of the leaves. This small germ has caused me a much greater emotion than the order of His Highness which turned aside the sword on the scaffold at the Buytenhof.'

'You hope, then?' said Rosa, smiling.

'Yes, yes, I hope.'

'And I, in my turn, when shall I plant my bulb?'

'Oh, the first favourable day I will tell you; but whatever you do, let nobody assist you, and don't confide your secret to anyone in the world; for you see, a connoisseur, by merely looking at the bulb, would be able to discover its value; and so, my dearest Rosa, be careful in locking up the third bulb which you still hold.'

'It is wrapped up in the same paper in which you put it, and just as you gave it me. I have laid it at the bottom of my chest under my point lace, which keeps it dry without pressing upon it. But good-night, my poor captive.'

'How? Already?'

'It must be, it must be.'

'Coming so late, and going so soon.'

'My father might grow impatient at not seeing me return, and that precious lover might suspect a rival.'

Here she listened uneasily.

'What is it?' asked Van Baerle.

'I thought I heard something.'

'What was it like?'

'Something like a step creaking on the staircase.'

'Surely,' said the prisoner, 'that cannot be Mynheer Gryphus, for he can always be heard at a distance.'

'No, it is not my father, I am quite sure, but—'

'But?'

'It might be Mynheer Jacob.'

Rosa ran towards the staircase, and a door was heard to close rapidly before the young damsel had descended the first ten steps.

Cornelius was very uneasy about it, but, after all, it was only a forerunner of greater troubles in store.

The following day passed without any remarkable incident. Gryphus made his three visits and discovered nothing. He never came at the same hours, as he hoped thus to discover the secrets of the prisoner. Van Baerle, therefore, had devised a contrivance, a sort of pulley, by means of which he was able to lower or to raise his jug below the ledge of tiles and stone before his window. The strings by which this was effected he had found means to cover with that moss which generally grows on tiles, or in the crannies of high buildings.

Gryphus suspected nothing, and the device succeeded for eight days. One morning, however, when Cornelius, absorbed in the contemplation of his bulb, from which a germ of vegetation was beginning to peep forth, had not heard old Gryphus coming upstairs, as a gale of wind was blowing which shook the whole tower, the door suddenly opened.

Gryphus, perceiving an unknown and consequently a forbidden object in the hands of his prisoner, pounced upon it with the same rapidity as a hawk on its prey.

As ill luck would have it, his coarse, hard hand, the same which he had broken and which Cornelius van Baerle had set so well, grabbed at the jug on the spot where the bulb was lying in the soil.

'What have you got here?' he roared. 'Ah! have I caught you?' and with this he grubbed in the soil.

'I? nothing, nothing,' cried Cornelius, trembling.

'Ah! have I caught you? A jug, and earth in it. There is some criminal secret at the bottom of all this.'

'Oh, my good Mynheer Gryphus,' said Van Baerle, imploringly, and as anxious as the partridge robbed of her young by the reaper.

In fact, Gryphus was beginning to dig the soil with his crooked fingers.

'Take care, take care,' said Cornelius, growing quite pale.

'Care of what! zounds! of what!' roared the jailer.

'Take care, I say, you will crush it, Mynheer Gryphus!'

And with a rapid and almost frantic movement he snatched the jug from the hands of Gryphus, and hid it like a treasure under his arms.

But Gryphus, obstinate, like an old man, and more and more convinced that he was discovering here a conspiracy against the Prince of Orange, rushed up to his prisoner with raised stick; seeing, however, the unflinching resolution of the captive to protect his flower-pot, he was convinced that Cornelius trembled much less for his head than for his jug.

He therefore tried to wrest it from him by force.

'Halloa!' said the jailer, furious. 'This is black rebellion.'

'Leave me my tulip,' cried Van Baerle.

'Ah, yes, your tulip,' replied the old man; 'I know your tricks.'

'But I declare—'

'Let go,' repeated Gryphus, stamping his foot, 'let go, or I will call the guard.'

'Call whoever you like, but you shall not have this simple plant except with my life.'

Gryphus, exasperated, plunged his finger a second time into the soil, and now he drew out the bulb, which certainly looked quite black; and while Van Baerle, quite happy to have saved the vessel, did not suspect that the adversary had possessed himself of its precious contents, Gryphus hurled the softened bulb with all his force on the flags, where, almost immediately after, it was crushed to atoms under his heavy shoe.

Van Baerle saw the work of destruction, got a glimpse of the juicy remains of his darling bulb, and, guessing the cause of the ferocious joy of Gryphus, uttered a cry of agony which would have melted the heart even of that ruthless jailer who some years before killed Pellisson's spider.

The idea of striking down this spiteful bully passed like lightning through the brain of the tulip-fancier. The hot blood rushed to his brow, and seemed like fire in his eyes, which blinded him; he raised in his two hands the heavy jug with all the now useless earth which remained in it. One instant more and he would have flung it on the bald head of old Gryphus.

But a cry stopped him, a cry of fearful agony, uttered by poor Rosa, who, trembling and pale, with her arms raised to heaven, made her appearance behind the grated window, and thus came between her father and her friend.

Gryphus then understood the danger with which he had been threatened, and he broke out in a volley of the most terrible abuse.

'Indeed,' said Cornelius to him, 'you must be a very mean and spiteful fellow to rob a poor prisoner of his only consolation—a tulip bulb.'

'For shame, father,' Rosa chimed in, 'it is indeed a crime that you have committed.'

'Ah, is that you, my little chatterbox?' the old man cried, boiling with rage and turning towards her; 'mind your own business.'

'Alas! unfortunate wretch that I am,' continued Cornelius, overwhelmed with grief.

'After all, it is but a tulip,' Gryphus resumed, as he began to be a little ashamed of himself. 'You may have as many tulips as you like; I have hundreds of them in my loft.'

'To the devil with your tulips!' cried Cornelius;

'you are worthy of each other; had I a hundred thousand millions of them, I would gladly give them for the one which you have just destroyed!'

'Ah! indeed,' Gryphus said triumphantly. 'It was not your tulip that you cared for. There was some witchcraft in that false bulb, perhaps some means of correspondence with conspirators against His Highness who has granted you your life. I always said they were wrong in not cutting your head off.'

'Father, father!' cried Rosa.

'Well, it's all right, all right,' repeated Gryphus, growing warm; 'I have destroyed it, and I'll do the same again, as often as you repeat the trick. Didn't I tell you, my fine fellow, that I would make your life a hard one?'

'A curse on you!' Cornelius exclaimed, quite beyond himself with despair, as he gathered, with his trembling fingers, the remnants of that bulb on which he had rested so many joys and so many hopes.

'We shall plant the other to-morrow, my dear Mynheer Cornelius,' said Rosa, in a low voice, understanding the intense grief of the unfortunate tulip-fancier, and who, with the pure love of her innocent heart, poured these kind words, like a drop of balm, on the bleeding wounds of Cornelius.

CHAPTER XVIII

ROSA'S LOVER

ROSA had scarcely pronounced these consolatory words when a voice was heard from the staircase asking Gryphus how matters were going on.

'Do you hear, father?' said Rosa.

'What?'

'Mynheer Jacob calls you, he is uneasy.'

'There was such a noise,' said Gryphus; 'wouldn't you have thought that this confounded doctor was murdering me; these scholars are always troublesome fellows.'

Then pointing with his finger towards the staircase he said to Rosa, 'Just lead the way, will you?'

After this, he locked the door and called out, 'I shall be with you in a moment, friend Jacob.'

Poor Cornelius, thus left alone with his bitter grief, muttered to himself,—

'Ah! you old hangman, it is me you have trodden under foot. I shall not survive it!'

And certainly the unfortunate prisoner would have fallen ill but for the counterpoise which Providence had granted to his grief, and which was called Rosa.

In the evening she came back. Her first words announced to Cornelius that henceforth her father would no longer make any objection to his cultivating flowers.

'And how do you know that?' the prisoner asked, with a doleful look.

'I know it, because he has said so.'

'To deceive me, perhaps.'

'No, he repents.'

'Ah! yes, but too late.'

'This repentance is not of himself.'

'And who put it into him?'

'If you only knew how his friend scolded him.'

'Ah, Mynheer Jacob; so he has not left yet?'

'Well, he certainly leaves us as little as he can help.'

Saying this, she smiled in such a way that the

little cloud of jealousy which had darkened the brow of Cornelius speedily vanished.

'How did it occur?' asked the prisoner.

'Well, being asked by his friend, my father told at supper the whole story of the tulip, or rather of the bulb, and of his own fine exploit of crushing it.'

Cornelius heaved a sigh, which might have been called a groan.

'Had you only seen Mynheer Jacob at that moment!' continued Rosa. 'I really thought he would set fire to the castle; his eyes were like two flaming torches, his hair stood on end, and he clenched his fist for a moment; I thought he would have strangled my father.'

'"You have done that," he cried, "you have crushed the bulb?"

'"Indeed I have."

'"It is infamous," said Mynheer Jacob, "it is odious! You have committed a great crime!"

'My father was quite dumfounded.

'"Are you mad too?" he asked his friend.'

'Oh! what a worthy man is this Mynheer Jacob,' muttered Cornelius, 'an honest soul, an excellent heart, that he is.'

'In truth he treated my father most rudely; he was really quite in despair, repeating, over and over again,—

'"Crushed, crushed the bulb; my God, my God! crushed!"

'Then, turning towards me, he asked, "But it was not the only one that he had?"'

'Did he ask that?' inquired Cornelius, with some anxiety.

'"You think it was not the only one?" said my father. "Very well, we shall search for the others."

'"You will search for the others?" cried Jacob, taking my father by the collar; but he immediately loosed him. Then turning towards me, he continued asking, "And what did that poor young man say?"

'I did not know what to answer, as you had so strictly enjoined me never to allow anyone to guess the interest which you are taking in the bulb. Fortunately, my father saved me from the difficulty by chiming in,—

'"What did he say? He was simply like a madman."

'I interrupted him, saying, "Was it not natural that he should be furious, when you were so unjust and brutal, father?"

'"Well, now! are you mad too," cried my father; "what a terrible misfortune is it to crush a tulip-bulb? You may buy a hundred of them in the market of Gorcum."

'"Perhaps some less precious one than that was!" I incautiously replied.'

'And what did Jacob say or do at these words?' asked Cornelius.

'At these words, I must say, his eyes seemed to flash fire.'

'But,' said Cornelius, 'that was not all; I am sure he said something.'

'"So then, my pretty Rosa," he said, with a voice as sweet as honey, "so you think the bulb was valuable."

'I saw that I had made a blunder.

'"What do I know?" I said carelessly; "I don't understand anything about tulips. I only know—as unfortunately it is our lot to live with prisoners—that for them any pastime is of value. This poor Mynheer van Baerle amused himself with this bulb, and I think it very cruel to take from him the only thing that he seemed to find pleasure in."

'" But, first of all," said my father, "where did he get this bulb?"

'I turned my eyes away to avoid my father's look, and encountered those of Jacob.

'It was as if he had tried to read my thoughts at the bottom of my heart.

'Some little show of anger sometimes saves an answer. I shrugged my shoulders, turned my back, and advanced towards the door.

'But I was kept by something which I heard, although it was uttered in a very low voice only.

'Jacob said to my father,—

'" It would not be so difficult to ascertain that."

'" How so?"

'" You need only search his person; and if he has the other bulbs, we shall find them, as there usually are three bulbs!"

'Three bulbs!' cried Cornelius. 'Did he say that I have three?'

'The word certainly struck me just as much as it does you. I turned round. They were both of them so deeply engaged in their conversation that they did not observe my movement.

'" But," said my father, "perhaps he has not got his bulbs about him."

'" Then bring him down under some pretext and I will search his cell in the meanwhile."'

'Halloa, halloa!' said Cornelius, 'but this Mr Jacob of yours is a villain, it seems.'

'I am afraid he is.'

'Tell me, Rosa,' continued Cornelius, with a pensive air.

'What?'

'Did you not tell me that on the day when you prepared your border this man followed you?'

'Yes. So he did.'

'That he glided like a shadow behind the elder-trees?'

'Certainly.'

'That he watched you intently.'

'Indeed he did.'

'Rosa,' said Cornelius, growing quite pale.

'Well?'

'It is not you he is in love with.'

'With whom else, then?'

'He was after my bulb, and is in love with my tulip!'

'You don't say so!—and yet it is very possible,' said Rosa.

'Will you make sure of it?'

'In what manner?'

'Oh! it would be very easy.'

'Tell me.'

'Go to-morrow into the garden; manage matters so that Jacob may know, as he did the first time, that you are going there, and that he may follow you. Feign to put the bulb in the ground; leave the garden; but look through the keyhole of the door and watch him. See what he does.'

'And then?'

'What then? We must lay plans.'

'Oh!' said Rosa with a sigh, 'you are very fond of your bulbs.'

'To tell the truth,' said the prisoner, sighing likewise, 'since your father crushed that unfortunate bulb, I feel as if part of my own self had been paralysed.'

'Then why not accept my father's proposition?' said Rosa.

'Which proposition?'

'Did not he offer you tulip-bulbs by hundreds?'

'Indeed he did.'

'Accept two or three, and along with them you may grow the third bulb.'

'Yes, that would do very well,' said Cornelius, knitting his brow, 'if your father were alone; but there is that Mynheer Jacob, whom I mistrust.'

'But only think! you are depriving yourself, as I can see, of a very great pleasure.'

She pronounced these words with a smile, which was not altogether without a tinge of irony.

Cornelius reflected for a moment; he evidently was struggling against some vehement desire.

'No!' he cried at last, with the stoicism of a Roman of old, 'no, it would be a weakness, it would be folly, it would be a cowardice! If I thus gave up the only and last resource which we possess, to the uncertain chances of the bad passions of anger and envy, I should never deserve to be forgiven. No, Rosa, no; to-morrow we will decide upon the spot for your tulip; you will plant it according to my instructions; and as to the third bulb'—Cornelius here heaved a deep sigh— 'I will watch over it, as a miser over his first or last piece of gold; as the mother over her child; as the wounded over the last drop of blood in his veins;—watch over it, Rosa! Some voice within me tells me that it will be our saving, that it will be a source of good to us.'

'Be easy, Mynheer Cornelius,' said Rosa, with a sweet mixture of melancholy and gravity; 'be easy, your wishes are commands to me.'

'And even,' continued Van Baerle, warming more and more with his subject, 'if you should perceive that your steps are watched, and that your speech has excited the suspicion of your father and of that detestable Jacob, Rosa, don't hesitate for one moment to sacrifice me, who am only still living through you, me, who have no one in the world but you ; sacrifice me, don't come to see me any more.'

Rosa felt her heart sink within her, and her eyes were filling with tears.

'Alas!' she said.

'What is it?' asked Cornelius.

'I see one thing.'

'What do you see?'

'I see,' she said, bursting out in sobs, 'I see that you love your tulips with such love as to have no more room in your heart left for any other affection.'

Saying this, she fled.

Cornelius, after this, passed one of the worst nights he had ever had in his life.

Rosa was vexed with him, and with good reason. Perhaps she would never return to see him, and then he would have no more news either of Rosa or of his tulips.

We must confess, to the shame and disgrace of our hero and of floriculture, that of his two affections he felt most strongly inclined to regret the loss of Rosa ; and when, at about three in the morning, he fell asleep, overcome with fatigue, and harassed by remorse, the grand black tulip yielded precedence in his dreams to the sweet blue eyes of the fair Frisian maid.

CHAPTER XIX

THE MAIDEN AND THE FLOWER

BUT poor Rosa, in her secluded chamber, did not know of whom or of what Cornelius was dreaming.

From what he had said she was more ready to believe that his dreams were of the black tulip, and not of her; and yet Rosa was mistaken.

But as there was no one to tell her so, and as the words of Cornelius's thoughtless speech had fallen upon her heart like drops of poison, she did not dream, she only wept.

During the whole of that terrible night the poor girl did not close an eye, and before she rose in the morning she had come to the resolution that she would appear at the grated window no more.

But as she knew with what ardent desire Cornelius looked forward to the news about his tulip and as, notwithstanding her determination not to see him any more, for her pity was fast growing into love, she did not, on the other hand, wish to drive him to despair, so she resolved to continue the reading and writing lessons by herself; and, fortunately, she had made sufficient progress to dispense with the help of a master when the master was not Cornelius.

Rosa therefore applied herself most diligently to reading poor Cornelius de Witte's Bible, on the second fly-leaf of which the last will of Cornelius van Baerle was written.

'Alas!' she muttered, when perusing this document, which she never finished without a tear, the pearl of love, rolling from her limpid eyes on her blanched cheeks; 'alas! at that time I thought that he did love me.'

Poor Rosa! she was mistaken. Never had the love of the prisoner been more sincere than at the time at which we are now arrived, when, in the contest between the black tulip and Rosa, the tulip had had to yield to her the first and foremost place in Cornelius's heart.

But Rosa was not aware of it.

Having finished her reading, she took a pen and began with as laudable diligence the far more difficult task of writing.

As, however, Rosa was already able to write a legible hand, when Cornelius so uncautiously opened his heart, she did not despair of progressing quickly enough to pen an account of his tulip to the prisoner after eight days.

She had not forgotten one word of the directions given to her by Cornelius, whose speeches she treasured in her heart, even when they did not take the shape of directions.

He, on his part, awoke deeper in love than ever. The tulip, indeed, was still a luminous and prominent object in his mind; but he no longer looked upon it as a treasure to which he ought to sacrifice everything, and even Rosa, but as a marvellous combination of nature and art, with which he would have been happy to adorn the bosom of the one he loved so dearly.

Yet during the whole of that day he was haunted by a vague uneasiness, at the bottom of which was the fear lest Rosa should not come in the evening to pay him her usual visit. This thought took more and more hold of him, until at the approach of evening his whole mind was absorbed in it.

His heart beat rapidly as the darkness closed in. The words which he had said to Rosa on the evening before, and which had so deeply afflicted her, now came back to his mind more vividly than ever; and he asked himself how he could have told his gentle comforter to sacrifice him to his tulip, that is to say, to give up, if needs be, seeing him, whereas to him the sight of Rosa had become a necessity of life.

In his cell Cornelius heard the chimes of the
clock of the fortress. It struck seven, it struck
eight, it struck nine. Never did the metal voice
vibrate more forcibly through the heart of any man
than did the last stroke, marking the ninth hour,
through the heart of Cornelius.

All was then silent again. Cornelius put his
hand on his heart to repress, as it were, its violent
palpitation, and listened.

The noise of Rosa's footstep, the rustling of her
gown on the staircase, were so familiar to his ear
that she had no sooner mounted one step than he
used to say to himself,—

'Here she comes.'

This evening no sound broke the silence of the
corridor ; the clock struck nine, and a quarter ; the
half hour, then a quarter to ten, and at last its
deep tone announced, not only to the inmates of
the fortress, but also to all the inhabitants of Lœwestein, that it was ten.

This was the hour at which Rosa generally used
to leave Cornelius. The hour had struck, but Rosa
had not come.

Thus, then, his foreboding had not deceived
him. Rosa, in her vexation, shut herself up in her
room and left him to himself.

'Alas!' he thought, 'I have deserved all this.
She will come no more, and she is right to stay
away ; in her place I should do just the same.'

Nevertheless, Cornelius listened, waited and
hoped until midnight ; then he threw himself, in
his clothes, upon his bed.

It was a long and sad night for him, and the
day brought him no hope.

At eight in the morning the door of his cell
opened, but Cornelius did not even turn his head ;
he had heard the heavy step of Gryphus in the

corridor, and this step had satisfied the prisoner that his jailer was alone.

Thus Cornelius did not even look at Gryphus.

And yet he would have been so glad to have drawn him out, and to inquire about Rosa. He even very nearly made this inquiry, strange as it would have appeared to her father. To tell the truth, there was a selfish hope to hear from Gryphus that his daughter was ill.

Except on extraordinary occasions, Rosa never came during the day. Cornelius, therefore, did not really expect her as long as the day lasted. Yet his sudden starts, his listening at the door, his rapid glances, at every little noise, towards the grated window, showed clearly that the prisoner entertained some latent hope that Rosa would, somehow or other, look in.

On the second visit of Gryphus, Cornelius, contrary to all his former habits, asked the old jailer, with the most winning voice, about her health, but Gryphus contented himself with giving the laconic answer,—

'She's all right.'

At the third visit of the day Cornelius changed his former inquiry.

'I hope nobody is ill at Lœwestein?'

'Nobody,' replied the jailer, even more laconically, shutting the door on the nose of the prisoner.

Gryphus, being little used to this sort of civility on the part of Cornelius, began to suspect that his prisoner was about to try and bribe him.

Cornelius now was alone once more; it was seven o'clock in the evening, and the anxiety of yesterday returned with increased intensity.

But the hours passed away without bringing the sweet vision which lighted up through the grated window the cell of poor Cornelius; and

which, in retiring, left light enough in his heart
to last until it came back again.

Van Baerle passed the night in an agony of
despair. On the following day, Gryphus appeared
to him even more hideous, brutal and hateful
than usual; in his mind, or rather in his heart,
there had been some hope that it was the old man
who prevented his daughter from coming.

In his wrath he could have strangled Gryphus,
only that such a proceeding would have separated
him from Rosa for ever.

The evening closed in, and his despair changed
into melancholy, which was the more gloomy,
because in spite of himself he thought of his poor
tulip. It was now just that week in April when,
the most experienced gardeners say, tulips ought
to be planted. He had said to Rosa,—

'I will tell you the day when you are to put
the bulb in the ground.'

The following evening would be the time. The
weather was propitious; the air, although still
damp, began to be tempered by those pale rays
of the April sun which, being the first, appear
so congenial, although so pale. Should Rosa allow
the right moment for planting the bulb to pass
by? If, in addition to the grief of seeing her no
more, he should have to deplore the misfortune of
seeing his tulip fail on account of its having been
planted too late, or perhaps not at all!

These two vexations combined might well make
him leave off eating and drinking.

This was the case on the fourth day.

It was pitiful to see Cornelius, dumb with grief,
and pale from utter prostration, stretch out his
head through the iron bars of his window, at the
risk of not being able to draw it back again, to
try and get a glimpse of the garden on the left

spoken of by Rosa, who had told him that its para-
pet overlooked the river. He hoped that perhaps
he might see, in the light of the April sun, Rosa
or the tulip, his two lost loves.

In the evening Gryphus took away his breakfast and dinner for he had scarcely touched them.

On the following day he did not touch them at
all, and Gryphus carried back the dishes just as
he had brought them.

Cornelius had remained in bed the whole day.

'Well,' said Gryphus, coming down from the
last visit, 'I think we shall soon get rid of our
scholar.'

Rosa was startled.

'Nonsense,' said Jacob, 'what do you mean?'

'He doesn't drink, he doesn't eat, he doesn't
leave his bed. Like Mynheer Grotius he will
leave in a chest; only the chest will be a coffin.'

Rosa turned as pale as death.

'Ah!' she said to herself, 'he is bothering about
his tulip.'

And rising with a heavy heart, she returned to
her chamber, where she took a pen and paper, and
during the whole of that night busied herself with
tracing letters.

On the following morning, when Cornelius got
up to drag himself to the window, he perceived a
paper which had been slipped under the door.

He pounced upon it, opened it and read the
following words—in a handwriting which he could
scarcely recognise as that of Rosa, so much had
she improved during her short absence of seven
days :—

'Be easy, your tulip is doing well.'

Although these few words of Rosa's somewhat

soothed the grief of Cornelius, yet he nevertheless felt the irony which underlay them. Rosa, then, was not ill, she was offended; she had not been forcibly prevented from coming, but had voluntarily stayed away. Thus Rosa, being at liberty, found in her own will sufficient strength not to come and see him who was dying with grief at not having seen her.

Cornelius had paper and a pencil which Rosa had brought to him. He guessed that she expected an answer, but that she would not come before the evening to fetch it. He therefore wrote on a piece of paper, similar to that which he had received,—

'It was not my anxiety about the tulip that has made me ill, but grief at not seeing you.'

After Gryphus had made his last visit of the day, and darkness had set in, he slipped the paper under the door, and listened with the most intense attention; but he neither heard Rosa's footsteps, nor the rustling of her gown.

He only heard a voice as feeble as the breath of a zeyphr and sweet as a kiss, which whispered through the wicket one word,—

'To-morrow.'

That to-morrow was the eighth day. For eight days Cornelius and Rosa had not seen each other.

CHAPTER XX

THE EVENTS OF EIGHT DAYS

ON the following evening, at the usual hour, Van Baerle heard someone scratch at the wicket, just as Rosa had been in the habit of doing in the heyday of their friendship.

Cornelius being, as may easily be imagined, not far from the door, was surprised to see who was waiting again for him with her lamp in her hand.

She was startled to see him so sad and pale, and said,—

'Are you ill, Mynheer Cornelius?'

'Yes, I am,' he answered, 'suffering in mind and in body.'

'I saw that you did not eat,' said Rosa; 'my father told me that you remained in bed all day, so I wrote to you to ease your mind concerning the fate of the most precious object of your anxiety.'

'And I,' said Cornelius, 'I have answered. Seeing you return, my dear Rosa, I thought you had received my letter.'

'It is true I have received it.'

'You cannot this time excuse yourself with not being able to read. Not only do you read very fluently, but you have also made marvellous progress in writing.'

'Indeed I have not only received, but also read, your note. Therefore I have come to see whether there might not be some means of restoring you to health.'

'Restore me to health?' cried Cornelius; 'but have you any good news to tell me?'

Saying this, the poor prisoner looked at Rosa, his eyes sparkling with hope.

Whether she did not, or would not, understand his meaning, Rosa answered gravely,—

'I have only to speak to you about your tulip, which, as I well know, is always uppermost in your mind.'

Rosa pronounced these few words in a freezing tone, which cut deeply into the heart of Cornelius.

He did not suspect what lay hidden under this appearance of indifference with which the poor girl affected to speak of her rival, the black tulip.

'Oh!' muttered Cornelius, 'again! again! Have I not told you, Rosa, that I thought but of you; that it was you alone whom I regretted, you whom I missed, you whose absence I felt more than the loss of liberty and of life itself?'

Rosa smiled with a melancholy air.

'Ah!' she said, 'your tulip has been in great danger.'

Cornelius trembled involuntarily, and allowed himself to be caught in the trap, if ever the remark was meant as such.

'Danger!' he cried, quite alarmed, 'what danger?'

Rosa looked at him with gentle compassion; she felt that what she wished was beyond the power of this man, and that he must be taken as he was, with his little foible.

'Yes,' she said, 'you have guessed the truth. That amorous swain, Jacob, did not come on my account.'

'But what did he come for?' Cornelius anxiously asked.

'He came for the sake of the tulip.'

'Alas!' said Cornelius, growing even paler at this piece of information than he had been when Rosa, a fortnight before, had told him that Jacob was coming for her sake.

Rosa saw this alarm, and Cornelius guessed, from the expression of her face, in what direction her thoughts were running.

'Oh! pardon me, Rosa,' he said, 'I know you, and I am well aware of the kindness and sincerity of your heart. To you God has given the ability and power to defend yourself, but to my poor tulip, when it is in danger, God has given no strength whatever.'

Rosa, without replying to this excuse, continued,—

'From the moment when I first knew that you were uneasy on account of the man who followed me, and in whom I had recognised Jacob, I was even more uneasy myself. On the day, therefore, after that on which I saw you last, and on which you said—'

Cornelius interrupted her.

'Once more, pardon me, Rosa!' he cried. 'I was wrong in saying to you what I said. I have asked your pardon for that unfortunate speech before. I ask it again; shall I always ask it in vain?'

'On the following day,' Rosa continued, 'remembering what you had told me about the stratagem which I was to employ to ascertain whether that odious man was after the tulip or after me—'

'Yes, yes, odious. Tell me,' he said, 'you hate him, don't you?'

'I do hate him,' said Rosa, 'as he is the cause of all the unhappiness I have suffered these eight days.'

'You, too, have been unhappy, Rosa? I thank you a thousand times for the kind confession.'

'Well, on the day after that unfortunate one, I went down into the garden, and proceeded towards the border, where I was to plant your tulip, looking round all the while to see whether I was again followed as I was before.'

'Yes?' Cornelius asked.

'Well, then, the same shadow glided between the gate and the wall, and once more disappeared behind the elder-trees.'

'Intending not to see, I stooped over the border, in which I dug with a spade, as if I were going to plant the bulb.'

'And he—what did he do during all this time?'

'I saw his eyes glisten through the branches of the tree like those of a tiger.'

'You see, you see!' cried Cornelius.

'Then, after having finished my make-believe work, I retired.'

'But only behind the garden-door, I dare say, so that you might see through the keyhole what he was going to do when you had left?'

'He waited for a moment, very likely to make sure of my not coming back; after which he sneaked out from his hiding-place, and approached the border by a roundabout way. At last, having reached the spot where the ground was newly turned, he stopped with a careless air, looking about in all directions, and scanning every corner of the garden, every window of the neighbouring houses, and even the sky; after which, thinking himself quite unobserved, quite isolated, and out of everybody's sight, he pounced upon the bed, plunged both his hands into the soft mould, took up a handful and gently sifted it between his fingers to see whether the bulb was in it, and repeated the same thing twice or three times, until at last he perceived that he was outwitted. Then, keeping down the agitation which was evidently raging in his breast, he took up the rake and smoothed the ground, so as to leave it in the same state as he had found it; and, quite abashed and rueful, walked back to the door, affecting the unconcerned air of an ordinary visitor to the garden.'

'Oh! the wretch,' muttered Cornelius, wiping the cold sweat from his brow. 'Oh! the wretch. I guessed his intentions. But the bulb, Rosa;

what have you done with it? It is already rather late to plant it.'

'The bulb? It has been in the ground for these six days.'

'Where? and how?' cried Cornelius. 'Good Heaven! what imprudence. Where is it? In what sort of soil is it? In what aspect? Good or bad? Is there no risk of having it filched by that detestable Jacob?'

'There is no danger of its being stolen,' said Rosa, 'unless Jacob will force the door of my chamber.'

'Oh! then it is with you in your bedroom?' said Cornelius, somewhat relieved. 'But in what soil? in what vessel? You don't let it grow, I hope, in water, like those good ladies of Haarlem and Dort, who imagine that water could replace the earth?'

'You may make yourself comfortable on that score,' said Rosa, smiling; 'your bulb is not growing in water.'

'I breathe again.'

'It is in a good sound stone-pot, just about the size of the jug in which you had planted yours. The soil is composed of three parts of common mould, taken from the best spot of the garden, and one of the sweepings of the road. I have heard you and that detestable Jacob, as you call him, so often talk about the soil best suited for growing tulips that I know it as well as the first gardener of Haarlem.'

'And now, what is the aspect, Rosa?'

'At present it has the sun all day long, that is to say, when the sun shines. But when it once peeps out of the ground I shall do as you have done here, dear Mynheer Cornelius, I shall put it out in my window, on the eastern side, from eight in the morning until eleven, and in my window, towards the west, from three to five in the afternoon.'

'That's it, that's it,' cried Cornelius; 'and you are a perfect gardener, my pretty Rosa. But I am afraid the nursing of my tulip will take up all your time.'

'Yes, it will,' said Rosa, 'but never mind. Your tulip is my daughter. I shall devote to it the same time as I should to a child of mine, if I were a mother. Only by becoming its mother,' Rosa added, smilingly, 'can I cease to be its rival.'

'My kind and pretty Rosa!' muttered Cornelius, casting on her a glance in which there was much more of the lover than of the gardener, and which afforded Rosa great consolation.

Then, after a silence of some minutes, during which Cornelius had grasped through the openings of the grating for the receding hand of Rosa, he said,—

'Do you mean to say that the bulb has now been in the ground for six days?'

'Yes, six days, Mynheer Cornelius,' she answered.

'And it does not yet show leaf?'

'No; but I think it will to-morrow.'

'Well, then, to-morrow you will bring me news about it, and about yourself, won't you, Rosa? I care very much for the daughter, as you called it just now, but I care much more for the mother.'

'To-morrow?' said Rosa, looking at Cornelius, askance, 'I don't know whether I shall be able to come to-morrow.'

'Good Heavens!' said Cornelius, 'why can't you come to-morrow?'

'Mynheer Cornelius, I have lots of things to do.'

'And I have only one,' muttered Cornelius.

'Yes,' said Rosa, 'to love your tulip.'

'To love you, Rosa.'

Rosa shook her head, after which followed a pause.

'Well'—Cornelius at last broke the silence—'well, Rosa, everything changes in the realm of nature; the flowers of spring are succeeded by other flowers; and the bees, which so tenderly caressed the violets and the wallflowers, will flutter with just as much love about the honeysuckles, the rose, the jessamine, and the carnation.'

'What does all this mean?' asked Rosa.

'You have abandoned me, Rosa, to seek your pleasure elsewhere. You have done well, and I will not complain. What claim have I to your fidelity?'

'My fidelity!' Rosa exclaimed, with her eyes full of tears, and without caring any longer to hide from Cornelius this dew of pearls dropping on her cheeks, 'my fidelity! Have I not been faithful to you?'

'Do you call it faithful to desert me and to leave me here to die?'

'But, Mynheer Cornelius,' said Rosa, 'am I not doing everything for you that could give you pleasure? Have I not devoted myself to your tulip?'

'You are bitter, Rosa; you reproach me with the only unalloyed pleasure which I have had in this world.'

'I reproach you with nothing, Mynheer Cornelius, except, perhaps, with the intense grief which I felt when people came to tell me at the Buytenhof that you were about to be put to death.'

'You are displeased, Rosa, my sweet girl, because I love flowers.'

'I am not displeased with your loving them, Mynheer Cornelius, only it makes me sad to think that you love them better than you do me.'

'Oh! my dear, dear Rosa, see how my hands tremble; look at my pale cheek, hear how my heart beats. It is for you, my love, not for the black tulip. Destroy the bulb, destroy the germ of that flower, extinguish the gentle light of that innocent and delightful dream to which I have accustomed myself, but love me, Rosa, love me; for oh, I feel deeply that I love you, and only you.'

'Yes, after the black tulip,' sighed Rosa, who at last no longer coyly withdrew her warm fingers from the grating as Cornelius most affectionately kissed them.

'Above and before everything in this world, Rosa.'

'May I believe you?

'As you believe in your own existence.'

'Well, then, be it so; but loving me does not bind you to much.'

'Unfortunately it does not bind me more than I am bound, but it binds you, Rosa, you.'

'To what?'

'First of all, not to marry.'

She smiled.

'Ah,' she said, 'you are all tyrants. You worship a certain beauty; you think of nothing but her. Then you are condemned to death, and while on your way to the scaffold you devote to her your last sigh; and now you expect poor me to sacrifice all my dreams and my ambitions.'

'But who is the beauty you are talking of, Rosa?' said Cornelius, trying in vain to remember a woman to whom Rosa might possibly be alluding.

'The dark beauty, with a slender waist, small feet, and a noble head; in short, I am speaking of your flower.'

Cornelius smiled.

'That is an imaginary lady love, at all events;

whereas—without counting that amorous Mynheer Jacob—you, by your own account, are surrounded by all sorts of swains eager to make love to you. Do you remember, Rosa, what you told me of the students, officers and clerks of the Hague? Are there no clerks, officers or students at Lœwestein?

'Indeed there are, and lots of them.'

'Who write letters?'

'Who write letters.'

'And now that you know how to read?'—

Here Cornelius heaved a sigh at the thought that, poor captive as he was, to him alone Rosa owed the faculty of reading the love-letters which she received.

'As to that,' said Rosa, 'I think that in reading the notes addressed to me, and passing the different swains in review who send them to me, I am only following your instructions.'

'How so? My instructions?'

'Indeed, your instructions, sir,' said Rosa, sighing in her turn. 'Have you forgotten the will written by your hand in the Bible of Cornelius de Witte? I have not forgotten it; for now, as I know how to read, I read it every day over and over again. In that will you bid me to love and marry a handsome young man of twenty-six or eight years. I am on the look-out for that young man, and as the whole of my day is taken up with your tulip, you must leave me the evenings to find him.'

'But, Rosa, the will was made in the expectation of death, and, thanks to Heaven, I am still alive.'

'Well, then, I shall not be after the handsome young man, and I shall come and see you.'

'That's it, Rosa, come! come!'

'Upon one condition.'

'Granted beforehand!'

'That the black tulip shall not be mentioned for the next three days.'

'It shall never be mentioned any more, if you wish it, Rosa.'

'No, no,' the damsel said, laughing, 'I will not ask for impossib. ties.'

And, saying this, she brought her fresh cheek, as if unconsciously, so near the iron grating that Cornelius was able to touch it with his lips.

Rosa uttered a little scream, which, however, was full of love, and disappeared.

CHAPTER XXI

BULB NO. TWO

THAT night was beautiful and a happy one; and the whole of the next day happier still.

During the past few days the prison had been heavy, dark and lowering, as it were, with all its weight on the unfortunate captive. Its walls were black, its air chilling, the iron bars seemed to exclude every ray of light.

But when Cornelius awoke, a beam of the morning sun was playing about the iron bars; pigeons were hovering above with outspread wings, and others were lovingly cooing on the roof near the still closed window.

Cornelius ran to the window and opened it. It seemed to him as if new life, and joy, and liberty itself were entering with the sunbeams into his cell, which, so dreary of late, was now cheered and irradiated by the light of love.

When Gryphus, therefore, entered the prisoner's cell, he no longer found him morose and lying in bed, but standing at the window, and singing a little ditty.

'Halloa!' exclaimed the jailer.

'How are you this morning?' asked Cornelius.

Gryphus looked at him with a scowl.

'And how is the dog, and Mynheer Jacob, and the pretty Rosa?'

Gryphus ground his teeth, saying,—

'Here is your breakfast.'

'Thank you, friend Cerberus,' said the prisoner; 'you are just in time, I am very hungry.'

'Oh! you are hungry, are you?' said Gryphus.

'And why not?' asked Van Baerle.

'The conspiracy seems to thrive,' remarked Gryphus.

'What conspiracy?'

'Oh, I know, my fine scholar, be careful; we shall be on our guard.'

'Be on your guard, friend Gryphus; be on your guard as long as you please; my conspiracy as well as my person is entirely at your service.'

'We'll see about that at noon.'

Saying this, Gryphus went out.

'At noon?' repeated Cornelius; 'what does that mean? Well, let us wait until the clock strikes twelve, and we shall see.'

It was very easy for Cornelius to wait for twelve at mid-day, for was he not already waiting for nine at night.

It struck twelve, and he heard on the staircase, not only the steps of Gryphus, but also those of three or four soldiers who were coming up with him.

The door opened, Gryphus entered, led his men in, and shut the door after them.

' There, now search ! '

They searched not only the pockets of Cornelius, but even his person ; yet they found nothing.

They then searched the sheets, the mattress, and the straw of his bed ; and again they found nothing.

How Cornelius rejoiced that he had not taken the third bulb under his own care. Gryphus would have been sure to ferret it out in the search, and would then have treated it as he did the first.

And, certainly, never did prisoner look with greater complacency at a search made in his cell than Cornelius exhibited.

Gryphus retired with the pencil and the two or three leaves of white paper which Rosa had given to Van Baerle ; this was the only trophy brought back from the expedition.

At six Gryphus came again, but alone ; Cornelius tried to propitiate him, but Gryphus growled, showed a large tooth like a tusk, which he had in the corner of his mouth, and went out backwards like a man who is afraid of being attacked from behind.

Cornelius burst out laughing, to which Gryphus answered through the grating,—

' Let him laugh that wins.'

The winner that day was Cornelius—Rosa came at nine.

She was without a lantern. She no longer needed a light, for she knew how to read. Moreover, the light might betray her, as Jacob was dodging her steps more than ever. And, lastly, the light would have shown her blushes.

Of what did the young people speak that evening? Of those matters of which lovers speak at the house doors in France ; or from a balcony into the street in Spain ; or down from a terrace into a garden in the East.

They spoke of those things which give wings to the hours; they spoke of everything except the black tulip.

At last, when the clock struck ten, they parted as usual.

Cornelius was happy, as thoroughly happy as a tulip-fancier could be who had not spoken about his tulip.

He found Rosa pretty, good, graceful and charming.

But why did Rosa object to the tulip being spoken of?

This was indeed a great defect in Rosa.

Cornelius confessed to himself, sighing, that woman was not perfect.

Part of the night he thought of this imperfection; that is to say, as long as he was awake he thought of Rosa.

After having fallen asleep he dreamed of her.

But the Rosa of his dreams was by far more perfect than the Rosa of real life. Not only did the Rosa of his dreams speak of the tulip, but she also brought him a black one in a china vase.

Cornelius then awoke trembling with joy, and muttering,—

'Rosa, Rosa, I love you.'

And as it was already day he thought it right not to fall asleep again, and he continued following up the line of thought in which his mind was engaged when he awoke.

Ah! if Rosa had only talked about the tulip, Cornelius would have preferred her to Queen Semiramis, to Queen Cleopatra, to Queen Elizabeth, to Queen Anne of Austria; that is to say, to the greatest or most beautiful queens whom the world has seen.

There was one consolation—of the seventy-two

hours during which Rosa would not allow the
tulip to be mentioned, thirty-six had passed already; and the remaining thirty-six would pass
quickly enough, eighteen with waiting for the
evening's interview, and eighteen with rejoicing in
its remembrance.

Rosa came at the same hour, and Cornelius
submitted most heroically to the pangs which
the compulsory silence concerning the tulip gave
him.

His fair visitor, however, was well aware that to
command on the one hand people must yield on
another; she, therefore, no longer drew back her
hands from the grating, and even allowed Cornelius
tenderly to kiss her beautiful golden tresses.

Poor girl! she had no idea that these playful
little lovers' tricks were much more dangerous than
speaking of the tulip was; but she became aware
of the fact as she returned with a beating heart,
with glowing cheeks, dry lips and moist eyes.

And on the following evening, after the first exchange of salutations, she retired a step, looking
at him with a glance, the expression of which
would have rejoiced his heart could he but have
seen it.

' Well,' she said, ' she has come up.'

' She has come up! Who? What?' asked
Cornelius, who did not venture on a belief that
Rosa would, of her own accord, have abridged the
term of his probation.

' She? Well! my daughter, the tulip,' said
Rosa.

' What!' cried Cornelius, ' you give me permission then?'

' I do,' said Rosa, in the tone of an affectionate
mother who grants a pleasure to her child.

' Ah, Rosa!' said Cornelius, putting his lips to

the grating with the hope of touching a cheek, a hand, a forehead—anything, in short.

He touched something much better—two warm and half-open lips.

Rosa uttered a slight scream.

Cornelius understood that he must make haste to continue the conversation. He guessed that this unexpected kiss had frightened Rosa.

'Is it growing up straight?' he asked.

'Straight as a rocket,' said Rosa.

'How high?'

'At least two inches.'

'Oh, Rosa, take good care of it, and we shall soon see it grow quickly.'

'Can I take more of it?' said she; 'indeed, I think of nothing else but the tulip.'

'Of nothing else, Rosa? Why, now, I shall grow jealous in my turn.'

'Oh, you know that to think of the tulip is to think of you; I never lose sight of it. I see it from my bed; on my awaking, it is the first object that meets my eyes; and on falling asleep the last on which they rest. During the day I sit and work by its side, for I have never left my chamber since I put it there.'

'You are right, Rosa, it is your dowry, you know.'

'Yes, and thanks to it I may marry a young man of twenty-six or twenty-eight years, whom I shall fall in love with.'

'Hush, you naughty girl.'

That evening Cornelius was one of the happiest of men. Rosa allowed him to press her hand in his, and to keep it as long as he chose, besides which he talked of his tulip to his heart's content.

From that hour, every day marked some progress in the growth of the tulip and in the affections of the two young people.

At one time the leaves had expanded, and at another the flower itself had formed.

Great was the joy of Cornelius at this news, and his questions succeeded each other with a rapidity which gave proof of their importance.

'Formed!' exclaimed Cornelius, 'is it really formed?'

'It is,' repeated Rosa.

Cornelius trembled with joy, so much so that he was obliged to hold by the grating.

'Good Heavens!' he exclaimed.

Then turning again to Rosa, he continued his questions.

'Is the oval regular? the cyclinder full? and are the points very green?'

'The oval is almost one inch long, and tapers like a needle; the cyclinder swells at the sides, and the points are ready to open.'

Two days after Rosa announced that they were open.

'Open, Rosa!' cried Cornelius. 'Is the involucre open? If so, you may see and already distinguish—'

Here the prisoner paused, anxiously taking breath.

'Yes,' answered Rosa, 'one may already distinguish a thread of different colour, as thin as a hair.'

'And what is the colour?' asked Cornelius, trembling.

'Oh,' answered Rosa, 'it is very deep.'

'Brown?'

'Darker than that.'

'Darker, my good Rosa, darker? Thank you. Dark as ebony?—dark—?'

'Black, like the ink with which I wrote to you.'

Cornelius uttered a cry of mad joy.

Then suddenly stopping, and clasping his hands, he said,—

'Oh, there is not an angel in heaven that may be compared to you, Rosa!'

'Indeed!' said Rosa, smiling at his enthusiasm.

'Rosa, you have worked with such ardour; you have done so much for me. Rosa, my tulip is about to flower, and it will flower black. Rosa! Rosa! you are the most perfect being on earth.'

'After the tulip, though.'

'Ah! be quiet, you little rogue, be quiet; for shame, do not spoil my pleasure! But tell me, Rosa; as the tulip is so far advanced, it will flower in two or three days at the latest?'

'To-morrow or the day after.'

'Ah, and I shall not see it,' cried Cornelius, starting back, 'I shall not kiss it, as a wonderful work of the Almighty, as I kiss your hand and your cheek, Rosa, when by chance they are near the grating.'

Rosa drew near, not by accident, but intentionally, and Cornelius kissed her tenderly.

'Well, I will cut it, if you so wish.'

'Oh, no, no, Rosa! When it is open, place it carefully in the shade, and immediately send a message to Haarlem, to the President of the Horticultural Society, that the grand black tulip is in flower. I know well it is far to Haarlem, but with money you will find a messenger; have you any money, Rosa?'

Rosa smiled.

'Oh! yes,' she said.

'Enough?' asked Cornelius.

'I have three hundred guilders.'

'Oh! if you have three hundred guilders you must not send a messenger, Rosa, but you must go to Haalem yourself.'

'But what, in the meanwhile, is to become of the flower?'

'Oh, you must take the flower with you. You understand that you must not part from it for an instant.'

'But when I am not parting from it I am parting from you, Mynheer Cornelius.'

'Ah! that's true, my sweet Rosa. Oh, Lord! how wicked men are! What have I done to offend them, and why have they deprived me of my liberty? You are right, Rosa, I cannot live without you. Well, you will send someone to Haarlem —that's settled; really, the matter is wonderful enough for the President to put himself to some trouble. He will come himself to Lœwestein to see the tulip.'

Then, suddenly checking himself, he said with a faltering voice,—

'Rosa, Rosa, if after all it should not be black!'

'Oh, surely, surely you will know to-morrow, or the day after.'

'And to wait until evening to know it, Rosa! I shall die with impatience. Could we not agree about a signal?'

'I shall do better than that.'

'What will you do?'

'If it opens at night I shall come and tell you myself. If it is day, I shall pass this way and slip you a note either under the door or through the grating during the time between my father's first and second visit.'

'Dear Rosa, let it be so. One word from you, announcing this news, will be a double happiness.'

'There, it's ten o'clock,' said Rosa, 'I must leave you.'

'Yes, yes,' said Cornelius, 'go, Rosa, go,'

Rosa withdrew, almost melancholy, for Cornelius had all but sent her away.

Surely he did so in order that she might watch over his black tulip?

CHAPTER XXII

THE FLOWER BLOOMS

CORNELIUS passed a pleasant night, though in great agitation. Every instant he fancied he heard the gentle voice of Rosa calling him. He woke several times with a start, went to the door, and looked through the grating, but no one was behind it, and the corridor was empty.

Rosa, no doubt, was watching too, but, happier than he, she watched over the tulip; she had before her eyes that noble flower, that wonder of wonders, which not only was unknown, but was not even thought possible until that day.

What would the world say when it was known that the black tulip was found, that it existed, and that it was the prisoner Van Baerle who had it?

How Cornelius would have spurned the offer of his liberty in exchange for his tulip!

Day came without any news; the tulip was not yet in flower.

The day passed like the night. Night came, and with it Rosa, joyous and cheerful as a bird.

'Well?' asked Cornelius.

'Well, all is going on prosperously. This night, without any doubt, our tulip will be in flower.'

'And will it flower black?'

'Black as jet.'

'Without a speck of any other colour?'

'Without one speck.'

'Good Heavens! my dear Rosa, I have been dreaming all night, in the first place of you' (Rosa made a sign of incredulity), 'and then of what we must do.'

'Well?'

'Well, and I have decided. The tulip once being in flower, and it being quite certain that it is perfectly black, you must find a messenger.'

'If it is no more than that, I have a messenger quite ready.'

'Is he safe?'

'One for whom I will answer—he is one of my lovers.'

'I hope not Jacob.'

'No, be happy; it is the ferryman of Lœwestein, a smart young man of twenty-five.'

'The deuce!'

'Don't be alarmed,' said Rosa, smiling, 'he is still under age, as you have yourself fixed it at from twenty-six to twenty-eight.'

'Well, do you think you may rely on this young man?'

'As I can on myself; he would throw himself into the Waal or the Meuse if I bade him.'

'Well, Rosa, this lad may be at Haarlem in ten hours. You will give me paper and pencil, and, perhaps better still, pen and ink, and I will write, or rather, on second thoughts, you will, for if I did it, being a poor prisoner, people might, like your father, see a conspiracy in it. You will write to

the President of the Horticultural Society, and I
am sure he will come.'

'But if he tarries?'

'Well, let us suppose that he delays one day, or
even two; but it is impossible. A tulip-fancier like
him will not tarry one hour, not one minute, not
one second, to set out to see the eighth wonder of
the world. But as I said, if he tarried one, or even
two days, the tulip will still be in its full splendour.
The flower once being seen by the President, and
the protocol being drawn up, all will be complete ;
you will keep a duplicate of the protocol, and
intrust the tulip to him. Ah! if we had been able
to carry it ourselves, Rosa, it would never have left
my hands but to pass into yours; but this is a
dream which we must not entertain,' continued
Cornelius with a sigh ; 'the eyes of strangers will
see it flower to the last. And above all, Rosa,
before the President has seen it, don't let it be seen
by anyone. Alas! if anyone saw the black tulip,
it would be stolen.'

'Oh !'

'Did you not tell me yourself what you appre-
hended from the detestable Jacob? People will
steal one guilder, why not a hundred thousand?'

'I shall watch ; never fear.'

'But if it opened while you are here?'

'The whimsical little thing would indeed be
quite capable of playing such a trick,' said Rosa.

'And if on your return you find it open?'

'Well?'

'Oh, Rosa whenever it opens, remember that
not a moment must be losing in apprising the
President.'

'And you as well. Yes, I understand.'

Rosa sighed, without any bitter feeling, but
rather like a woman who begins to understand

a weakness of her lover, and to accustom herself
to it.

'I will return to your tulip, Mynheer van Baerle,
and as soon as it opens I will give you news,
which, being done, the messenger shall start at once.'

'Rosa, Rosa, I don't know to what wonder under
the sun I shall compare you.'

'Compare me to the black tulip, and I promise
you I shall feel very much flattered. Good-night,
then, till we meet again, Mynheer Cornelius.'

'Oh, say good-night, *my friend*.'

'Good-night, my friend,' said Rosa, a little
consoled.

'Say my very dear friend.'

'Oh, my friend.'

'Dearest, I entreat you say dearest, Rosa,
dearest.'

'Dearest, yes, dearest,' said Rosa, with a beating
heart, beyond herself with happiness, as their lips
met in ecstasy.

During part of the night Cornelius, with his
heart full of joy and delight, remained at his
window, gazing at the stars, and listening to every
sound.

Then casting a glance from time to time towards
the lobby,—

'Down there,' he said, 'is my Rosa, watching
like myself, and waiting from minute to minute;
down there, under Rosa's eyes, is the mysterious
flower, which lives, which expands, which opens;
perhaps Rosa holds at this moment the stem of
the tulip between her delicate fingers. Touch it
gently, Rosa. Perhaps she touches its expanding
calyx with her lips. Touch it cautiously, Rosa,
your lips are burning. Yes, perhaps at this
moment the two objects of my dearest love caress
each other with only God to see.'

At that moment a star blazed in the southern sky, and shot across the horizon, falling down, apparently, on the fortress of Lœwestein.

Cornelius felt a thrill run through his frame.

'Ah!' he said, 'God's sending a soul into my flower.'

And as if he had guessed aright, almost at that very moment the prisoner heard in the corridor a step, light as a sylph's, and the rustling of a gown, and a well-known voice, which said to him,—

'Cornelius, my friend, my very dear friend, and very happy friend, come, come quickly.'

Cornelius darted with one spring from the window to the door, his lips met those of Rosa, who told him, with a kiss,—

'It is open, it is black, here it is.'

'How, here it is!' exclaimed Cornelius.

'Yes, yes, we ought, indeed, to run some little risk for so great joy ; here it is, take it.'

With one hand she raised to the level of the grating a dark lantern, while with the other she held to the same height the marvellous tulip.

Cornelius uttered a cry, and felt ready to faint.

'Oh!' murmured he, 'my God, my God, here thou dost reward me in my captivity. Oh, I thank Thee that thou hast allowed two such flowers to grow at the grating of my prison.'

The tulip was beautiful, splendid, magnificent; its stem was more than eighteen inches high, it rose from out of four green leaves, which were as smooth and straight as lance-shafts. The whole of the flower was as black and shining as jet.

'Rosa,' said Cornelius, almost gasping, 'Rosa, there is not one moment to lose in writing the letter.'

'It is written, my dearest Cornelius,' said Rosa.

'Indeed?'

'While the tulip opened I wrote it myself, for I
did not wish to lose any time. Here is the letter,
tell me if you approve of it.'

Cornelius took the letter, and read, in a handwriting which was much improved even since the
last little note he had received from Rosa, as
follows :—

'MYNHEER PRESIDENT,—The black tulip is
about to open, perhaps in ten minutes. As soon
as it is open I shall send a messenger to you, with
the request that you will come and fetch it in
person from the fortress at Lœwestein. I am the
daughter of the jailer, Gryphus, almost as much
a captive as the prisoners of my father. I cannot,
therefore, bring to you this wonderful flower. This
is the reason why I beg you to come and fetch it
yourself.

'It is my wish that it should be called *Rosa
Barlæensis.*

'It has opened; it is perfectly black; come
Mynheer President, come.

'I have the honour to be, your humble servant,
                              'ROSA GRYPHUS.'

'That's excellent, dear Rosa, excellent. Your
letter is admirable! I could not have written it
with such beautiful simplicity. You will give the
committee all the information that will be asked of
you. They will then know how the tulip has been
grown, how much care and anxiety, and how many
sleepless nights it has cost. But, for the present,
not a minute must be lost, Rosa. The messenger,
the messenger.'

'What's the name of the President?'

'Give me the letter, I will direct it. Oh, he is
very well known, it is Mynheer van Systens, the

burgomaster of Haarlem ; give it me, Rosa, give
it me.'

And with a trembling hand Cornelius wrote the
address.

'To Mynheer Peter van Systens, Burgomaster,
and President of the Horticultural Society of
Haarlem.'

'Now, my Rosa, go, go,' said Cornelius, 'and let
us implore the protection of God who has so
kindly watched over us until now.'

CHAPTER XXIII

THE ENVIOUS RIVAL

At this time the poor young people were in great
need of protection.

They had never been so near the destruction of
their hopes as at this moment when they thought
themselves certain of their fulfilment.

Of course, Jacob is our old friend, or rather
enemy, Isaac Boxtel. This worthy had followed,
from the Buytenhof to Lœwestein, the object of
his love and the object of his hatred—the black
tulip and Cornelius van Baerle.

What no one but a tulip-fancier, and an envious
tulip-fancier at that, could have discovered—the
existence of the bulbs and the endeavours of the
prisoner—jealousy and hatred had enabled Boxtel
if not to discover, at least to guess.

We have seen him, more successful under the
name of Jacob than under that of Isaac, gain the
friendship of Gryphus, which for several months he

cultivated by means of the best gin ever distilled from the Texel to Antwerp, and he lulled the suspicion of the jealous turnkey by holding out to him the flattering prospect of his designing to marry Rosa.

Besides thus offering a bait to the ambition of the father, he managed, at the same time, to interest his zeal as a jailer, picturing to him in the blackest colours the learned prisoner whom Gryphus had in his keeping, and who, according to the sham Jacob, was in league with Satan, to the detriment of His Highness the Prince of Orange.

At first he had also made some way with Rosa; not, indeed, in her affections, but by talking to her of marriage and of love he thought he had lulled all the suspicions which he might otherwise have excited.

We have seen how his imprudence in following Rosa into the garden had unmasked him in the eyes of the young damsel, and how the instinctive fears of Cornelius had put the two lovers on their guard against him.

Naturally the first cause for uneasiness was aroused in Cornelius by the rage of Jacob when Gryphus crushed the first bulb. In that moment Boxtel's exasperation was the more fierce, as, though suspecting that Cornelius possessed a second bulb, he by no means felt sure of it.

From that moment he began to watch Rosa, not only following her to the garden, but also to the corridors as well.

Only as he now followed her in the night, and barefooted, he was neither seen nor heard, except once, when Rosa thought she saw something like a shadow on the staircase.

Her discovery, however, was made too late, as

Boxtel had heard from the mouth of the prisoner himself that a second bulb existed.

Taken in by the stratagem of Rosa, who had feigned to put it in the ground, and entertaining no doubt but that this little farce had been played in order to force him to betray himself, he redoubled his precaution, and employed every means suggested by his crafty nature to watch the others without being seen himself.

He saw Rosa conveying a large flower-pot of white earthenware from her father's kitchen to her bedroom. He saw Rosa washing her pretty little hands, begrimed as they were with the mould which she had handled, to give her tulip the best soil possible.

And at last he hired, just opposite Rosa's window, a little attic, distant enough to prevent him from being recognised by the naked eye, but sufficiently near to enable him, with the help of his telescope, to watch everything that was going on at Lœwestein in Rosa's room, just as at Dort he had watched the dry-room of Cornelius.

He had not been installed more than three days in his attic before all his doubts were removed.

From morning to sunset the flower-pot was in the window, and like those charming female figures of Mieris and Metzys, Rosa appeared at that window as in a frame, formed by the first budding sprays of the wild vine and the honeysuckle growing round her window.

Rosa watched the flower-pot with an interest which betrayed to Boxtel the real value of the object enclosed in it.

This object could not be anything but the second bulb, that is to say, the quintessence of all the hopes of the prisoner.

When the nights threatened to be too cold, Rosa took in the flower-pot.

This, of course, was in accordance with the instructions of Cornelius, who was afraid of the bulb being killed by frost.

When the sun became too hot, Rosa likewise took in the pot from eleven in the morning until two in the afternoon.

Another proof, for Cornelius was afraid lest the soil should become too dry.

But when the first leaves peeped out of the earth Boxtel was fully convinced, and his telescope left him no longer in any uncertainty. Before they had grown one inch in height all his doubts vanished.

Cornelius possessed two bulbs, and the second was entrusted to the love and care of Rosa.

For it may well be imagined that the tender secret of the two lovers had not escaped the prying curiosity of Boxtel.

The question, therefore, was how to get the second bulb from the care of Rosa.

Decidedly this was no easy task.

Rosa watched over her tulip as a mother over her child, or a dove over her eggs.

Rosa never left her room during the day, and, more than that, strange to say she never left it in the evening.

For seven days Boxtel in vain watched Rosa; she was always at her post.

This happened during the seven days of misunderstanding, when Cornelius was so unhappy, being deprived at the same time of all news of Rosa and of his tulip.

Would the differences between Rosa and Cornelius last for ever?

This would have made the theft much more

difficult than Mynheer Isaac had at first antici-
pated.

We say theft, for Isaac had deliberately made
up his mind to steal the tulip; and as it grew in
the most profound secrecy, and as, moreover, his
word, being that of a renowned tulip-grower,
would any day be taken before that of an unknown
girl without any knowledge of horticulture, or
against that of a prisoner convicted of high
treason, he confidently hoped that, having once
got possession of the bulb, he would be certain to
obtain the prize; and then the tulip, instead of
being called *Tulipa nigra Barlæensis*, would go
down to posterity under the name of *Tulipa nigra
Boxtellensis* or *Boxtellea*.

Mynheer Isaac had not yet quite decided which
of these two names he would give to the tulip, but
as both meant the same thing, this was, after all,
not of much importance.

The thing was, to steal the tulip. But before
Boxtel could get the tulip, it was necessary that
Rosa should leave her room.

Great, therefore, was his joy when he saw the
usual evening meetings of the lovers resumed.

He, first of all, took advantage of Rosa's absence
to make himself fully acquainted with all the
peculiarities of the door of her chamber. The
lock was a double one, and in good order, and
Rosa always took the key with her.

Boxtel at first entertained the idea of stealing
the key, but it soon occurred to him that not only
would it be exceedingly difficult to abstract it
from her pocket, but that, when she discovered her
loss, she would not leave her room until the lock
was changed, and then Boxtel's first theft would
be useless.

He thought it, therefore, better to employ a

different expedient. He collected as many keys as he could, and tried all of them during one of those delightful hours which Rosa and Cornelius passed together at the grating of the cell.

Two of the keys fitted the lock, and one of them turned round once, but not the second time.

There was therefore not much to be done to this key.

Boxtel covered it with a slight coat of wax, and when he renewed the experiment, the obstacle which prevented the key from being turned a second time left its impression on the wax.

It cost Boxtel two days more to bring his key to perfection, with the aid of a small file.

Rosa's door thus opened without noise and without difficulty, and Boxtel found himself in her room alone with the tulip.

The first guilty act of Boxtel had been to climb over a wall in order to dig up the tulip; the second, to introduce himself into the drying-room of Cornelius through an open window; and the third, to enter Rosa's room by means of a false key.

Thus envy made Boxtel steep himself deeply in his career of crime.

Boxtel, as we have said, was alone with the tulip.

A common thief would have taken the pot under his arm and carried it off.

But Boxtel was not a common thief, and he reflected.

It was not yet certain, although very probable, that the tulip would flower black; if, therefore, he stole it now, he not only might be committing a useless crime, but the theft might be discovered before the time elapsed when the flower was due to open.

Therefore, being in possession of the key, he

could enter Rosa's chamber whenever he liked, and he thought it better to wait and to take it either an hour before or after opening, and to start on the instant to Haarlem, where the tulip would be before the judges of the committee before anyone else could put in a claim.

Should anyone then lay claim to it, Boxtel could, in his turn, charge that person with theft.

This was a deep-laid scheme, and quite worthy of its author.

So, every evening during that delighful hour which the two lovers passed together at the grated window, Boxtel entered Rosa's chamber to watch the progress which the black tulip was making towards flowering.

On the evening at which we have arrived he was making preparations to enter as usual ; but the two lovers, as we have seen, only exchanged a few words before Cornelius sent Rosa back to watch over the tulip.

Seeing Rosa enter her room ten minutes after she had left it, Boxtel guessed that the tulip had opened, or was about to open.

During that night, therefore, the great blow was to be struck. Boxtel presented himself before Gryphus with a double supply of Genièvre, that is to say, with a bottle in each pocket.

Gryphus being quickly fuddled, Boxtel was very nearly master of the house.

At eleven o'clock Gryphus was dead drunk. At two in the morning Boxtel saw Rosa leaving her chamber ; but evidently she held in her arms something which she carried with great care.

He did not doubt but that this was the black tulip which was in flower.

But what was she going to do with it ? Would she set out that instant to Haarlem with it herself ?

It was not likely that so young a girl would undertake such a journey alone during the night.

Was she only going to show the tulip to Cornelius? This was more probable.

He followed Rosa, therefore, with stockinged feet, walking on tiptoe.

He saw her approach the grated window. He heard her calling Cornelius. By the light of the dark-lantern he saw the tulip in full bloom, as black as the darkness in which he was hidden.

He heard the plan concerted between Cornelius and Rosa to send a messenger to Haarlem. He saw the lips of the lovers meet, and then heard Cornelius send Rosa away.

He saw Rosa extinguish the light, and return to her chamber. Ten minutes after he saw her leave the room again, and lock it twice.

Boxtel, who observed all this while hiding himself on the landing-place of the staircase above, descended step by step from his storey, as Rosa descended from hers; so that when she touched with her light foot the lowest step of the staircase, Boxtel touched, with a still lighter hand, the lock of Rosa's chamber.

And in that hand, it must be understood, he held the false key which opened Rosa's door as easily as did the real one.

Consequently it will be readily understood why the poor young people should be in great need of the protection of God.

CHAPTER XXIV

THE BLACK TULIP CHANGES MASTERS

CORNELIUS remained standing on the spot where Rosa had left him, almost overpowered by the weight of his twofold happiness.

Half an hour passed away. Already the first rosy rays of the sun entered through the iron grating of the prison, when Cornelius was suddenly startled at the noise of steps which came hurrying up the staircase, and of cries which approached nearer and nearer.

Almost at the same instant he saw before him the pale and distracted face of Rosa.

He started, and turned pale with fright.

'Cornelius, Cornelius!' she screamed, gasping for breath.

'Good Heaven! what is it?' asked the prisoner.

'Cornelius, the tulip.'

'Well?'

'How can I tell you?'

'Speak, speak, Rosa!'

'Some one has taken—stolen it from us.'

'Stolen—taken?' said Cornelius.

'Yes,' said Rosa, leaning against the door to support herself; 'yes, taken, stolen.'

And saying this, she felt her limbs failing her, and she sank on her knees.

'But how? tell me, explain to me.'

'Oh, it is not my fault, my friend.'

Poor Rosa! she no longer dared to call him 'My beloved one.'

'You left it alone then,' said Cornelius, ruefully.

'One minute only, to instruct our messenger,

who lives scarcely fifty yards off, on the banks of the Waal.'

'And during that time, notwithstanding all my injunctions, you left the key behind—unfortunate child!'

'No, no, no! that is what I cannot understand. The key was never out of my hands; I clenched it as if I were afraid it would take wings.'

'But how did it happen, then?'

'That's what I cannot make out. I had given the letter to my messenger; he started before I left his house; I came home, and my door was locked; everything in my room was as I had left it, except the tulip — that was gone. Someone must have found a key for my room, or had a false one made on purpose.'

She was nearly choking with sobs, and was unable to continue.

Cornelius, immovable and full of consternation, heard almost without understanding, and only muttered,—

'Stolen, stolen, stolen, I am lost!'

'Oh, Cornelius, forgive me, forgive me, it will kill me!'

Seeing Rosa's distress, Cornelius seized the iron bars of the grating, and furiously shaking them, called out,—

'Rosa, Rosa, we have been robbed, it is true, but shall we allow ourselves to be dejected for all that? No, no, the misfortune is great, but it may perhaps be remedied; Rosa, we know the thief!'

'Alas! what can I say about it?'

'Well, I say that it is none other than that infamous Jacob. Shall we allow him to carry to Haarlem the fruit of our labour, the pride of our sleepless nights, the child of our love? Rosa, we must pursue, we must overtake him!'

'But how can we do all this, my dear, without letting my father know that we were in communication with each other? How should I, a poor girl with so little knowledge of the world and its ways, be able to attain that which, perhaps, you might fail in yourself?'

'Rosa, Rosa, open this door to me, and you will see whether I will not find the thief—whether I will not make him confess his crime and beg for mercy.'

'Alas!' cried Rosa, sobbing, 'can I open the door for you? have I the keys? If I had had them, would not you have been free long ago?'

'Your father has them—your wicked father who has already crushed the first bulb of my tulip. Oh, the wretch, the wretch, he is an accomplice of Jacob!'

'Don't speak so loud, for Heaven's sake.'

'Oh, Rosa, if you don't open the door for me,' Cornelius cried, in his rage, 'I shall force these bars, and kill everything I find in the prison!'

'Be merciful, be calm, my dear.'

Rosa, in her fright, made vain attempts to check the furious outbreak which Cornelius made on the door.

'I tell you that I will kill that infamous Gryphus!' roared Cornelius. 'I tell you I will shed his blood, as he did that of my black tulip!'

The wretched prisoner was beginning to rave.

'Well, then, yes,' said Rosa, all in a tremble. 'Yes, yes, only be quiet. Yes, I will get the keys, I will open the door for you—yes, only be quiet, my own dear Cornelius.'

She did not finish her speech, as a growl by her side interrupted her.

'My father!' cried Rosa.

'Gryphus!' roared Van Baerle. 'Oh, you villain!'

Old Gryphus, in the midst of all the noise, had ascended the staircase without being heard.

He rudely seized his daughter by the wrist.

'So you will take my keys?' he said, in a voice choked with rage. 'Ah! this dastardly fellow, this monster, this gallows-bird of a conspirator is your own dear Cornelius, is he? So you have communications with prisoners of State. Very good, very good indeed.'

Rosa wrung her hands in despair.

'Ah!' Gryphus continued, passing from the madness of anger to the cool irony of a man who has got the better of his enemy. 'Ah! you innocent tulip-fancier, you gentle scholar, you will kill me and drink my blood! Very well! very well! And you have my daughter for an accomplice. Am I, forsooth, in a den of thieves—in a cave of brigands? Yes, but the governor shall know all to-morrow, and His Highness the Stadtholder the day after. We know the law; we shall have a second edition of the Buytenhof, Mynheer Scholar, and a good one this time. Yes, yes; just gnaw your paws like a bear in his cage, and you, my fine little lady, devour your dear Cornelius with your eyes. I tell you, my lambkins, you shall not much longer have the felicity of conspiring together. Away with you, unnatural daughter! And as to you, Mynheer Scholar, we shall see each other again. Just wait—we shall.'

Rosa, beyond herself with terror and despair, kissed her hands to her friend; then, suddenly struck with a bright thought, she rushed towards the staircase, saying,—

'All is not yet lost, Cornelius. Rely on me, my Cornelius.'

Her father followed her, growling.

As to poor Cornelius, he gradually loosened his

hold of the bars, which his fingers still grasped convulsively. His head was heavy, his eyes almost started from their sockets, and he fell heavily on the floor of his cell, muttering,—

'Stolen; it has been stolen from me!'

During this time Boxtel had left the fortress by the door which Rosa herself had opened. He carried the black tulip wrapped up in a cloak, and, throwing himself into a coach, which was waiting for him at Gorcum, he drove off, without, as may well be imagined, having informed his friend Gryphus of his sudden departure.

And now we will follow him to the end of his journey.

He proceeded but slowly, as a black tulip could not bear travelling post haste.

But Boxtel, fearing that he might not arrive early enough, procured at Delft a box, lined all round with fresh moss, in which he packed the tulip. The flower was so lightly pressed upon on all sides, with a supply of air from above, that the coach could now travel full speed without any possibility of injury.

He arrived next morning at Haarlem, fatigued but triumphant; and, to do away with every trace of the theft, he transplanted the tulip, and breaking the original flower-pot, threw the pieces into the canal. After which he wrote the President of the Horticultural Society a letter, in which he announced to him that he had just arrived at Haarlem with a perfectly black tulip; and, with his flower all safe, took up his quarters at a good hotel in the town, and there he waited.

CHAPTER XXV

PRESIDENT VAN SYSTENS

Rosa, on leaving Cornelius, had fixed on her plan, which was no other than to restore to Cornelius the stolen tulip, or never to see him again.

She had seen the despair of the prisoner, and she knew that it was derived from a double source, and that it was incurable.

On the one hand, separation became inevitable; Gryphus having, at the same time, surprised the secret of their love, and of their clandestine meetings.

On the other hand, all the hopes, on the fulfilment of which Cornelius van Baerle had rested his ambition for the last seven years, were almost crushed.

Rosa was one of those women who are dejected by trifles; but who, in great emergencies, are supplied by misfortune itself with the energy for combating, or with the resources for remedying it.

She went to her room, and cast a last glance around to see whether she had not been mistaken, and whether the tulip was not stowed away in some corner where it had escaped her notice. But she sought in vain; the tulip was still missing; the tulip was indeed stolen.

Rosa made up a little parcel of things indispensable for a journey; took her three hundred guilders, that is to say, all her fortune; fetched the third bulb from among her lace, where she had laid it up, and carefully hid it in her bosom; after which she locked her door twice, to disguise her flight as long as possible; and leaving the prison by the same exit which an hour before Boxtel had used, she went to a stable-keeper to hire a carriage.

The man had only a two-wheel chaise, and this was the vehicle which Boxtel had hired since last evening, and in which he was now driving along the road to Delft; for the road from Lœwestein to Haarlem, owing to the many canals, rivers and rivulets · intersecting the country, is exceedingly circuitous.

Not being able to procure a vehicle, Rosa was obliged to take a horse, with which the stable-keeper readily intrusted her, knowing her to be the daughter of the jailer of the fortress.

Rosa hoped to overtake her messenger, a kind-hearted and honest lad, whom she would take with her, and who might, at the same time, serve her as a guide and a protector.

And, in fact, she had not proceeded more than a league before she saw him hastening along one of the side paths of a very pretty road by the river. Setting her horse off at a canter she soon came up with him.

The honest lad was not aware of the important character of his message; nevertheless, he used as much speed as if he had known it; and in less than an hour he had already gone a league and a half.

Rosa took from him the note, which had now become useless, and explained to him what she wanted him to do for her. The boatman placed himself entirely at her disposal, promising to keep pace with the horse if Rosa would allow him to take hold of either the croup or the bridle. The two travellers had been on their way for five hours, and made more than eight leagues, and yet Gryphus had not the least suspicion of his daughter having left the fortress.

Moreover, the jailer, who was of a very spiteful and cruel disposition, chuckled within himself at the idea of having struck such terror into his daughter's heart.

But whilst he was congratulating himself on having such a nice story to tell to his boon companion, Jacob, that worthy was on his road to Delft; and, thanks to the swiftness of the horse, had already the start of Rosa and her companion by four leagues.

And whilst the affectionate father was rejoicing at the thought of his daughter weeping in her room, Rosa was making the best of her way towards Haarlem.

Thus, only the prisoner was where Gryphus thought him to be.

Rosa was so seldom with her father since she had taken care of the tulip, that at his dinner hour, that is to say, at twelve o'clock, he was reminded, for the first time, by his appetite, that his daughter was fretting rather too long.

He sent one of the under-turnkeys to call her; and when the man came back to tell him that he had called and sought her in vain, he resolved to go and seek her himself.

He first went to her room, but, loud as he knocked, Rosa answered not.

The locksmith of the fortress was sent for; he opened the door, but Gryphus no more found Rosa than she had found the tulip.

At that very moment she was entering Rotterdam.

Gryphus, therefore, had just as little chance of finding her in the kitchen as in her room, and just as little in the garden as in the kitchen.

There is no describing the anger of the jailer when, after having made inquiries about the neighbourhood, he heard that his daughter had hired a horse, and, like an adventuress, set out on a journey without saying where she was going.

Gryphus again went up in his fury to Van Baerle, abused him, threatened him, knocked all the miserable furniture of his cell about, and promised him all sorts of misery, even starvation and flogging.

Cornelius, without even hearing what his jailer said, allowed himself to be ill-treated, abused and threatened, remaining all the while sullen, immovable, dead to every emotion and fear.

After having sought for Rosa in every direction, Gryphus looked out for Jacob, and as he could not find him either, he began to suspect from that moment that Jacob had run away with her.

The damsel, in the meanwhile, after having stopped for two hours at Rotterdam, had started again on her journey. On that evening she slept at Delft, and on the following morning she reached Haarlem four hours after Boxtel had arrrived there.

Rosa, first of all, caused herself to be led before Mynheer van Systens, the President of the Horticultural Society of Haarlem.

She found that worthy gentleman in a situation which we must not pass over, for he was a very important man this day.

The President was drawing up a report to the Committee of the Society.

This report was written on large-sized paper, in the finest handwriting of the President.

Rosa was announced simply as Rosa Gryphus; but as her name, well as it might sound, was unknown to the President, she was refused admittance.

Rosa, however, was by no means disheartened, having vowed in her heart, in pursuing her cause, not to allow herself to be put down either by refusal, or abuse, or even brutality.

'Announce to the President,' she said to the

servant, 'that I come to speak to him about the black tulip.'

These words acted as an 'Open Sesame,' for she soon found herself in the office of the President, Van Systens, who gallantly rose from his chair to meet her.

He was a spare little man, resembling the stem of a flower, his head forming its calyx, and his two limp arms representing the double leaf of the tulip; the resemblance was rendered complete by his waddling gait, which made him very much like that flower when it bends under a breeze.

'Well, miss,' he said, 'you are come, I am told, about the affair of the black tulip.'

To the President of the Horticultural Society the *Tulipa nigra* was a first-rate power, which, in its character as queen of the tulips, might send ambassadors.

'Yes, sir,' answered Rosa, 'I come at least to speak of it.'

'Is it doing well, then?' asked Van Systens, with a smile of tender veneration.

'Alas! sir, I don't know,' said Rosa.

'How is that? Could any misfortune have happened to it?'

'A very great one, sir; yet not to it, but to me.'

'What?'

'It has been stolen from me.'

'Stolen! the black tulip!'

'Yes, sir.'

'Do you know the thief?'

'I have my suspicions, but I must not yet accuse anyone.'

'But the matter may very easily be ascertained.'

'How is that?'

'As it has been stolen from you, the thief cannot be far off.'

' Why not ? '

' Because I have seen the black tulip only two hours ago.'

' You have seen the black tulip ! ' cried Rosa, rushing up to Mynheer van Systens.

' As I see you, miss.'

' But where ? '

' Well, with your master, of course.'

' With my master ? '

' Yes, are you not in the service of Master Isaac Boxtel ? '

' I ? '

' Yes, you.'

' For whom do you take me, sir ? '

' And for whom do you take me ? '

' I hope, sir, I take you for what you are, that is to say, for the honourable Mynheer van Systens, burgomaster of Haarlem, and President of the Horticultural Society.'

' And what is it you told me just now ? '

' I told you, sir, that my tulip has been stolen.'

' Then your tulip is that of Mynheer Boxtel. Well, my child, you express yourself very badly. The tulip has been stolen, not from you, but from Mynheer Boxtel.'

' I repeat to you, sir, that I do not know who this Mynheer Boxtel is, and that I have now heard his name for the first time.'

' You do not know who Mynheer Boxtel is ; and you also had a black tulip ? '

' But is there another besides mine ? ' asked Rosa trembling.

' Yes—that of Mynheer Boxtel.'

' How is it ? '

' Black, of course.'

' Without speck ? '

' Without a single speck, or even point.'

'And you have this tulip? you have it deposited here?'

'No, but it will be, as it has to be exhibited before the Committee previous to the prize being awarded.'

'Oh, sir!' cried Rosa, 'this Boxtel, this Isaac Boxtel, who calls himself the owner of the black tulip—'

'And who is its owner?—'

'Is he not a very thin man?'

'Yes.'

'Bald?'

'Yes.'

'With sunken eyes?'

'I think he has.'

'Restless, stooping and bow-legged.'

'In truth you draw Mynheer Boxtel's portrait feature by feature.'

'And the tulip, sir? Is it not in a pot of white and blue earthenware, with yellowish flowers in a basket on three sides?'

'Oh, as to that, I am not quite sure; I looked more at the flower than at the pot.'

'Oh, sir! that's my tulip, which has been stolen from me. I come here to claim it before you and from you.'

'Oh! oh!' said Van Systens, looking at Rosa. 'What! you are here to claim the tulip of Master Boxtel? Well, I must say, you are cool enough.'

'Honoured sir,' said Rosa, a little put out by this apostrophe, 'I do not say that I am coming to claim the tulip of Mynheer Boxtel, but to claim my own.'

'Yours?'

'Yes, the one which I have myself planted and nursed.'

'Well, then, go and find out Mynheer Boxtel, at

the White Swan Inn, and you can then settle matters with him; as for me, considering that the cause seems to me as difficult to judge as that which was brought before King Solomon, and that I do not pretend to be as wise as he was, I shall content myself with making my report, establishing the existence of the black tulip, and ordering the hundred thousand guilders to be paid to its grower. Good-bye, my child.'

'Oh, sir, sir,' said Rosa, imploringly.

'Only, my child,' continued Van Systens, 'as you are young and pretty, and as there may be still some good in you, I'll give you good advice. Be prudent in this matter, for we have a court of justice, and a prison here at Haarlem; and, more-over, we are exceedingly particular, as far as the honour of our tulips is concerned—go, my child, go and find Mynheer Isaac Boxtel at the White Swan Inn.'

And Mynheer van Systens, taking up his fine pen, resumed his report, which had been interrupted by Rosa's visit.

CHAPTER XXVI

A MEMBER OF THE HORTICULTURAL SOCIETY

ROSA, beyond herself, and nearly mad with joy and fear at the idea of the black tulip being found again, started for the White Swan, followed by the boatman, a stout lad from Frisia, who was strong enough to knock down a dozen Boxtels single-handed.

He had been made acquainted in the course of the journey with the state of affairs, and was not afraid of any encounter ; only he had orders, in such a case, to spare the tulip.

But on arriving in the great market-place, Rosa at once stopped ; a sudden thought had struck her, just as Homer's Minerva seizes Achilles by the hair at the moment when he is about to be carried away by his anger.

'Good Heavens!' she muttered to herself, 'I have made a grievous blunder ; maybe I have ruined Cornelius, the tulip and myself. I have given the alarm, and perhaps awakened suspicion. I am but a woman ; these men may league themselves against me, and then I shall be lost. If I am lost, that matters nothing—but Cornelius and the tulip!'

She reflected for a moment.

'If I go to that Boxtel and do not know him ; if that Boxtel is not my Jacob, but another fancier who has also discovered the black tulip ; or if my tulip has been stolen by someone else, or has already passed into the hands of a third person ; if I do not recognise the man, only the tulip, how shall I prove that it belongs to me ? On the other hand, if I recognise this Boxtel as Jacob, who knows what will come out of it ? Whilst we are contesting with each other, the tulip will die.'

In the meanwhile, a great noise was heard, like the distant roar of the sea, at the other extremity of the market-place. People were running about, doors opening and shutting ; Rosa alone was unconscious of all this hubbub among the multitude.

'We must return to the President,' she muttered.

'Well, then, let us return,' said the boatman.

They took a small street, which led them straight to the mansion of Mynheer van Systens, who, with his best pen, in his finest hand, continued to draw up his report.

Everywhere on her way Rosa heard people speaking of the black tulip and the prize of a hundred thousand guilders. The news had spread like wildfire through the town.

Rosa had not a little difficulty in penetrating a second time into the office of Mynheer van Systens, who, however, was again moved by the magic name of the black tulip.

But when he recognised Rosa, whom in his own mind he had set down as mad, or even worse, he grew angry, and wanted to send her away.

Rosa, however, clasped her hands, and said with that tone of honest truth which generally finds its way to the hearts of men,—

'For Heaven's sake, sir, do not turn me away, listen to what I have to tell you, and if it be not possible for you to do me justice, at least you will not one day have to reproach yourself before God for having made yourself the accidental accessory to a bad action.'

Van Systens stamped his foot with impatience; it was the second time that Rosa had interrupted him in the midst of a composition which stimulated his vanity both as a burgomaster and as the president of the Horticultural Society.

'But my report!' he cried; 'my report on the black tulip!'

'Mynheer van Systens,' Rosa continued, with the firmness of innocence and truth, 'your report on the black tulip will, if you don't hear me, be based on crime or on falsehood. I implore you, sir, let this Mynheer Boxtel, whom I assert to be Mynheer Jacob, be brought here before you and me, and I swear that I will leave him in undisturbed possession of the tulip if I do not recognise the flower and its holder.'

'Well, I declare, here is a proposal,' said Van Systens.

'What do you mean?'

'I ask you what can be proved by your re-cognising them?'

'Oh, surely, mynheer,' said Rosa, in her despair, ' you are an honest man, sir; how would you feel if one day you found out that you had given the prize to a man for something which he not only had not produced, but which he had even stolen?'

Rosa's speech seemed to have brought a certain conviction into the heart of Van Systens, and he was going to answer her in a gentler tone, when a great noise was heard in the street, and loud cheers shook the house.

'What is this?' cried the burgomaster; 'what is this? Is it possible? have I heard right?'

And he rushed towards his ante-room, without any longer heeding Rosa, whom he left in his cabinet.

Scarcely had he reached his ante-room, when he cried out aloud, on seeing his staircase invaded up to the very landing-place by the multitude, which was accompanying, or rather following, a young man, simply clad in a coat of violet-coloured velvet, embroidered with silver; who, with a certain aristocratic slowness, ascended the shining white stone steps of the house.

In his wake followed two officers, one of the navy and the other of the cavalry.

Van Systens, having found his way through his frightened domestics, began to bow, almost to prostrate himself before his visitor, who had been the cause of all this stir.

'Monseigneur!' he called out, ' Monseigneur! What distinguished honour is Your Highness be-stowing for ever on my humble house by your visit!'

'Dear Mynheer van Systens,' said William of Orange, with a serenity which, with him, took the place of a smile, 'I am a true Hollander; I am fond of the water, of beer, and of flowers, sometimes even of that cheese, the flavour of which seems so grateful to the French; the flower which I prefer to all others is, of course, the tulip. I heard at Leyden that the city of Haarlem at last possessed the black tulip; and after having satisfied myself of the truth of news which seemed so incredible, I have come to know all about it from the President of the Horticultural Society.'

'Oh! Monseigneur, Monseigneur,' said Van Systens, 'what glory to the Society, if its endeavours are pleasing to Your Highness!'

'Have you got the flower here?' said the Prince, who, very likely, already regretted having made such a long speech.

'I am sorry to say we have not.'

'And where is it?'

'With its owner.'

'Who is he?'

'An honest tulip-grower of Dort.'

'His name?'

'Boxtel.'

'His quarters?'

'At the White Swan; I shall send for him, and if, in the meanwhile, Your Highness will do me the honour of stepping into my drawing-room, he will be sure—knowing that Your Highness is here —to lose no time in bringing his tulip.'

'Very well, send for him.'

'Yes, Your Highness, but—'

'What is it?'

'Oh! nothing of any consequence, Monseigneur.'

'Everything is of consequence, Mynheer van Systens.'

'Well, then, Monseigneur, if it must be said, a little difficulty has presented itself.'

'What difficulty?'

'This tulip has already been claimed by usurpers. You see it is worth a hundred thousand guilders.'

'Indeed!'

'Yes, Monseigneur, by usurpers, by forgers.'

'This is a crime, Mynheer van Systens.'

'So it is, Your Highness.'

'And have you any proofs of their guilt?'

'No, Monseigneur, the guilty woman—'

'The guilty woman, sir?'

'I ought to say the woman who claims the tulip, Monseigneur, is here in the room close by.'

'And what do you think of her?'

'I think, Monseigneur, that the bait of a hundred thousand guilders may have tempted her.'

'And so she claims the tulip?'

'Yes, Monseigneur.'

'And what proof does she offer?'

'I was just going to question her when Your Highness came in.'

'Question her, Mynheer van Systens, question her; I am the first magistrate of the country, I will hear the case, and administer justice.'

'I have found my King Solomon,' said Van Systens, bowing, and showing the way to the Prince.

His Highness was just going to walk ahead, but suddenly recollecting himself, he said,—

'Go before me and call me plain mynheer.'

The two then entered the cabinet.

Rosa was still standing at the same place, leaning on the window, and looking through the panes into the garden.

'Ah! a Frisian girl,' said the Prince, as he

observed Rosa's gold brocade head-dress and red petticoat.

At the noise of their footsteps she turned round, but scarcely saw the Prince, who seated himself in the darkest corner of the apartment.

All her attention, as may easily be imagined, was fixed on that important person who was called Van Systens, so that she had no time to notice the humble stranger who was following the master of the house, and who, for aught that she knew, might be somebody or nobody.

The humble stranger took a book down from the shelf, and made Van Systens a sign to commence the examination forthwith.

Van Systens, likewise, at the invitation of the young man in the violet coat, sat down in his turn, and, quite happy and proud of the importance thus cast upon him, began,—

'My child, you promise to tell me the truth, and the entire truth, concerning this tulip?'

'I promise.'

'Well, then, speak before this gentleman; this gentleman is one of the members of the Horticultural Society.'

'What am I to tell you, sir,' said Rosa, 'besides that which I have told you already?'

'Well, then, what is it?'

'I repeat the request which I have addressed to you before.'

'Which?'

'That you will order Mynheer Boxtel to come here with his tulip; if I do not recognise it as mine I will frankly say so; but if I do recognise it I will reclaim it, even if I must go before His Highness the Stadtholder himself, with my proofs in my hands.'

'You have, then, some proofs, my child?'

'God, who knows my good right, will assist me to some.'

Van Systens exchanged a look with the Prince, who, since the first words of Rosa, seemed to try to remember her, thinking it was not the first time that this sweet voice rang in his ears.

An officer went off to fetch Boxtel, and Van Systens, in the meanwhile, continued his examination.

'And with what do you support your assertion that you are the real owner of the black tulip?'

'With the very simple fact of my having planted and grown it in my own chamber.'

'In your chamber? Where was your chamber?'

'At Lœwestein.'

'You are from Lœwestein?'

'I am the daughter of the jailer of the fortress.'

The Prince made a little movement, as much as to say, 'Ah, I remember now.'

And, all the while feigning to be engaged with his book, he watched Rosa even with more attention than he had done before.

'And you are fond of flowers?' continued Mynheer van Systens.

'Yes, sir.'

'Then you are an experienced florist, I daresay?'

Rosa hesitated a moment; then, with a tone which came from the depth of her heart, she said,—

'Gentlemen, I am speaking to men of honour?'

There was such an expression of truth in the tone of her voice that Van Systens and the Prince answered simultaneously by an affirmative movement of their heads.

'Well, then, I am not an experienced florist: I am only a poor girl, one of the people, who, three months ago, knew neither how to read nor write. No, the black tulip has not been found by myself.'

'But by whom else?'

'By a poor prisoner of Lœwestein.'

'By a prisoner of Lœwestein?' repeated the Prince.

The tone of this voice startled Rosa, who was sure she had heard it before.

'By a prisoner of State, then,' continued the Prince, 'as there are none else there.'

Having said this, he began to read again, at least in appearance.

'Yes,' said Rosa, with a faltering voice, 'yes, by a prisoner of State.'

Van Systens trembled as he heard such a confession made in the presence of such a witness.

'Continue,' said William, dryly, to the President of the Horticultural Society.

'Ah, sir,' said Rosa, addressing the person whom she thought to be her real judge, 'I am going to incriminate myself very seriously.'

'Certainly,' said Van Systens, 'the prisoners of State ought to be kept in close confinement at Lœwestein.'

'Alas! mynheer!'

'And from what you tell me you took advantage of your position, as daughter of the jailer, to communicate with a prisoner of State about the cultivation of flowers.'

'So it is, sir,' Rosa murmured in dismay; 'yes, I am bound to confess, I saw him every day.'

'Unfortunate girl!' exclaimed Van Systens.

The Prince, observing the fright of Rosa, and the pallor of the President, raised his head, and said, in his clear and decided tone,—

'This does not concern the members of the Horticultural Society; they have to judge on the

black tulip, and have no cognisance to take of
political offences. Go on, young woman, go on.'

Van Systens, by means of an eloquent glance,
offered, in the name of the tulip, his thanks to the
new member of the Horticultural Society.

Rosa, reassured by this thread of encouragement
which the stranger held out to her, related all that
had happened for the last three months, all that
she had done, and all that she had suffered. She
described the cruelty of Gryphus ; the destruction
of the first bulb ; the grief of the prisoner ; the
precautions taken to insure the success of the
second bulb ; the patience of the prisoner, and his
anxiety during their separation ; how he was
about to starve himself because he had no longer
any news of his tulip ; his joy when she went to
see him again ; and lastly, their despair when they
found that the tulip, which had come into flower,
was stolen just one hour after it had opened.

All this was detailed with an accent of truth,
which, although producing no change in the
impassible mien of the Prince, did not fail to
take effect on Van Systens.

'But,' said the Prince, 'it cannot be long since
you knew the prisoner.'

Rosa opened her large eyes and looked at the
stranger, who drew back into the dark corner as if
he wished to escape her observation.

'Why, sir ?' she asked him.

'Because it is not yet four months since the
jailer Gryphus and his daughter were removed to
Lœwestein.'

'That is true, mynheer.'

'Otherwise, you must have solicited the transfer
of your father in order to be able to follow some
prisoner who may have been transported from the
Hague to Lœwestein.'

'Oh, mynheer,' said Rosa, blushing.

'Finish what you have to say,' said William.

'I confess I knew the prisoner at the Hague.'

'Happy prisoner!' said William, smiling.

At this moment, the officer who had been sent for Boxtel returned and announced to the Prince that the person whom he had been to fetch was following on his heels with his tulip.

CHAPTER XXVII

THE THIRD BULB

BOXTEL'S advent was scarcely announced, when he entered in person the drawing-room of Mynheer van Systens, followed by two men, who carried their precious burden in a box, and deposited it on a table.

The Prince, on being informed, left the cabinet, passed into the drawing-room, admired the flower, and silently resumed his seat in the dark corner, where he had himself placed his chair.

Rosa, trembling, pale and terrified, waited until she expected to be invited in her turn to see the tulip.

She now heard the voice of Boxtel.

'It is he!' she exclaimed.

The Prince made her a sign to go and look through the open door into the drawing-room.

'It is my tulip,' cried Rosa, 'I recognise it. Oh, my poor Cornelius!'

And saying this she burst into tears.

The Prince rose from his seat, went to the door, where he stood for some time with the full light falling upon his figure.

As Rosa's eyes now rested upon him, she felt more than ever convinced that this was not the first time she had seen the stranger.

'Mynheer Boxtel,' said the Prince, 'come in here, if you please.'

Boxtel eagerly approached, and finding himself face to face with William of Orange, started back.

'His Highness!' he called out.

'His Highness!' Rosa repeated in dismay.

Hearing this exclamation on his left, Boxtel turned round and perceived Rosa.

At the sight of her the whole frame of the thief shook as if under the influence of a galvanic shock.

'Ah!' muttered the Prince to himself, 'he is confused.'

But Boxtel, making a violent effort to control his feelings, was already himself again.

'Mynheer Boxtel,' said William, 'you seem to have discovered the secret of growing the black tulip?'

'Yes, Your Highness,' answered Boxtel, in a voice which still betrayed some confusion.

Of course his agitation might have been attributable to emotion which he might have felt on suddenly recognising the Prince.

'But,' continued the Stadtholder, 'here is a young damsel who also pretends to have found it.'

Boxtel, with a disdainful smile, shrugged his shoulders.

William watched all his movements with evident interest and curiosity.

'Then you don't know this young girl?' said the Prince.

'No, your Highness!'

'And you, child, do you know Mynheer Boxtel?'

'No; I don't know Mynheer Boxtel, but I know Mynheer Jacob.'

'What do you mean?'

'I mean to say that at Lœwestein the man who here calls himself Isaac Boxtel went by the name of Jacob.'

'What do you say to that, Mynheer Boxtel?'

'I say that this damsel lies, Your Highness.'

'You deny, therefore, having ever been at Lœwestein?'

Boxtel hesitated; the fixed and searching glance of the proud eye of the Prince prevented him from lying.

'I cannot deny having been at Lœwestein, Your Highness, but I deny having stolen the tulip.'

'You have stolen it, and that from my room,' cried Rosa, with indignation.

'I deny it.'

'Now listen to me. Do you deny having followed me into the garden on the day when I prepared the border where I was to plant it? Do you deny having followed me into the garden when I pretended to plant it? Do you deny that, on that evening, you rushed, after my departure, to the spot where you hoped to find the bulb? Do you deny having dug in the ground with your hands—but, thank God! in vain; as it was but a stratagem to discover your intentions. Say, do you deny all this?'

Boxtel did not deem it fit to answer these several charges, but, turning to the Prince, continued,—

'I have now for twenty years grown tulips at Dort, I have even acquired some reputation in this art; one of my hybrids is entered in the catalogue under the name of an illustrious personage. I have dedicated it to the King of Portugal. The truth of the matter is as I shall now tell Your Highness. This damsel knew that I had pro-

duced the Black Tulip, and in concert with a lover
of hers, in the fortress of Lœwestein, she formed
the plan of ruining me by appropriating to herself the prize of a hundred thousand guilders,
which, with the help of Your Highness's justice, I
hope to gain.'

'Bah!' cried Rosa, beyond herself with anger.

'Silence!' said the Prince.

Then, turning to Boxtel, he said,—

'And who is that prisoner to whom you allude
as the lover of this young woman?'

Rosa nearly swooned, for Cornelius was desig-
nated as a dangerous prisoner, and recommended,
by the Prince, to the especial surveillance of the
jailer.

Nothing could have been more agreeable to
Boxtel than this question.

'This prisoner,' he said, 'is a man whose name
in itself will prove to Your Highness what trust
you may place in his probity. He is a prisoner
of State, who was once condemned to death.'

'And his name?'

Rosa hid her face in her hands with a movement
of despair.

'His name is Cornelius van Baerle,' said
Boxtel, 'and he is godson of that villain, Cornelius de Witte.'

The Prince gave a start; his generally quiet
eye flashed, and a death-like paleness spread
over his impassible features.

He went up to Rosa, and, with his finger, gave
her a sign to remove her hands from her face.

Rosa obeyed, as if under mesmeric influence,
without having seen the sign.

'It was then to follow this man that you came
to me at Leyden to solicit for the transfer of your
father?'

Rosa hung down her head, and nearly choking, said,—

'Yes, Your Highness.'

'Go on,' said the Prince to Boxtel

'I have nothing more to say,' Isaac continued. 'Your Highness knows all. But there is one thing which I did not intend to say, because I did not wish to make this girl blush for her ingratitude. I went to Lœwestein, because I had business there. On this occasion I made the acquaintance of old Gryphus, and falling in love with his daughter, made an offer of marriage to her; and, not being rich, I committed the imprudence of mentioning to them my prospect of gaining a hundred thousand guilders, in proof of which I showed to them the black tulip. Her lover, having himself made a show at Dort of cultivating tulips to hide his political intrigues, they now plotted together for my ruin. On the eve of the day when the flower was expected to open the tulip was taken away by this young woman. She carried it to her room, whence I had the good luck to recover it, at the very moment when she had the impudence to despatch a messenger to announce to the members of the Horticultural Society that she had produced the Grand Black Tulip. But she did not stop there. There is no doubt but that, during the few hours which she kept the flower in her room, she showed it to some persons, whom she may now call as witnesses. But, fortunately, Your Highness has now been warned against this impostor and her witnesses.'

'Oh, my God! my God! what infamous falsehoods,' said Rosa, bursting into tears, and throwing herself at the feet of the Stadtholder, who, although thinking her guilty, felt pity for her dreadful agony.

'You have done very wrong, my child,' he said, 'and your lover shall be punished for having thus badly advised you. For you are so young, and have such an honest look, that I am inclined to believe the mischief to have been his doing and not yours.'

'Monseigneur! Monseigneur!' cried Rosa, 'Cornelius is not guilty.'

William started.

'Not guilty of having advised you; that's what you want to say is it not?'

'What I wish to say, Your Highness, is that Cornelius is as little guilty of the second crime imputed to him as he was of the first.'

'Of the first? And do you know what was his first crime? Do you know of what he was accused and convicted? Of having, as an accomplice of Cornelius de Witte, concealed the correspondence of the Grand Pensionary and the Marquis de Louvois.'

'Well, sir, he was ignorant of this correspondence being deposited with him; completely ignorant. I am as certain, as of my life, that if it were not so he would have told me; for how could that pure mind have harboured a secret without revealing it to me? No, no, Your Highness, I repeat it, and even at the risk of incurring your displeasure, Cornelius is no more guilty of the first crime than of the second; and of the second no more than of the first. Oh, would to Heaven that you knew my Cornelius, Monseigneur!'

'He is a De Witte!' cried Boxtel. 'His Highness knows only too much of him, having once granted him his life.'

'Silence!' said the Prince; 'all these affairs of State, as I have already said, are completely out of

the province of the Horticultural Society of
Haarlem.'

Then knitting his brow he added,—

'As to the tulip, make yourself easy, Mynheer
Boxtel, you shall have justice done to you.'

Boxtel bowed, with a heart full of joy, and received the congratulations of the President.

'You, my child,' William of Orange continued,
'you were going to commit a crime. I shall not
punish you; but the real evil-doer will pay
the penalty for both. A man of his name may
be a conspirator, and even a traitor, but he ought
not to be a thief.'

'A thief!' cried Rosa. 'Cornelius a thief! Pray,
Your Highness, do not say such a word; it would
kill him if he knew it. If theft there has been I
swear to you, sir, no one else but this man has
committed it.'

'Prove it,' Boxtel coolly remarked.

'I shall prove it. With God's help I shall.'

Then turning towards Boxtel, she asked,—

'The tulip is yours?'

'It is.

'How many bulbs were there of it?'

Boxtel hesitated for a moment, but, after a short
consideration, he came to the conclusion that she
would not ask this question if there were none
besides the two bulbs of which he had known
already. He therefore answered,—

'Three.'

'What has become of these bulbs?'

'Oh! what has become of them? Well, one
has failed; the second has produced the black
tulip.'

'And the third?'

'The third!'

'The third—where is it?'

'I have it at home,' said Boxtel, quite confused.

'At home? Where? At Lœwestein, or at Dort?'

'At Dort,' said Boxtel.

'You lie!' cried Rosa. 'Monseigneur,' she continued, whilst turning round to the Prince, 'I will tell you the true story of those three bulbs. The first was crushed by my father in the prisoner's cell, and this man is quite aware of it, for he himself wanted to get hold of it, and being baulked in his hope, he very nearly quarrelled with my father, who had been the cause of his disappointment. The second bulb, planted by me, has produced the Black Tulip; and the third and last'—saying this, she drew it from her bosom—'here it is, in the very same paper in which it was wrapped up together with the two others. When about to be led to the scaffold, Cornelius van Baerle gave me all the three. Take it, Monseigneur, take it.'

And Rosa, unfolding the paper, offered the bulb to the Prince, who took it from her hands and examined it.

'But, Monseigneur, this young woman may have stolen the bulb, as she did the tulip,' Boxtel said with a faltering voice, and evidently alarmed at the attention with which the Prince examined the bulb, and even more at the movements of Rosa, who was reading some lines written on the paper which remained in her hands.

Her eyes suddenly lighted up; she read, with breathless anxiety, the mysterious paper over and over again; and at last, uttering a cry, held it out to the Prince, and said,—

'Read, Monseigneur, for Heaven's sake, read!'

William handed the third bulb to Van Systens, took the paper and read.

No sooner had he looked at it than he began to stagger; his hand trembled, and very nearly let the paper fall to the ground, and the expression of pain and compassion in his features was really frightful to see.

It was that fly-leaf, taken from the Bible, which Cornelius de Witte had sent to Dort by Craeke, the servant of his brother John, to request Van Baerle to burn the correspondence of the Grand Pensionary with the Marquis de Louvois.

This request, as the reader may remember, was couched in the following terms:—

'AUGUST 20, 1672.

'MY DEAR GODSON,—Burn the parcel which I have entrusted to you. Burn it without looking at it and without opening it, so that its contents may remain unknown to yourself. Secrets of this description are death to those with whom they are deposited. Burn it, and you will have saved John and Cornelius de Witte.—Farewell, and love me,

'CORNELIUS DE WITTE.'

This slip of paper offered the proofs both of Van Baerle's innocence and of his claim to the property of the tulip.

Rosa and the Stadtholder exchanged one look only.

That of Rosa was meant to express, 'There, you can judge for yourself.'

That of the Stadtholder signified, 'Say nothing, and wait.'

The Prince wiped the cold sweat from his forehead and slowly folded up the paper, whilst his thoughts were wandering in that labyrinth, without a goal and without a guide, which is called remorse and shame for the past.

Soon, however, raising his head with an effort, he said, in his usual voice,—

'Go, Mynheer Boxtel, justice shall be done, I promise you.'

Then, turning to the President, he added,—

'You, my dear Mynheer van Systens, take charge of this young woman and of the tulip. Good-bye.'

All bowed, and the Prince left, among the deafening cheers of the crowd outside.

Boxtel returned to his inn, rather puzzled and uneasy, tormented by misgivings about the paper which William had received from the hand of Rosa, and which His Highness had read, folded up, and so carefully put in his pocket. What was the meaning of all this?

Rosa went up to the tulip, tenderly kissed its leaves, and, with a heart full of happiness and confidence in the ways of God, broke out in the words,—

'Thou knowest best for what end my good Cornelius was led to teach me to read.'

CHAPTER XXVIII

THE SONG OF THE FLOWERS

WHILST the events we have described were taking place, the unfortunate Van Baerle, forgotten in his cell in the fortress of Lœwestein, suffered at the hands of Gryphus all that a prisoner can suffer when his jailer has formed the determination of playing the part of hangman.

Gryphus, not having received any tidings of

Rosa or Jacob, persuaded himself that all that had happened was the devil's work, and that Satan himself was responsible for the presence on earth of Doctor Cornelius van Baerle.

The result was that one fine morning, the third after the disappearance of Jacob and Rosa, he went up to the cell of Cornelius in even a greater rage than usual.

The latter, leaning with his elbows on the window-sill, and supporting his head with his two hands, whilst his eyes wandered over the distant, hazy horizon, where the windmills of Dort were lazily turning their sails, was seeking for strength in the fresh air to keep down his tears and to fortify himself in his philosophy.

The pigeons were still there, but of hope there was none; there was no future to look forward to.

Alas! Rosa, being watched, was no longer able to come. Could she not write? and if so, could she convey her letters to him?

No, no. He had seen, during the two preceding days, too much fury and malignity in the eyes of old Gryphus to expect that his vigilance would relax, even for one moment. Moreover, had not she to suffer torments even worse than those of seclusion and separation? Did this brutal, blaspheming, drunken bully take revenge on his daughter, like the ruthless fathers of the Greek drama? and when the Geneva had heated his brain, would it not give to his arm, which had been only too well set by Cornelius, the strength of two men?

The idea that Rosa might, perhaps, be ill-treated, nearly drove Cornelius mad.

He then felt his own powerlessness. He asked himself whether God was just in inflicting so much tribulation on two innocent creatures. And certainly in these moments he began to doubt the wisdom of Providence.   Misfortune is apt to make a man humble.

Van Baerle had thoughts of writing to Rosa— but where was she?

He also proposed writing to the Hague to be beforehand with Gryphus, who, he had no doubt, would denounce him and bring more miseries on his head.

But how should he write?   Gryphus had taken the paper and pencil from him ; and even if he had both, he could hardly expect Gryphus to despatch his letter.

Then Cornelius revolved in his mind all those little artifices resorted to by unfortunate prisoners.

He had thought of an attempt to escape, a thing which never entered his head while he could see Rosa every day ; but the more he thought of it the more clearly he saw the impracticability of such an attempt.   His was one of those noble natures which abhor everything that is common, and who often lose a good chance through not taking the way of the vulgar, that high road of mediocrity which leads to success.

'How is it possible,' said Cornelius to himself, 'for me to escape from Lœwestein, as Grotius did? Has not every precaution been taken since?   Are not the windows barred?   Are not the doors of double and even of treble strength, and the sentinels ten times more watchful?   And have not I, besides all this, an Argus doubly dangerous, for he has the jealous eyes of hatred?   I am losing my reason since I have lost the joy and company of Rosa, and especially since I have lost my tulip.   Undoubtedly, one day or other, Gryphus will attack me in a manner painful to my self-respect, or to my love, or even offer me personal violence.   I don't know how it is, but since my imprisonment I feel a strange and almost irresistible pugnacity grow upon me. Well, some day I shall certainly dash at the throat of that old villain and strangle him.'

Cornelius, at these words, stopped for a moment, biting his lips, and staring before him; then, eagerly returning to an idea which seemed to possess a strange fascination for him, he continued his soliloquy,—

'Well, once having strangled him, why should I not take his keys from him? why not go down the stairs as if I had done the most virtuous action? why not go and fetch Rosa from her room? why not tell her all, and jump from her window into the Waal? I am expert enough as a swimmer to save both of us. Rosa! but, oh, Heavens! Gryphus is her father. Whatever may be her affection for me, she will never approve of my having strangled her father, brutal and malicious as he has been. It will not do, Cornelius, my fine fellow—it is a bad plan. But then, what is to become of me, and how shall I find Rosa again?'

Such were the cogitations of Cornelius three days after the sad scene of separation from Rosa, at the moment when we find him standing at the window.

And at that very moment Gryphus entered.

He held in his hand a huge stick; his eyes glistened with spiteful thoughts, a malignant smile played round his lips, and the whole of his carriage, and even all his movements, betokened bad and malicious intentions.

Cornelius heard him enter, and guessed that it was he, but did not turn round, as he knew well that Rosa was not coming after him.

There is nothing more galling to angry people

than the coolness of those upon whom they wish to vent their venom.

The expense being once incurred, one does not like to lose it; one's passion is roused, and one's blood boiling, so it would be labour lost not to have at least a nice little disturbance.

Gryphus, therefore, on seeing that Cornelius did not stir, tried to attract his attention by a loud—

'Umph, umph.'

Cornelius was humming between his teeth the 'Song of Flowers,' a sad but very charming piece.

The placid melancholy of the song was still further heightened by its calm and sweet melody, which exasperated Gryphus.

He struck his stick on the stone pavement of the cell, and yelled out,—

'Halloa! my singing master, don't you hear me?'

Cornelius turned round, merely saying,—

'Good morning,' and then began his song again.

This maddened Gryphus, who roared out,—

'Ah, you accursed sorcerer! you are making game of me, I believe.'

Cornelius was in no wise abashed, so he went on singing.

Gryphus went up to the prisoner, and said,—

'But you don't see that I have taken means to humble your confounded pride, and to compel you to confess your crimes.'

'Are you mad, my dear Mynheer Gryphus?' asked Cornelius.

And as he now for the first time observed the frenzied features, the flashing eyes and foaming mouth of the old jailer, he said,—

'The devil—surely he is mad.'

Gryphus flourished his stick above his head, but

Van Baerle moved not, and remained standing
with his arms akimbo.

'It seems your intention to threaten me, Mynheer
Gryphus.'

'Yes, indeed, I threaten you,' cried the jailer.

'And with what?'

'First of all, look what I have in my hand.'

'I think that's a stick,' said Cornelius, calmly,
'but I don't suppose you will threaten me with
that.'

'Oh, you don't suppose. And why not?'

'Because any jailer who strikes a prisoner is
liable to two penalties; the first laid down in
Article 9 of the regulations at Lœwestein :—

'"Any jailer, inspector or turnkey who lays
hands upon a prisoner of State will be dismissed."'

'Yes, who lays hands,' said Gryphus, mad with
rage; 'but there is not a word about a stick in the
regulation.'

'And the second,' continued Cornelius, 'which is
not written in the regulation, but which is to be
found elsewhere,—

'"Whosoever takes up the stick will be thrashed by
the stick."'

Gryphus, growing more and more exasperated
by the calm and sententious tone of Cornelius,
brandished his cudgel, but at the moment when
he raised it, Cornelius rushed at him, snatched it
from his hands, and put it under his own arm.

Gryphus fairly bellowed with rage.

'There, there, my good man,' said Cornelius,
'don't run the chance of losing your place.'

'Ah! you sorcerer, I'll make you pay for this,'
roared Gryphus.

'Oh, very good.'

'Don't you see that my hand is empty?'

'Yes, I see it, and I'm glad of it.'

'You know that it is not generally so when I come upstairs in the morning.'

'It's true, you generally bring me the worst soup and the most miserable rations one can secure. But that's not a punishment to me; I eat only bread, and the worse the bread is to your taste, Gryphus, the better it is to mine.'

'How so?'

'Oh, it's a very simple thing.'

'Well, tell me,' said Gryphus.

'Very willingly. I know that in giving me bad bread you think you injure me.'

'Certainly, I don't give it you to please you, you brigand.'

'Well, then, I, who am a sorcerer, as you know, change your bad into excellent bread, which I relish more than the best cake; and then I have the double pleasure of eating something that gratifies my palate, and of doing something that puts you in a passion.'

Gryphus answered with a growl.

'Oh, you confess, then, that you are a sorcerer.'

'Oh, indeed, yes. I don't say it before all the world, because they might burn me for it, but as we are alone, I don't mind telling you.'

'Well, well, well,' answered Gryphus; 'but if a sorcerer can change black bread into white, won't he die of hunger if he has no bread at all?'

'What's that?' said Cornelius.

'Therefore, I think I won't bring you any bread at all, and we shall see how it will be after eight days.'

Cornelius grew pale.

'And,' continued Gryphus, 'we'll begin this very day! As you are such a clever sorcerer, why, you had better change the furniture of your room into

bread; as to myself, I shall pocket the eighteen
sous which are paid to me for your board.'

'But that's murder,' cried Cornelius, carried away
by the first impulse of the very natural terror with
which this horrible mode of death inspired him.

'Well,' Gryphus went on in his jeering way, 'as
you are a sorcerer, you will live notwithstanding.'

Cornelius resumed his easy manner again, and
said,—

'Have not you seen me make the pigeons come
here from Dort?'

'Well?' said Gryphus.

'Well, a pigeon is a very dainty morsel, and a
man who eats one every day would not starve, I
think.'

'And what about the fire?' said Gryphus.

'Fire! surely you know that I'm in league with
the devil. Do you think the devil will leave me
without fire? Why, fire is his natural element.'

'A man, however healthy his appetite may be,
would not eat a pigeon every day. Wagers have
been made to do so, and those who made them
gave them up.'

'Well, but when I am tired of pigeons I shall
make the fish of the Waal and of the Meuse come
up to me.'

Gryphus open his large eyes to their greatest
extent, quite bewildered.

'I am rather fond of fish,' continued Cornelius;
'you never let me have any. Well, I shall take
advantage of this attempt on your part to starve
me, and regale myself with fish.'

Gryphus nearly fainted with anger and with
fright, but he soon rallied and said, putting his
hand in his pocket,—

'Well, if you force me to it,' and with these
words he drew forth a clasp-knife and opened it.

'Halloa, a knife!' said Cornelius, preparing to
defend himself with his stick.

CHAPTER XXIX

IN WHICH VAN BAERLE SETTLES ACCOUNTS
WITH GRYPHUS

FOR a while the two remained silent, Gryphus on
the offensive, and Van Baerle on the defensive.

Then, as the situation might be prolonged to an
indefinite length, Cornelius, anxious to learn something more of the cause of this extraordinary
behaviour of the jailer, asked a question.

'Well, what is it you want?'

'I'll tell you what I want,' answered Gryphus.
'I want you to restore to me my daughter Rosa.'

'Your daughter?' cried Van Baerle.

'Yes, my daughter Rosa, whom you have taken
from me by your devilish magic. Now, will you
tell me where she is?'

And the attitude of Gryphus became more and
more threatening.

'Is not Rosa at Lœwestein?' cried Cornelius.

'You know well she is not. Once more, will
you give me back my daughter?'

'I see,' said Cornelius, 'this is a trap you are
laying for me.'

'Now, for the last time, will you tell me where
my daughter is?'

'Guess it, you rogue, if you don't know it.'

'Only wait, only wait,' growled Gryphus, white
with rage, and with quivering lips, as his brain

began to turn. 'Ah, you will not tell me anything? Well, I'll unlock your teeth!'

He advanced a step towards Cornelius, and said,
showing him the weapon which he held in his
hand,—

'Do you see this knife? Well, I have killed
more than fifty black cocks with it, and I vow I'll
kill their master, the devil, as well as them.'

'But, you blockhead,' said Cornelius, 'will you
really kill me?'

'I shall open your heart, to learn from it the
place where you have hidden my daughter.'

Saying this, Gryphus, in his frenzy, rushed
towards Cornelius, who had barely time to retreat
behind his table to avoid the first thrust. Gryphus
continued, with horrid threats, to brandish his huge
knife, and as, although out of the reach of his
weapon, yet, as long as it remained in the madman's hand the ruffian might fling it at him—
Cornelius lost no time, and, availing himself of the
stick, which he held tight under his arm, dealt the
jailer a vigorous blow on the wrist of the hand
which held the knife.

The knife fell to the ground, and Cornelius put
his foot on it.

Then, as Gryphus seemed bent upon engaging in
a struggle which the pain in his wrist, and shame
for having allowed himself to be disarmed, would
have made desperate, Cornelius took a decisive
step, belabouring his jailer with the most heroic
self-possession, and deliberately choosing the spot
for each blow.

Very soon Gryphus howled and begged for
mercy. But, before begging for mercy, he had
lustily roared for help, and his cries had roused all
the functionaries of the prison. Two turnkeys, an
inspector and three or four guards, made their

appearance all at once, and found Cornelius still using the stick, with the knife under his foot.

At the sight of these witnesses, who could not know all the circumstances which had provoked and might justify his offence, Cornelius felt that he was irretrievably lost.

In fact, appearances were sadly against him.

In one moment Cornelius was disarmed, and Gryphus raised and supported; and, bellowing with rage and pain, he was able to take account of the bruises which were beginning to swell like the hills dotting the slopes of a mountain-ridge on his back and shoulders.

A full statement of the violence practised by the prisoner against his jailer was immediately drawn up, and as it was made on the depositions of Gryphus, it certainly could not be said to lack force; the prisoner being charged with neither more nor less than an attempt to murder, for a long time premeditated, in open rebellion.

Whilst the charge was made out against Cornelius, Gryphus, whose presence was no longer necessary after having made his depositions, was taken down by his turnkeys to his lodge, groaning, and covered with bruises.

During this time, the guards who had seized Cornelius busied themselves in charitably informing their prisoner of the usages and customs of Lœwestein, which, however, he knew as well as they did. The regulations had been read to him at the moment of his entering the prison, and certain articles in them remained fixed in his memory.

Among other things, they explained to him how these regulations had been carried out to its full extent in the case of a prisoner named Mathias, who in 1668, that is to say, five years before, had

committed a much less violent act of rebellion than
that of which Cornelius was guilty. He had found
his soup too hot, and thrown it at the head of the
chief turnkey, who, in consequence of this ablution,
had been put to the inconvenience of having his
skin come off as he wiped his face.

Mathias was taken within twelve hours from his
cell, then led to the jailer's lodge, where he was
registered as leaving Lœwestein, then taken to the
Esplanade, from which there is a very fine prospect
over a wide expanse of country. There they
fettered his hands, bandaged his eyes, and allowed
him to say his prayers.

Hereupon he was invited to go down on his
knees, and the guards of Lœwestein, twelve in
number, at a sign from a sergeant, each very
cleverly lodged a musket ball in his body.

In consequence of this proceeding, Mathias in-
continently did then and there die.

Cornelius listened with the greatest attention to
this delightful recital, and then said,—

' Ah! ah! within twelve hours, you say ? '

' Yes, the twelfth hour had not even struck, if I
remember right,' said the guard, who had told him
the story.

' Thank you,' said Cornelius.

The guard still had the smile on his face with
which he accompanied, and, as it were, accentuated
his tale, when footsteps and a jingling of spurs
were heard ascending the staircase.

The guards fell back to allow an officer to pass,
who entered the cell of Cornelius, at the moment
when the clerk of Lœwestein was still making out
his report.

' Is this No. 11 ? ' he asked.

' Yes, Captain,' answered a non-commissioned
officer.

'Then this is the cell of the prisoner, Cornelius van Baerle ? '

'Exactly, Captain.'

'Where is the prisoner ? '

'Here I am, sir,' answered Cornelius, growing rather pale, notwithstanding all his courage.

'You are Doctor Cornelius van Baerle ? ' asked he, this time addressing the prisoner himself.

'Yes, mynheer.'

'Then follow me.'

'Oh! oh!' said Cornelius, whose heart felt oppressed by the first dread of death. 'What quick work they make here in the fortress of Lœwestein. And the rascal talked to me of twelve hours!'

'Now, what did I tell you ? ' whispered the communicative guard into the ear of the culprit.

'A lie.'

'How so ? '

'You promised me twelve hours.'

'Ah, yes, but here comes to you an aide-de-camp of His Highness, even one of his most intimate companions, Van Decken. Zounds ! they did not grant such an honour to poor Mathias.'

'Come, come !' said Cornelius, drawing a long breath. 'Come, I'll show to these people that an honest burgher, godson of Cornelius de Witte, can, without flinching, receive as many musket-balls as that Mathias.'

Saying this, he passed proudly before the clerk, who, being interrupted in his work, ventured to say to the officer,—

'But, Captain van Decken, the protocol is not yet finished.'

'It is not worth while finishing it,' answered the officer.

'All right,' replied the clerk, philosophically putting up his paper and pen into a greasy and well-worn writing-case.

'It was written,' thought poor Cornelius, 'that I should not, in this world, give my name either to a child, to a flower, or to a book, the three things by which a man's memory is perpetuated.'

However, he followed the officer with a resolute heart, carrying his head erect.

Cornelius counted the steps which led to the Esplanade, regretting that he had not asked the guard how many there were of them, which the man in his officious complaisance would not have failed to tell him.

What the poor prisoner was most afraid of during this walk, which he considered as leading him to the end of the journey of life, was to see Gryphus and not to see Rosa. What savage satisfaction would glisten in the eyes of the father, and what sorrow dim those of the daughter!

But although he looked to the right and to the left, he saw neither Rosa nor Gryphus.

On reaching the Esplanade, he bravely looked about for the guards who were to be his executioners, and in reality saw a dozen soldiers assembled. But they were not standing in line, or carrying muskets, but talking together so gaily, that Cornelius felt almost shocked. It was hardly a time even for soldiers to joke.

Suddenly Gryphus appeared, limping, staggering, and supporting himself on a crooked stick, at his lodge gate; his old eyes, grey as those of a cat, were lit up with a gleam of inexpressible hatred. He then began to pour forth such a torrent of foul abuse and disgusting imprecations against Cornelius that the latter, addressing the officer, said,—

'I do not think it very becoming, sir, that I

should be thus insulted by this man, especially at a moment like this.'

'Well! but think,' said the officer, laughing, 'it is quite natural that this worthy fellow should bear you a grudge—you seem to have beaten him very soundly.'

'But, sir, it was only in self-defence.'

'Never mind,' said the captain, shrugging his shoulders like a true philosopher, 'let him talk; what does it matter to you now?'

The cold sweat stood on the brow of Cornelius at this answer, which he looked upon somewhat in the light of brutal irony, especially as coming from an officer of whom he had heard it said that he was attached to the person of the Prince.

The unfortunate tulip-fancier then felt that he had no more resources, and no more friends, and resigned himself to his fate.

'God's will be done,' he muttered, bowing his head; then, turning towards the officer, who seemed complacently to wait until he had finished his meditations, he asked,—

'Mynheer, may I know where I am to go?'

The officer pointed to a carriage drawn by four horses, which reminded him very strongly of that which, under similar circumstances, had before attracted his attention at the Buytenhof.

'Enter,' said the officer.

'Ah!' muttered Cornelius to himself, 'it seems they are not going to treat me to the honours of the Esplanade.'

He uttered these words loud enough for the chatty guard, who was at his heels, to overhear him.

That kind soul very likely thought it his duty to give Cornelius some new information; for approaching the door of the carriage, whilst the officer, with one foot on the step, was still giving some orders, he whispered to Van Baerle,—

'Condemned prisoners have sometimes been taken to their own town, to be made an example of, and they have then been executed before the door of their own house. It's all according to circumstances.'

Cornelius thanked him by a sign, and muttered to himself,—

'Well, here is a fellow who never misses giving consolation whenever an opportunity presents itself. In truth, my friend, I'm very much obliged to you. Good-bye.'

And the carriage drove off.

'Ah! you villain, you brigand,' roared Gryphus, clenching his fists at the victim, who was escaping from his clutches. 'To think of his going without having restored my daughter to me!'

'If they take me to Dort,' thought Cornelius, 'I shall see, as I pass my house, whether my poor beds have all been spoiled.'

CHAPTER XXX

WHEREIN IS HINTED THE SORT OF PUNISHMENT THAT WAS AWAITING CORNELIUS VAN BAERLE

THE carriage rolled on during the whole day; it passed on the right of Dort, went through Rotterdam, and reached Delft. At five o'clock in the evening they had travelled at least twenty leagues.

Cornelius addressed some questions to the officer,

who was at the same time his guard and his companion; but, cautious as were his inquiries, he had the disappointment of receiving no answer.

Cornelius regretted that he had no longer by his side that chatty soldier, who would talk without being pressed.

From him he would doubtless have had many pleasant details, and exact explanations, concerning this third strange part of his adventures, as he had received concerning the two first.

The travellers passed the night in the carriage. On the following morning, at dawn, Cornelius found himself beyond Leyden, having the North Sea on his left, and the Zuyder Zee on his right.

Three hours after, they entered Haarlem.

Cornelius was not aware of what had passed at Haarlem, of course, but it will be necessary for us to take up the thread.

We have seen that Rosa and the tulip, like two orphan sisters, had been left by the Prince William of Orange at the house of the President van Systens.

Rosa did not hear again from the Stadtholder until the evening of the day on which she had seen him face to face.

One evening an officer called at Van Systens's house. He came from His Highness, with a request for Rosa to appear at the Town Hall.

There, in the large council room, into which she was ushered, she found the Prince writing.

He was alone, with a large Frisian greyhound at his feet, who gazed steadily at his master, as if the faithful animal were wishing to do what no man could do—read his thoughts in his face.

William continued his writing for a moment; then, raising his eyes, and seeing Rosa standing near the door, he said, without laying down his pen,—

'Come here, my child.'

Rosa advanced a few steps towards the table.

'Sit down,' he added.

Rosa obeyed, for the Prince was fixing his eyes upon her; but he had scarcely turned them again to his paper, when she bashfully retired.

The Prince finished his letter.

During this time, the greyhound went up to Rosa, surveyed her, and began to make friends.

'Ah!' said William to his dog, 'it's easy to see that she is a countrywoman of yours, and that you recognise her.'

Then, turning towards Rosa, and fixing on her his scrutinising, and, at the same time, impenetrable, glance, he said,—

'Now, my child.'

The Prince was scarcely twenty-three, and Rosa eighteen or twenty. He might, therefore, perhaps, better have said my sister.

'My child,' he said, with that strangely-commanding accent, which chilled all those who approached him, 'we are alone; let us speak together.'

Rosa began to tremble; and yet there was nothing but kindness in the expression of the Prince's face.

'Monseigneur,' she stammered.

'You have a father at Lœwestein?'

'Yes, Your Highness.'

'You do not love him?'

'I do not—at least, not as a daughter ought to do, Monseigneur.'

'It is not right not to love one's father, but it is right not to tell a falsehood at any time.'

Rosa cast her eyes on the ground.

'What is the reason of your not loving your father?'

'He is a wicked man.'

'In what way does he show his wickedness?'

'He ill-treats the prisoners.'

'All of them?'

'All.'

'But don't you bear him a grudge for ill-treating some one in particular?'

'My father ill-treats in particular Mynheer van Baerle, who—'

'Who is your lover?'

Rosa started back a step.

'Whom I love, Monseigneur,' she answered proudly.

'Since when?' asked the Prince.

'Since the day when I first saw him.'

'And when was that?'

'The day after that on which the Grand Pensionary John and his brother Cornelius met with such an awful death.'

The Prince compressed his lips and knit his brow, and his eyelids dropped so as to hide his eyes for an instant. After a momentary silence, he resumed the conversation.

'But what is the use of loving a man who is doomed to live and die in prison?'

'It will lead, if he lives and dies in prison, to my aiding him in life and to death with resignation.'

'And would you accept the lot of being the wife of a prisoner?'

'As the wife of Mynheer van Baerle I should, under any circumstances, be the proudest and happiest woman in the world; but—'

'But what?'

'I dare not say, Monseigneur.'

B.T.   I 2

' There is something like hope in your voice—
what do you hope ? '

She raised her moist and beautiful eyes, and
looked at William with a glance full of meaning,
which was calculated to stir up in the recesses of
his heart the clemency which was slumbering
there.

' Ah ! I understand you,' he said.

Rosa, with a smile, clasped her hands.

' You hope in me ? ' said the Prince.

' Yes, Monseigneur.'

' Umph ! '

The Prince sealed the letter which he had just
written, and summoned one of his officers, to
whom he said,—

' Captain van Decken, carry this despatch to
Lœwestein ; you will read the orders which I give
to the Governor ; execute them as far as they
apply to you.'

The officer bowed, and; a few minutes afterwards, the gallop of a horse was heard resounding
in the vaulted archway.

' My child,' continued the Prince, ' the feast of
the tulip will be on Sunday next, that is to say,
the day after to-morrow. Make yourself neat with
these five hundred guilders, as I wish that day to
be a great day for you.'

' How does Your Highness wish me to be
dressed ? ' faltered Rosa.

' Wear the costume of a Frisian bride,' said
William, ' it will suit you very well indeed.'

CHAPTER XXXI

HAARLEM

HAARLEM, the great horticultural city, was in high feather, and the fifteenth of May 1673 was a great day for the good city. It was about to celebrate a threefold festival. In the first place, the black tulip had been produced ; secondly, the Prince William of Orange, as a true Dutchman, had promised to be present at the ceremony of its inauguration ; and, thirdly, it was a point of honour with the States to show to the French, at the conclusion of so disastrous a war as that of 1672, that the flooring of the Batavian Republic was solid enough for its people to dance upon to the accompaniment of the cannon of their fleets.

The Horticultural Society of Haarlem had shown itself worthy of its fame, by giving a hundred thousand guilders for the bulb of a tulip. The town, which did not wish to remain behind-hand, voted a like sum, which was placed in the hands of its leading citizens to solemnise the auspicious event.

And so, on the Sunday fixed for this ceremony, there was such a stir among the people, and such an enthusiasm among the townsfolk, that even a cynical Frenchman, who laughs at everything at all times, could not have helped admiring the character of those honest Hollanders, who were equally ready to spend their money for the construction of a man-of-war, as they were to reward the grower of a new flower, destined to bloom for one day, and to serve during that day to divert the ladies, the learned and the curious.

At the head of the municipal authorities and of

the Horticultural Committee shone Mynheer van
Systens, dressed in his richest habiliments.

The worthy man had done his best to resemble
his favourite flower, in the sombre yet chaste
elegance of his garments ; and we are bound to
record, to his honour, that he had perfectly succeeded in his object.

Jet-black velvet and purple silk, with linen of
dazzling whiteness, composed the festive dress of
the President, who marched at the head of his
Committee, carrying an enormous nosegay, like
that which, a hundred and twenty-one years
later, Monsieur de Robespierre displayed at the
festival of ' The Supreme Being.'

Quite different from the French tribune, whose
heart was so full of hatred and ambitious vindic-
tiveness, the honest President carried in his bosom
a heart as simple as the flowers which he held in
his hand.

Behind the Committee, who were as gay as a
field of wild flowers, and as fragrant as a garden
in spring, marched the learned societies of the
town, the magistrates, the military, the nobles
and the peasants.

The people, even among the respected republicans of the Seven Provinces, had no place
assigned to them in the procession ; they merely
lined the streets.

It is the true place for the multitude, which,
with good philosophic spirit, waits until the
triumphal pageants have passed, that they may
know what to say, and sometimes to know what
to do as well.

This time, however, there was no question either
of the triumph of Pompey or of Cæsar ; neither
were they celebrating the defeat of Mithridates,
nor of the conquest of Gaul. The procession was

as placid as the passing of a flock of sheep, and as inoffensive as a flight of birds sweeping through the air.

Haarlem had no other conquerors save its gardeners. In worshipping flowers, Haarlem idolised the florist.

In the centre of this pacific and fragrant *cortège* the black tulip was seen, borne on a litter which was covered with white velvet and fringed with gold.

It was arranged that the Prince Stadtholder himself should give the prize of a hundred thousand guilders, a matter in which all were interested, and it was thought that perhaps he would make a speech, which interested more particularly his friends and enemies.

The whole population of Haarlem, reinforced by that of the neighbourhood, had arranged itself along the beautiful avenues of trees, with the fixed resolution, this time, to applaud neither the heroes of war nor those of science, but merely the conqueror of nature, who had forced her to produce an absolutely black tulip.

Nothing, however, is more fickle than such a resolution of the people. When a crowd is once in the humour to cheer, it is just the same as when it begins to hiss. It never knows when to stop.

They began, therefore, by cheering Van Systens and his nosegay, then the corporations, then followed a cheer for the people ; and at last, and for once with great justice, there was one for the excellent music with which the gentlemen of the town council generously treated the assemblage at every halt.

All eyes were on the look-out for the hero of the day—of course, we mean the grower of the tulip.

This hero made his appearance at the conclusion

of the reading of the report which we have seen
Van Systens drawing up with such conscientious-
ness ; and he produced almost a greater sensation
that the Stadtholder himself.

There walked the hero, covered with flowers
down to his girdle ; well combed and brushed and
entirely dressed in scarlet, a colour which contrasted
strongly which his black hair and yellow complexion.

This beaming personage, radiant with intoxicated
joy, who had the distinguished honour of making
the people forget the speech of Van Systens, and
even the presence of the Stadtholder, was Isaac
Boxtel, who saw, carried on his right before him,
the black tulip, his pretended daughter ; and on
his left, in a large purse, the hundred thousand
guilders in glittering gold pieces, towards which he
was constantly squinting in his determination not
to lose sight of them for one moment.

Another quarter of an hour and the Prince will
arrive, and the procession will halt for the last
time. The tulip being placed on its throne, the
Prince, yielding precedence to this rival in the
public adoration, will take a magnificently-blazoned
parchment, on which is written the name of the
grower ; and His Highness, in a loud and audible
tone, will proclaim him to be the discoverer of a
marvel : that Holland, by Boxtel's instrument-
ality, has forced nature to produce a black flower,
which shall henceforth be called *Tulipa nigra
Boxtellea.*

From time to time, however, Boxtel withdrew
his eyes for a moment from the tulip and the purse
and scanned the crowd with apprehension, for,
more than anything, he dreaded to encounter the
pale face of the pretty Frisian girl.

She would have been as a spectre spoiling the

joy of the festival for him, just as Banquo's ghost disturbed the repose of Macbeth.

And yet, this robber, this wretch, who had stolen what was the boast of a man, and the dowry of a woman, did not consider himself a thief. He had so intently watched this tulip, followed it so eagerly from the drawer in Cornelius's drying-room to the scaffold of the Buytenhof, and from the scaffold to the fortress of Lœwestein ; he had seen it bud and grow in Rosa's window, and so often warmed the air round it with his breath that he felt as if no one had a better right to call himself its producer than he had ; and anyone who would now take the black tulip from him would have appeared to him as a veritable highwayman.

But he did not see Rosa, therefore his joy was unspoiled.

In the centre of a circle of magnificent trees, which were decorated with garlands and inscriptions, the procession halted, amidst the sounds of lively music ; and the young damsels of Haarlem made their appearance to escort the tulip to the raised seat which it was to occupy on the platform, by the side of the gilded chair of His Highness the Stadtholder.

And the proud tulip, elevated on its pedestal, soon overlooked the assembled crowd of people, who clapped their hands, and made the old town of Haarlem re-echo with their tremendous cheers.

CHAPTER XXXII

A LAST REQUEST

At this solemn moment, and while the cheers were at their heartiest, a carriage was speeding along the road which skirted the green on which the scene occurred ; it now pursued its way slowly, on account of the flocks of children who were pushed out of the avenue by the crowd of men and women.

This carriage, covered with dust, and creaking on its axles, the result of a long journey, enclosed the unfortunate Van Baerle, who was quite dazzled and bewildered by this festive splendour and bustle.

Notwithstanding the unreadiness which his companion had shown in answering his questions concerning his fate, he ventured once more to ask what all this meant.

'As you may see, sir,' replied the officer, 'it is a *fête*.'

'Ah, a *fête*,' said Cornelius, in the sad tone of indifference of a man to whom no joy remains in this world.

Then, after some moments' silence, during which the carriage had proceeded a few yards, he asked once more,—

'Is it the *fête* of the patron saint of Haarlem ? for I see so many flowers.'

'It is indeed a *fête* in which flowers play a principal part.'

'Oh, the sweet scents ! oh, the beautiful colours !' cried Cornelius.

'Stop, that the gentleman may see,' said the officer, with that frank kindliness which is peculiar to military men, to the soldier who was acting as postillion.

'Oh, thank you, mynheer, for your kindness,' replied Van Baerle, in a melancholy tone; 'the joy of others pains me, please spare me this pang.'

'Just as you wish. Drive on! I ordered the driver to stop because I thought it would please you, as you are said to love flowers, and especially that, the festival of which is celebrated to-day.'

'And what flower is that?'

'The tulip.'

'The tulip!' cried Van Baerle. 'Is to-day the *fête* of the tulip?'

'Yes, mynheer, but as this spectacle is disagreeable to you, let us drive on.'

The officer was about to give the order to proceed, but Cornelius stopped him, a painful thought having struck him.

'Mynheer, is the prize given to-day?' he asked falteringly.

'Yes, the prize for the black tulip.'

Cornelius's cheek blanched, his whole frame trembled, and the cold sweat stood on his brow.

'Alas! mynheer,' he said, 'all these good people will be as unfortunate as myself, for they will not see the solemnity which they have come to witness, or at least they will see it incompletely.'

'What is it you mean to say?'

'I mean to say,' replied Cornelius, throwing himself back in the carriage, 'that the black tulip will not be found, except by one whom I know.'

'In that case,' said the officer, 'the person whom you know has found it, for the thing which the whole of Haarlem is looking at at this moment is neither more nor less than the black tulip.'

'The black tulip!' cried Van Baerle, thrusting half his body out of the carriage window. 'Where is it? where is it?'

'Over there, on the throne, don't you see?'

'I do see it.'

'Come along, mynheer,' said the officer. 'Now, we must drive off.'

'Oh! have pity, have mercy, sir,' said Van Baerle, 'don't take me away. Let me look once more. Is what I see down there the black tulip? Quite black? Is it possible? Oh, sir, have you seen it? It must have specks, it must be imperfect, it can only be dyed black; ah, if I were there! I should see it at once. Let me alight, let me see it close, I beg of you.'

'Are you mad, sir? How could I allow such a thing?'

'I implore you.'

'But you forget that you are a prisoner.'

'It is true I am a prisoner, but I am a man of honour, and I promise you on my word that I will not run away, I will not attempt to escape—only let me see the flower.'

'But my orders, sir, my orders.' And the officer again made the driver a sign to proceed.

Cornelius stopped him once more.

'Oh, be forbearing, be generous, my whole life depends upon your pity. Alas! perhaps it will not be much longer. You don't know, sir, what I suffer. You don't know the struggle going on in my heart and mind; for after all,' Cornelius cried in despair, 'if this were my tulip, if it were the one which has been stolen from Rosa! Oh! I must alight, sir! I must see the flower. You may kill me afterwards, if you like, but I will see it, I must see it.'

'Be quiet, miserable man, and come quickly back into the carriage, for here is the escort of His Highness the Stadtholder, and if the Prince observed any disturbance, or heard any noise, it would be ruin to me as well as to you.'

Van Baerle, more afraid for his companion than himself, threw himself back into the carriage, but he could only keep quiet for half a minute, and the first twenty horsemen had scarcely passed when he again leaned out of the carriage window, gesticulating imploringly towards the Stadtholder at the very moment when he passed.

William, impassive and retiring as usual, was proceeding to the square to fulfil his duty as chairman. He held in his hand the roll of parchment which, on this festive day, had become his baton.

Seeing the man gesticulate with imploring mien, and perhaps also recognising the officer who accompanied him, His Highness ordered his carriage to stop.

In one instant his snorting steeds stood still, at a distance of about six yards from the carriage in which Van Baerle was caged.

'What it this?' the Prince asked the officer, who at the first order of the Stadtholder had jumped out of the carriage, and was respectfully approaching him.

'Monseigneur,' he cried, 'this is the prisoner of State whom I have fetched from Lœwestein, and whom I have brought to Haarlem according to Your Highness's command.'

'What does he want?'

'He entreats for permission to stop here for a moment.'

'To see the black tulip, Monseigneur,' said Van Baerle, clasping his hands, 'and when I have seen it, when I have seen what I desire to know, I am quite ready to die, if die I must; but in dying I shall bless Your Highness's mercy for having allowed me to witness the glorification of my work.'

It was, indeed, a curious spectacle to see these

two men, at the windows of their several carriages ;
the one, surrounded by his guards, and all-powerful,
the other a prisoner and miserable ; the one going
to mount a throne, the other believing himself to
be on his way to the scaffold.

William, looking with his cold glance on
Cornelius, listened to his anxious and urgent
request.

Then, addressing himself to the officer, he
said,—

' Is this person the mutinous prisoner who has
attempted to kill his jailer at Lœwestein ? '

Cornelius heaved a sigh and hung his head.
His good-tempered, honest face turned pale and
red at the same instant. These words of the all-
powerful Prince, who, by some secret messenger,
unavailable to other mortals, had already been
apprised of his crime, seemed to him to forebode
not only his doom, but also the refusal of his last
request.

He did not try to make a struggle, or to defend
himself; and he presented to the Prince the affecting spectacle of despairing innocence, like that of
a child ; a spectacle which was fully understood
and felt by the great mind and the great heart of
him who observed it.

' Allow the prisoner to alight, and let him see
the black tulip ; it is well worth being seen once.'

' Thank you, Monseigneur, thank you,' said
Cornelius, nearly swooning with joy, and staggering on the steps of his carriage ; had not the
officer supported him, our poor friend would have
made his thanks to His Highness prostrate on his
knees full length in the dust.

After having granted this permission, the Prince
proceeded on his way over the green amidst the
most enthusiastic acclamations.

He soon arrived at the platform, and the thunder
of cannon shook the air. .

***

CHAPTER XXXIII

CONCLUSION

VAN BAERLE, led by four guards, who pushed
their way through the crowd, sidled up to the
black tulip, towards which his gaze was attracted
with increasing interest, the nearer he approached
to it.

He saw it at last; that unique flower, which he
was to see once, and no more. He saw it at the
distance of six paces, and was delighted with its
perfection and gracefulness; he saw it surrounded
by young and beautiful girls, who formed, as it
were, a guard of honour for this queen of ex-
cellence and purity. And yet, the more he
ascertained with his own eyes the perfection of
the flower, the more wretched aud miserable he
felt. He looked all around for some one to whom
he might address only one question; but his eyes
everywhere met strange faces, and the attention of
all was directed towards the chair of state, on
which the Stadtholder had seated himself.

William rose, casting a tranquil glance over the
enthusiastic crowd, and his keen eye rested by
turns on the three extremities of a triangle, formed
opposite to him by three person with very different
interests and emotions.

At one of the angles stood Boxtel, trembling
with impatience, and quite absorbed in watching

the Prince, the guilders, the black tulip and the
crowd.

At the other was Cornelius, panting for breath,
silent, with all his attention, his eyes, his life, his
heart, his love, concentrated on the black tulip—
his own child.

At the third, standing on a raised step among
the maidens of Haarlem, was a beautiful Frisian
girl, dressed in fine scarlet woollen cloth, embroidered with silver, and covered with a lace veil,
which fell in rich folds from her head-dress of gold
brocade ; in one word, Rosa, who, faint and with
swimming eyes, was leaning on the arm of one of
the officers of William.

The Prince then slowly unfolded the parchment,
and said, in a calm clear voice, which, although
low, made itself perfectly heard amid the respectful silence which all at once fell upon the fifty
thousand spectators,—

' You all know what has brought us here.

' A prize of one hundred thousand guilders has
been promised to whosoever should grow the black
tulip.

' The black tulip has been grown ; here it is
before your eyes, coming up to all the conditions
required by the programme of the Horticultural
Society of Haarlem.

' The history of its production, and the name of
its grower, will be inscribed in the book of honour
of the city.

' Let the person approach to whom the black
tulip belongs.'

In uttering these words, the Prince, to judge of
the effect they produced, surveyed, with his eagle
eye, the three extremities of the triangle.

He saw Boxtel rushing forward ; he saw
Cornelius make an involuntary movement ; and,

lastly, he saw the officer, who was taking care of Rosa, lead, or rather push, her forward towards him.

At the sight of Rosa a double cry arose on the right and left of the Prince.

Boxtel, thunderstruck, and Cornelius, in joyful amazement, both exclaimed,—

'Rosa! Rosa!'

'This tulip is yours, is it not, my child?' said the Prince.

'Yes, Monseigneur,' stammered Rosa, whose striking beauty excited a general murmur of applause.

'Oh!' muttered Cornelius, 'she has then belied me when she said this flower was stolen from her. Oh! that is why she left Lœwestein. Alas! am I then forgotten, betrayed by her whom I thought my best friend on earth?'

'Oh!' sighed Boxtel, 'I am lost.'

'This tulip,' continued the Prince, 'will therefore bear the name of its producer, and figure in the catalogue under the title, *Tulipa nigra Rosa Barlæ-ensis*, which will henceforth be the name of this damsel.'

And at the same time William took Rosa's hand and placed it in that of a young man who rushed forth, pale and beyond himself with joy, to the foot of the throne, greeting alternately the Prince and his bride; and who, with a grateful look to Heaven, returned his thanks to the Giver of all this happiness.

At the same moment there fell at the feet of the President van Systens another man, struck down by a very different emotion.

Boxtel, crushed by the failure of his hopes, lay senseless on the ground.

When they raised him, and examined his pulse and his heart, he was quite dead.

This incident did not much disturb the festival, as neither the Prince nor the President seemed to mind it much.

Cornelius started back in dismay, when in the thief, in the pretended Jacob, he recognised his neighbour, Isaac Boxtel, whom, in the innocence of his heart, he had not for one instant suspected of such a base action.

Then, to the sound of trumpets, the procession marched back without any change in its order, except that Boxtel was now dead and that Cornelius and Rosa were walking triumphantly side by side and hand in hand.

When they arrived at the Hotel de Ville, the Prince, pointing with his finger to the purse with the hundred thousand guilders, said to Cornelius,—

'It is difficult to say by whom this money is gained, by you or by Rosa; for if you have found the black tulip, she has nursed it and brought it into flower. It would, therefore, be unjust to consider it as her dowry; it is the gift of the town of Haarlem to the tulip.'

Cornelius wondered what the Prince meant, and waited. The latter continued,—

'I give to Rosa the sum of a hundred thousand guilders, which she has fairly earned, and which she can offer to you. They are the reward of her love, her courage, and her honesty. As to you, mynheer, thanks to Rosa again, who has furnished the proofs of your innocence—'

And, saying these words, the Prince handed to Cornelius that fly-leaf of the Bible on which was written the letter of Cornelius de Witte, and in which the third bulb had been wrapped.

'As to you, it has come to light that you were imprisoned for a crime which you did not commit. This means that you are not only free, but that your property will be restored to you, as the property of an innocent man cannot be confiscated. Cornelius van Baerle, you are the godson of Cornelius de Witte, and the friend of his brother John. Remain worthy of the name you have received from one of them, and of the friendship you have enjoyed from the other. The two De Wittes, wrongly judged, and wrongly punished in a moment of popular error, were two great citizens, of whom Holland is now proud.'

The Prince, after these last words, which, contrary to his custom, he pronounced with a voice full of emotion, gave his hands to the lovers to kiss while they were kneeling before him.

Then he said, with a sigh,—

' Alas! you are happy, who, dreaming perhaps of the true glory of Holland and her forms, especially her true happiness, do not attempt to acquire for her anything except the true colours of a tulip.'

And hastily glancing towards that point of the compass where France lay, as if he saw new clouds gathering there, he entered his carriage and drove off.

Cornelius started on the same day for Dort with Rosa, who sent her lover's old housekeeper as a messenger to her father to inform him of all that had taken place.

Old Gryphus was by no means willing to be reconciled to his son-in-law. He had not forgotten the blows which he received in that famous encounter. To judge from the weals which he counted, he said they amounted to forty-one; but at last, in order, as he declared, not to be less generous than His Highness the Stadtholder, he consented to make his peace.

Appointed to watch over the tulips, the old man

made the most reckless keeper of flowers in the whole of the Seven Provinces.

It was indeed a sight to see him watching the obnoxious moths and butterflies, killing slugs and driving away the hungry bees.

As he had heard Boxtel's story, and was furious at having been the dupe of the pretended Jacob, he destroyed the sycamore behind which the envious Isaac had spied into the garden. Boxtel's ground being in the market, it had been bought by Cornelius and absorbed into his own garden.

Rosa grew more beautiful in mind as well as body, and after two years of married life she could read and write so well that she was able to undertake by herself the education of two beautiful children which she bore her husband in 1674 and 1675, both in May, the month of flowers.

As a matter of course, one was a boy, the other a girl, the former being called Cornelius, the other Rosa.

Van Baerle remained faithfully attached to Rosa, and to his tulips. The whole of his life was devoted to the happiness of his wife and the culture of flowers, in the latter of which occupations he was so successful that he originated a large number of varieties, which duly found a place in the catalogue of Holland.

The two principal ornaments of his drawing-room were the two leaves from the Bible of Cornelius de Witte, set in large golden frames. One of them contained the letter in which his godfather enjoined him to burn the correspondence of the Marquis de Louvois, and the other was his own will, in which he bequeathed to Rosa his bulbs, under condition that she should marry a young man of from twenty-six to twenty-eight years, who loved her, and whom she loved, a condition which was fulfilled to the letter, although, or rather because, Cornelius refused to die.

To ward off any envious attempts of another Isaac Boxtel, he wrote over his door the lines which Grotius had, on the day of his flight, cut in the wall of his prison,—

'Sometimes one's sufferings have been so great that one need never say, " I am too happy." '

THE END

PRINTED BY WILLIAM BRENDON AND SON, LTD., PLYMOUTH, ENGLAND